Where the River Meets the Skye

FELICITY SNOW

One of the MCs in this story has a history of SA. I have done my best to portray his situation with care and sensitivity, and have had some amazing sensitivity readers who have helped me along the way. Please know that if you too are a survivor of SA, I know there is no one right way to deal with that trauma. I hope you find comfort in River's story. I hope you find hope. I hope you find healing for yourself and peace despite all that you have been through.

This story also deals heavily with chronic pain and illness. It is not an easy one to read, nor was it an easy one to write, but it is very personal to me, because it's my own in many ways. This was a story I wrote to help me cope with the reality of living with chronic health issues. And while this story does have an HEA, it has a lot of grief and heartache, and the HEA may not be your typical one, because sometimes we don't heal completely and we don't get the answers we want. But if we're blessed enough to have a partner or a friend by our side on the journey, it can make each day a little bit easier. This applies both to those who deal with chronic health issues and those who have a history of trauma. In many cases they are intertwined.

If you are thinking to yourself as you read that there is no way one person could deal with so many health issues one right after the other, I promise you there is. Everyone's journey is different and this is not exaggerated. So many people live with the reality of chronic pain and illness every single day, without getting better.

My intention with this story is not to elicit pity or sympathy, but rather to educate, inform and enlighten. If you are not someone who deals with the reality of chronic health issues, of being in pain or being sick day after day, year after year, of never knowing how you will be feeling from one day to the next, of spending more time in a hospital or a drs office than you do at home, know how blessed you are. If you are someone who struggles, or you are taking care of someone who struggles, while also trying to hold down a job and take care of a home and even raise children, please know that you are not alone. I hope you see yourself in River and Skye's story. I hope that you find hope, encouragement, comfort, and healing. I hope that you Rise.

CONTENT WARNINGS

Mentions and discussions of past SA, including a brief on page flashback, passing of a minor character, brief mentions of self harm

Acknowledgments

To my amazing beta and sensitivity readers, Hawthorne Gray, Donatella Coluzzi, Wren Vale, Rebecca Louise, Rae Simmons and Becky Wenzel. Thank you so much for all of your help and support on this story. And to my street team for spreading the word about River and Skye. I couldn't do this without you!

A special thank you as well to my amazing editor Jen Sharon for making my work shine, and to Dr. Rachel D. Miller on instagram at holdthevisiontherapy for her guidance on this project

"People with chronic illness aren't faking being sick. They're actually faking being well." ~Anonymous

CHAPTER 1
Skye

Skyelar Mckenzie walked in the front door of his condo and set his messenger bag on the chair next to him. His keys went in the small square basket on the table next to the door, before he kicked his shoes off, and ran his fingers through his blond waves. His feet were aching from standing all day in those stupid dress shoes, and his low back was complaining, too. At twenty eight he was still fairly young, but some days he felt closer to forty.

Stretching his back, he heard it pop, then rubbed the back of his neck with his hand. He'd gotten home a little later than usual today. The teachers meeting (that should have been an email) had taken much longer than necessary, he'd gotten a flat tire on the way home, and he was most definitely not looking forward to the stack of papers he still had to grade. When he glanced at the clock on the wall it read half past six, but his body told him that it was so much later.

God, he was getting old. He could remember ten years ago, staying up until two in the morning and still making it to his ten am classes, partying night after night. How the hell had he been able to do that? Now he was ready for bed by ten most nights. Midnight if he was being really wild.

His roommate wasn't home yet. His keys weren't in the basket next to Skye's, nor were his shoes by the door. His car wasn't in the driveway either, which was odd because River was always home by six thirty. Skye decided he would give it a few more minutes and then text his friend.

River was pretty much Skye's polar opposite, but despite their vast differences, they'd been best friends and roommates since their freshman year of college.

River considered exercising a *hobby* and loved to go running, biking, and rock climbing. He *enjoyed* eating vegetables, which Skye still couldn't understand. He could spend hours outside, relaxing, reading, or scrolling through his phone, soaking up the sun, whereas Skye had discovered his allergy to bugs and dirt a long time ago. It was definitely a thing. He was positive.

River also enjoyed decorating, so Skye had let him take over in that department when they'd moved in together five years ago. He hadn't a clue about such things. If left up to him, the walls of their condo would still be barren. But River had made it a home, with the art on the walls, throw pillows, blankets, and little knick-knacks on the side tables and shelves, along with photos of the two of them and their families scattered about.

Skye smiled as he walked into his bedroom and slipped off his tie. He stripped off his dress clothes and changed into sweatpants and a T-shirt as his mind wandered back to that first meeting with River all those years ago.

~

TEN YEARS AGO

Skye was expecting the tall, dark-haired guy, whom he was assuming was his roommate, to introduce himself when he entered the dorm room and started making noise as he unpacked. But the young man just kept pulling things out of his suitcase and setting them aside on his bed, or carrying them to the closet. It took Skye a second to realize that he had earbuds in and probably couldn't hear him, so he made his way over to where his roommate was setting some folded clothes in the dresser it looked like they would be sharing, and tapped his shoulder.

The young man practically jumped out of his skin, his clothes falling to the floor, eyes wide with alarm. And if Skye wasn't mistaken, he actually looked a bit panicked.

"Woah, hey," Skye said, when the other boy reached into his pocket and pulled his phone out, pressing what Skye assumed was the pause button on whatever he was listening to. He pulled the earbuds out of his ears. "I just wanted to introduce myself." Skye held his hand out for the boy to shake, but the boy just blinked and stared, his face having gone slightly pale. He didn't take Skye's hand, just knelt down to pick his clothes up off the floor. Since Skye was the one who made him drop them, and because he wasn't an asshole, he crouched down to help.

The young man took the T-shirts and jeans Skye handed him, and Skye saw the blush that crept up his roommate's face as he set a couple of pairs of underwear in his arms as well. His eyes met Skye's behind black framed glasses, and they were such a vibrant shade of blue that Skye couldn't help but get lost in them for a moment. This boy was gorgeous. Thick hair that was so dark it was almost black, a slender but toned frame, with the perfect amount of bicep peaking out under the sleeve of his black, form fitting T-shirt, thick full lips and high cheekbones. And God, if those glasses didn't just add to his sex appeal. Once they stood, Skye noticed that his roommate was maybe an inch or two shorter than his own six feet.

"Sorry I scared you," Skye said, as the young man pushed his glasses up on his nose with one finger and then continued laying his clothes in the dresser drawer. "I'm Skye."

The boy glanced at him. "River." The word was so quiet,

Skye almost missed it. River seemed more tense and on edge than anyone Skye had ever met. He smiled at the other boy, trying to help him relax, but when he moved closer to clap River on the shoulder, River flinched, and Skye lowered his hand.

"You all right?" The poor guy seemed terrified. But if there was one thing Skye was good at, it was relating to people and getting them to come out of their shells, and he was determined to do it with River, too.

"Need some help unpacking?" he asked. "Maybe if we both work on it, it will go faster. I can help with your things and then you can help me get the rest of my shit out of my car. Is this everything of yours?"

River nodded, looking a little flustered but still not speaking. "You okay with me touching your stuff?" The boy hesitated, but then nodded again.

"What do you say you take the first three dresser drawers, and I'll take the bottom three?" Another nod. Skye didn't give a shit about what closet or bed he had, and River had already started putting his things in the closet near the window at the back of the room, so Skye would take the one at the front of the room.

Skye moved towards River's bed to get some more of his clothes, and saw a large leather bound book with the words 'Holy Bible' inscribed on the front in silver letters. It looked worn and well used. He'd never been a religious person himself. Never wanted to have anything to do with it honestly, after hearing his entire life that who he was as a person was a sin, and that he was going to hell for liking men. Any kind of religion that taught you to hate people or to hide who you are, couldn't be a good one. But when he looked over at River, the other boy didn't strike him as the kind of person who would hate anyone, or be unkind to anyone.

"You religious?" Skye asked, holding up the Bible. River nodded again. "Not gonna be a problem that I'm gay, is it?" To Skye's surprise River actually gave a small smile, then shook his head. "Good, cause that isn't changing no matter what this book says."

River stepped towards him cautiously and extracted the Bible from his hands, setting it on his desk next to his laptop. Then he nodded to the suitcase filled with clothes, toiletries, more books, and other random stuff as if to tell Skye to get a move on already.

Skye smiled and handed him things, and they worked on unpacking together. Skye didn't say anything for a while and the dark haired boy actually seemed to relax around him a little more. "You have family here?" Skye asked eventually.

River nodded.

"Where are they?" Skye looked around the small room like he might have somehow missed them.

"It's just my aunt," River murmured, his voice soft, but deeper than Skye had anticipated. "She's talking something over with the registrar."

"Hey, you do talk." Skye grinned at him. "Not so bad, is it?" River gave a soft smile, his cheeks flushed, and Skye counted that as a win. He promised himself that he would get one of River's genuine smiles, or even a laugh out of him before too long.

"My mom wanted to come but she had to stay home with my brother. He wasn't feeling well. And she was super busy with work. My parents started a beer company a ways back and things get pretty crazy sometimes." Skye didn't know why he was telling River his life story but he'd never been comfortable in silence for too long and he thought maybe it would help his roommate loosen up a little. He seemed so tightly wound, like he was sure something was going to jump out at him any minute.

River looked, for a moment, like he wanted to ask Skye something, but then decided against it and went back to unpacking.

"Mind if we play some music?" Skye asked after another minute. They'd gotten all the things in the dresser and River was moving to setting things up in his closet as Skye did the same. "We can listen to whatever you were listening to when I came in here."

River flushed again. Skye noticed that he did that a lot. "I don't think you would like it," the boy said softly.

"Oh, why not?"

"It's worship music." Skye cringed, but managed to get a laugh out, and he noticed that River smiled a little.

"Yeah, maybe not," Skye agreed, and the other boy's smile widened. God, he looked good when he smiled, an adorable dimple on his left cheek, his eyes lighting up behind his glasses. And the fact that he wasn't trying to shove anything about his religion or his faith down Skye's throat was kind of awesome. He would not handle that well.

"You okay with my stuff?" Skye asked, taking out his phone and scrolling. "We can do my chill section." Skye grinned at his roommate and winked, and the other boy's cheeks flushed yet again. Fuck, why was that so adorable?

River shrugged, his lips pursed like there was something he wanted to say again but wasn't sure if he should.

Just as Skye was about to press the play button he heard, "I'm sorry."

His gaze lifted to meet his roommate's. He blinked. "For what?"

"For all the Christians who ever hurt you and made you feel bad about who you are." The other boy glanced down and shuffled his feet, hands in his pockets. His sapphire eyes met Skye's again. They were warm and sincere when he said, "There's nothing wrong with you. I...uh, I just want you to know that."

Fuck. Skye was not crying. He absolutely refused to cry in front of some guy he'd just met. But he was stunned. River's words were more life-giving and liberating than he could have imagined. And yes, damn it, there were definitely tears stinging at the corners of his eyes.

He'd never had someone apologize for mistreating him for his sexuality before, especially when they hadn't personally been the one to do the harm. And while he'd been out for a while, it hadn't all been sunshine and rainbows. His mom and brother had accepted him right away. Coming out to them had been the hardest thing he had ever done. Skye had known he was gay since his freshman year of high school, but it had taken him another year before finally gathering the courage to tell them, and he'd cried like a baby when he had.

But they hadn't batted an eyelash. They'd just hugged him and told him they loved him, and wanted him to be himself. When Skye had asked his mom what she thought his dad would have said, she'd just smiled and said, "He would have said he loves you and that he's proud of you." It had gone better than Skye could have imagined, and he'd wished he'd told them sooner to keep from carrying all that guilt, fear, and shame for so long.

It had given him the courage to come out to a group of friends at school, all guys. Unfortunately when they found out, they hadn't had the same positive reaction. They hadn't called him names, or harassed him, but they had ignored him, and made it very clear he wasn't welcome in their company anymore. Which may have actually been worse. He'd been afraid to come out to anyone for a long time after that. It had taken meeting the right people, forming new friendships, and the love and support of his family to realize that who he was was nothing to be ashamed of. He had been very open about his sexuality since, and refused to hide who he was or let others make him feel like shit for who he was attracted to.

"Uh, thank you," he said. "So, uh, you, you really don't mind?" River frowned and it made Skye laugh. "Sorry, I just, I'm not sure what to make of the Christian guy telling me I'm not going to hell for liking dick."

River's face flushed and Skye realized that maybe he wasn't used to such crass language. Well, for Skye it wasn't crass, but he had no idea how sheltered his roommate might be. Had he ever even had sex? Seen a woman naked? Was he a virgin? He was *too fucking gorgeous to have never been laid, that was for damn sure. If he had any interest in Skye at all he would not say no to fucking his roommate senseless.*

"Maybe that not all Christians are assholes," River replied, crossing his arms over his chest.

Skye smirked, pretty damn proud of himself for actually getting his roommate fired up over something enough to talk, and show some sass.

He shrugged. "All the Christians I've ever heard open their mouths are."

River narrowed his eyes. "Except me."

Skye couldn't help it when his lips quirked into a small smile. "Except you."

"So, if I'm bringing anyone back to the room for a good time I'll just put a sock on the door or something. You cool with that?" They both moved around again as they continued to unpack. Skye's unpacking was a bit more haphazard, while River had things neatly organized and stacked perfectly. Skye had a feeling being roommates with River was going to be an adjustment for both of them, but found himself not minding.

River shrugged. "As long as it's not every night."

Skye laughed. "Same goes for you. I don't want to walk in and see tits bouncing and hear those girly moans." River coughed and Skye grinned. Virgin or not, River was definitely a bit shy when it came to sex.

River shook his head, seeming to shrink back into himself. His voice had gone soft again when he said, "That won't be a problem."

"Why not? Don't like girls?" Skye winked at his roommate again, that adorable flush back in an instant as River cleared his throat.

"No, I..." he cleared it again and ran his long, slender fingers through those thick, dark strands. "I like girls, I just...I'm not..." Jesus, he was flustered.

"You're a virgin?" River's face paled as he swallowed again,

then rubbed his palms on his jeans, letting out a deep breath, and Skye wondered if he had overstepped. He hadn't meant to make his roommate uncomfortable. Shit. "Hey, it's not a problem. I'm not gonna judge you for being a virgin any more than you are judging me for being gay, okay?"

Those blue eyes met his again, darker this time, like the depths of the ocean. Skye's heart sank when he saw the pain behind them. "Can we not talk about this, please?"

Now it was Skye's turn to flush. "Sure, yeah. I'm sorry." Was River embarrassed or ashamed about being a virgin?

"You said you had more stuff to carry in?" River asked, and Skye was thankful for the change of subject. He nodded and grabbed his keys, River close behind him as they made their way to the parking lot.

Skye couldn't help noticing the way River's eyes lit up when he saw Skye's car.

"Oh, wow." His roommate's smile was genuine as he stared. God, that was a sexy smile. Full, and bright, and absolutely beautiful. It suited him and Skye knew right then and there that he wanted to see more of it.

"She's a 1969 Newport," Skye said proudly. "She used to be my dad's, but my mom kept her maintained after he died and I got her after I got my license."

River's eyes met his. "You lost your dad?"

Skye nodded. "It was a long time ago. I was four and I barely remember him."

"I'm sorry," River said, and Skye could tell he meant it, in a way that maybe even suggested that he knew what it was like to lose a parent. And then Skye remembered that River had come here with his aunt.

His chest tightened, emotions washing over him that he hadn't felt in a long time. He'd always missed his dad, wondered what his life would have been like if Jacob Mckenzie were still around, and had always wanted to make his father proud even after he'd been gone for years. "Thank you."

River turned back to the car, his smile back, but not quite as wide. "She's beautiful," he murmured, running his fingers gently over the hood. Skye smiled, filled with pride once again.

"You have a car?" he asked. River shook his head.

"We drove my aunt's station wagon here, but she's taking it back with her when she leaves."

"So you won't have a car on campus?"

"Nah, but it's okay. I'll have my bike, and I don't mind walking. It's good exercise."

Skye couldn't believe the words that came out of his mouth next. "You're welcome to borrow her, if you need to get somewhere, church or whatever."

River's eyes widened as their gazes met. "Are you sure?" He seemed stunned, and honestly Skye was pretty fucking stunned himself, but yeah, he was sure.

He shrugged. Normally he wouldn't let another soul drive his car, but for some reason he didn't have a problem with lending it to River. There was just something about him that Skye trusted, and letting River get behind the wheel of his baby, that didn't bother him at all.

River gave Skye that breathtaking smile again. "Thanks."

～

PRESENT DAY

Hey, what's your ETA? Skye texted as he walked out of his bedroom. ***Are you coming home for dinner?***

He couldn't help but smile at how ridiculously domestic it sounded. But honestly, that's what living with River was like. They'd developed a comfortable routine over the years. Skye enjoyed cooking and did pretty much all of it. River hated cooking, so he did the cleanup afterwards instead. Skye took care of the maintenance on the condo and both of their cars because he was good at it, and River knew shit all about cars.

He took care of the dishwasher, the vacuuming, mopping, dusting, etc. and both men did their own laundry, and cleaned their own bathrooms, because River had informed Skye, when they first moved in, that he was not going anywhere near Skye's bathroom without a hazmat suit. Skye, for his part, thought River was being a bit dramatic with that particular statement. His bathroom really wasn't that bad, it just wasn't pristine, like River's.

All in all though, it was a pretty sweet arrangement, and the best part was that Skye was living with his best friend.

River had come out of his shell some in the past several years that Skye had known him. He was still shy and reserved around strangers and didn't enjoy big crowds, but he was much more relaxed and at ease around Skye than he had been when they first met. When it was just him and River, or if they were hanging out with their friends Nick and Jenna, Skye got to see the real River; the River with the contagious laughter and a smile that lit up the room. The fun, sarcastic River that liked to joke and make people laugh. The tender, sweet River who was the first to comfort someone who was hurting. River didn't trust easily but he loved fiercely, and if you were fortunate enough to make it into his small group of friends, you would have a loyal, faithful, amazing friend in return.

Depends, River texted back a moment later. ***What are you making***? *Smile emoji*

Haven't decided yet, Skye replied. ***Depends on if you'll be here.***

I think I'm gonna go out with my coworkers when I get off, actually. They've been inviting me for a while and I feel bad that I haven't taken them up on it yet.

Where are you going?

Jake's.

Jake's was the local hangout. They would go there at least twice a month with Nick and Jenna, who they had met in college. Even though River never drank due to the antidepressants he was on that didn't mix well with alcohol, he still enjoyed the atmosphere, the food, and the people. ***Enjoy yourself. And don't do anything I wouldn't do.*** *winky face emoji.* ***I'll see you later.***

Since River wasn't coming home for dinner, Skye decided to keep it simple. He cooked a hot dog on the stove and grabbed some greasy potato chips that he knew he wouldn't be able to eat with his roommate there, without getting a lecture.

He took a seat on the couch in front of the television, turned Star Trek Voyager on, on Netflix, and pulled the lever on the side of the couch to recline the seat.

Their mismatched furniture was certainly nothing to brag about, but it worked for them. Mostly garage sale finds and a few odds and ends from Ikea, along with one or two pieces of furniture that River had made himself, like the bookshelf that stood in the corner, and the two end tables that sat on either side of the sofa.

With River's carpentry skills, Skye had always wondered why he hadn't started his own business. His work was beautiful and Skye knew he could make a decent living with his talent.

But River had said that he wanted to help people, so he'd chosen physical therapy as a vocation instead, and Skye had to admit, he did seem to enjoy his work, and he was good at it. He'd spent an extra three years in school after undergrad to get his degree in PT, so he'd certainly wanted it badly enough, and he'd worked as a physical therapist in town for the past two years. Skye couldn't be more proud of him.

He enjoyed his work, too, though if you had ever told him when he was younger that he'd be teaching middle school history in a small town in rural Indiana he would have laughed in your face. Yet, here he was. And yes, the students were a handful sometimes, but despite how exhausting teaching was, it was just as rewarding, and he felt like he was making a difference in his students' lives, however small. And if any of them were struggling like he had been at that age, whether with their sexuality or something else, Skye hoped to be a source of support and encouragement for them.

It was rough at that age, making friends, figuring out who you were, wanting so badly to fit in and belong. He still wouldn't say all these years later that even he had it completely figured out, but he'd become more comfortable with his sexuality, partly because of River. River had accepted and befriended him without question and that had made his college years much easier than his high school ones, having a roommate who was so supportive. Still, none of Skye's students had ever known he was gay in the four years he'd had his job. Not because Skye was ashamed of who he was, but because it had never really come up. It was still just a close circle of coworkers who knew, plus Jenna, Nick, and River, and Skye's mom and younger brother.

Thinking of his brother made Skye think of his girlfriend and how they would probably be engaged soon. He was incredibly happy for them both but also a tad bit jealous if he was being honest. Jaden was twenty-four and would be starting a family soon and Skye was twenty-eight and still waiting for Mr. Right to come along.

He'd hooked up with plenty of guys over the years, dated a few times, but nothing that lasted. He wasn't sure if it was because he wasn't ready for a real relationship, or if none of those guys had been the one.

He finished his meal and set his plate aside on the end table. A sigh escaped him as he thought of all the papers he still had to grade before the evening was over. He really should just stop assigning homework. Grabbing the bag off of the chair he'd thrown it on earlier, he dragged it back over to the couch, plopping himself down once again. Pulling out the papers on the American Revolution, he groaned when he saw the very first one. "Seriously, guys, how hard is it to write your name on the top?"

After the process of elimination and doing his best to try and place the student's handwriting, he wrote *Chris* on the top himself, with a question mark next to it.

He wasn't sure how long he worked on grading papers, but after getting up once to use the bathroom and another time to get a quick snack and try to clear his head a little with an episode of *Queer Eye*, he noticed that his shoulder was starting to ache, as was his upper back.

He graded a few more papers, but when the pain grew worse he put his things down and started to rotate his arm and shoulder back and forth, wincing at the tightness in his traps. "That's not normal."

"What's not normal?" A deep voice said, and Skye turned to see River tossing his keys into the basket by the door just as he had done earlier, then sliding off his shoes and leaving them on the mat. "You okay?"

"Yeah, just sore, I guess." Skye winced and rubbed his shoulder. "You're home already, huh?"

"It's nine-thirty." River gestured to the clock.

"Huh. Guess I was grading papers longer than I thought." He continued rubbing at his shoulder, trying to ease the tension, and grimacing as he did.

"Do you want me to rub it?" River asked. When Skye gave him a smirk, River just rolled his eyes. "Your shoulder, Skye."

Skye chuckled. "Yeah, that'd be awesome."

River slid his jacket off and tossed it on a chair, putting those glorious biceps on display. Skye was not drooling. He wasn't. Yes, he was still insanely attracted to his best friend. River knew it, too. Skye hadn't exactly been subtle over the years about how gorgeous he thought River was. He may have innocently flirted with him on occasion, and River may have caught Skye checking him out a time or two. Maybe.

"Get on the floor then. And take your shirt off."

"Ooh, I like it when you get bossy," Skye teased. He grabbed the hem of his T-shirt and pulled it up and over his head, tossing it aside as River made his way over to him. Then he pushed the leg rest of the couch in and slid onto the floor.

"Oh brother," River mumbled, sitting himself down on the couch behind Skye and gently starting to massage his upper back and shoulders. "Are you hard up or something?"

"Not particularly," Skye said with a laugh.

"Really?" River asked, and Skye could hear him smiling. "'Cause you're sounding pretty horny to me. How long has it been since you got laid?"

Skye chuckled. "Too damn long, honestly." It had been months, in fact, since Skye had seen any action, but he wasn't really interested in finding any, either, and the *why* part of that was bugging him, so he tried not to think about it too hard. Normally on a Friday night he'd be at a bar or a club, finding a guy to bring home or to go home with, but lately he'd found himself preferring to spend his evenings alone with River, and having sex with a random guy just didn't appeal to him like it used to.

"Well, maybe you should fix that soon so you can stop hitting on me," River teased. He started digging his thumb into the knot next to Skye's shoulder.

"Ow, ow, ow," Skye repeated, tensing up and leaning forward to get away from the torture.

"Man, you're tight," River said as Skye winced. "Relax, Skye, or it won't help. Try to breathe through it. You've got a nasty trigger point here."

"Riv, can you take off the ring?" Skye asked.

"Oh, sorry." His hands left Skye's back and Skye found that he missed the touch immediately, but a second later they were there again, ring gone, resting on the coffee table now. The ring River had worn for the last twelve years. The one that told him to "Rise." It reminded River that he was tougher than any battle he faced. That no matter what life threw at him, he could and would rise above it.

Skye did his best to relax his shoulders and closed his eyes. Moments later he felt the knot start to loosen. He let out a deep breath and hung his head as River's expert hands moved further up his traps. God, it felt good. River's hands were strong and warm, and soft, and they were practically putting Skye to sleep.

"God, River, you have magic hands," he murmured as he felt them on both sides of his upper back now, and the base of his neck, releasing tension he hadn't even realized he'd been carrying.

"I take it you're feeling better, then?"

Skye nodded, but just barely. He was really starting to doze off now.

"I think we need to get you to bed." River's hands left Skye's back once again, and the other man stood. He reached down and grabbed Skye's arm, pulling him to his feet. Skye didn't even care that he was tenting in his pants from the massage. He'd received his share of massages from River over the years and knew it was normal. He wobbled a little bit but River kept him steady as he walked Skye to his room and tucked him into bed.

"Thanks, Riv," Skye mumbled into his pillow, almost incoherently as River turned off the bedside lamp.

"Goodnight, Skye," River said, and left the room, closing the door behind him.

CHAPTER 2

Skye

Skye wasn't sure how much later it was when he woke to a warm body sidling up next to him, and River's strong arm draped over his waist. The other man buried his nose in Skye's neck, and Skye became immediately more alert when he felt River trembling against him, his breath hitching.

Fuck.

Skye sat up and turned on the lamp on his nightstand. When he looked over at his roommate, his heart shattered at the sight of the tears sliding down River's cheeks.

"Hey." Skye's voice was soft as he laid down and pulled River to him. The other man's body shook as he sobbed.

River didn't share Skye's bed very often but when he did it was because he'd had another nightmare. They were less frequent now than they had been in college, but they still happened and he had a tough time getting back to sleep afterwards. Skye had told his friend a long time ago that he could wake him when he was having a hard time. River hated to do it because he didn't want to inconvenience Skye or make him lose sleep, but Skye didn't give a fuck about that. And he'd never seen his roommate as an inconvenience, even with all of his struggles and heartache. He just wanted River to be okay.

"I'm so sorry," he said as he held his friend and ran his fingers through his dark hair. "You're safe, angel." His heart ached for his best friend. And his anger returned every single time he thought about what those bastards had done to him. How they had robbed him, humiliated him, violated him, in the worst possible way.

Skye couldn't think of anyone more worthy or deserving of everything good the world had to offer than River. River deserved peace, joy, and hope in abundance. He deserved love. He deserved the sun, the moon and all the stars.

His roommate had a history, one that burdened him and was not of his choosing. There were a lot of scars there. Deep ones. Ones that might never fade. But Skye did what he could, when he could, to make sure River knew that he was there for him. So now, he held him and let him cry, let him feel, let him grieve what had been taken from him all those years ago.

~

TEN YEARS AGO

"So, your aunt seems pretty nice," Skye said. It was mid October and he and River were sitting on their beds, facing each other, both working on class assignments. "Do you live with her?" River's aunt Jodi had just left a few hours earlier after visiting for Parent's Weekend and had headed back to Cincinnati.

"Yeah, since I was ten," River replied.

Skye hesitated before asking, "Are your parents around?"

There was a long pause and Skye was afraid he'd put his foot in his mouth. "Sorry, I shouldn't have asked that. Sometimes my mouth just runs away with me."

"No, it's okay." River seemed a little hesitant but his eyes met Skye's. "They died in a car accident when I was ten. I went to live with my aunt after that."

"Oh, shit. That must have been hard. I know how tough it was losing my dad. I can't imagine losing both of my parents."

"Yeah, it sucked pretty bad." River let out a heavy breath. "Still does sometimes."

"Do you like living with your aunt, though? She seems pretty cool."

River gave him a soft smile. "I mean, I would have preferred my parents, but yeah, she is pretty cool. It was hard, though, moving to Cincinnati. I grew up around here and once my parents died I had to move away from everything I'd known, start over in a new school and everything, new church. That was hard. I really missed my friends."

"Yeah, I can imagine. You made new friends, though, right?" Skye couldn't imagine River not having friends. The guy was funny, kind, and compassionate. Who wouldn't want to be friends with him?

River shrugged. "A few. But it wasn't easy. I was kinda nerdy, and quiet. Didn't always fit in. And I really missed my parents so I think the emotional struggle of that just made it harder for me to connect with other kids. I didn't want to talk about it, and they didn't really understand. Kinda made me more of an outcast. I got really depressed, actually." He tapped his pencil on his notebook and bit his lower lip, his gaze not meeting Skye's. River was definitely what Skye would consider shy, but Skye had managed to bring him out of his shell a bit already and really enjoyed talking to him. It sounded like he hadn't had it easy though, and that unsettled Skye.

"But you're better now?" he asked, hopefully. He hated the idea of River suffering, hurting. They'd had their share of deep conversations and they'd grown pretty close in the short time they'd known each other. But this was the first time they had talked about River's family and his past. Skye had no idea his roommate had been through so much as a kid.

River shrugged. "My aunt got me into grief counseling when she saw what a hard time I was having, and that helped some. So middle school was easier. I had a good home, with my aunt. I never felt unwanted or unloved with her, so yeah, things got better, for a while."

Skye swallowed a lump in his throat and the back of his neck prickled. "For a while? What does that mean? Did something else happen?" His pulse quickened. River's gaze met Skye's briefly, but it was long enough for Skye to notice the pain in those beautiful sapphire eyes, the truth in them, before they fell to his lap again and he gripped the ring on his middle finger, twisting it around. Skye couldn't tell, but he thought River might be shaking slightly. Shit. Did he scare him? Did he overstep?

"Sorry," Skye apologized, seeing that his roommate was clearly uncomfortable. "That's not my business." Maybe he was pushing the limits of social boundaries. They hadn't known each other all that long. Two months, really, but it felt longer, in a good way. He enjoyed River's company, enjoyed his friendship, and he hated to see that he was hurting, or that his past might be tainted in some way. Skye desperately wanted to help. That's what he did. He helped. Especially when it came to people he cared about. And yeah, he cared about River.

They had spent a lot of time together over the past couple of months, doing homework together, playing video games, watching movies, talking about theology and religion, and politics, and River had never pushed any of his beliefs on Skye, but had always done his best to answer any questions Skye had without sounding pompous or assholish, or making Skye feel inferior. He'd offered to take Skye to church once and when Skye had politely declined River hadn't brought it up again. They had joined the Gay-Straight Alliance on campus together and had attended several of the events and made some awesome friends together.

But Skye wouldn't push River into saying anything he wasn't ready to say, so he just went back to doing his homework.

A minute later he heard sniffles and looked up to see River wiping his eyes from behind his glasses. Fuck. Skye was so stupid. So goddamn fucking stupid. Why did he have to open his big fat mouth? Even if something did happen, River was under no obligation whatsoever to talk to Skye about it. God, why couldn't he keep his mouth shut?

"Shit, Riv." Skye scooted off of his bed and moved over to sit on River's bed next to his feet. River drew his legs up and wrapped his arms around them, continuing to wipe tears from his eyes even as more fell. "Fuck, I'm so sorry. I'm such an idiot."

River shook his head and then buried his face in his arms as he sobbed, his shoulders shaking. Skye moved up the bed until he was sitting next to River, then wrapped his arms around his roommate. River stiffened slightly, but then relaxed in Skye's grip. "I'm here. You don't have to tell me anything you don't want to, but I'm here." To Skye's surprise River leaned into him, his head resting on Skye's shoulder, his tears sliding underneath the collar of Skye's shirt as he sobbed.

"I tried...but I couldn't...and they..." River was trembling as the words left his lips, his chest heaving. His eyes met Skye's and they were filled with so much grief and anguish.

Skye's stomach clenched as he felt the color draining from his face. Holy fuck. "Shit, River, I'm so sorry." He held River tighter, not knowing what else to say, or do. But River kept talking, so Skye kept listening.

"Some seniors in my high school when I was a sophomore." River had tears spilling down his cheeks as his body shook. "They knew I was a Christian, and a virgin, and they started out just making fun of me for it, calling me the "righteous kid," and that was annoying but I could tolerate it because saving myself for marriage was more important to me than their opinion, but then they took that away from me, Skye." His chest heaved again and he sucked in a breath. "Like a cruel prank. They ganged up on me, and I couldn't do anything. I felt so helpless, and I tried

to fight, and call for help but there were three of them and they just..." He sobbed harder, burying his face in Skye's shoulder. "They gagged me, and they kept saying that I would thank them when it was over and that they were doing me a favor. They humiliated me and treated it like a game." He shook even harder now, his body racked with sobs.

Skye's head was spinning from what River had told him. He felt nauseated, horrified, and enraged. "Fucking bastards," he snarled. He wanted to rage, to throw things. He wanted to find whoever those sick fucks were and rip their fucking throats out. Instead, he ran his fingers through River's hair as his roommate's tears soaked his shirt, and he sucked in harsh breaths. He didn't know what to say. What did you say when someone you cared about told you that they had been robbed of their innocence? "River, I can't even imagine. I'm so fucking sorry."

When River didn't stop shaking or crying, Skye squeezed him tighter. River melted into him even as his breath hitched. "You're safe," Skye said. "I promise. You're safe with me." He held his roommate tighter as his sobs diminished, and he noticed that River was starting to breathe more evenly now. No wonder he'd been so put off when Skye had asked him about his virginity the day they had met. Fuck, now he really felt like a grade A dick.

River lifted his head and wiped away his tears. "Thank you for trusting me enough to tell me," Skye told him. "You don't ever have to talk about anything if you don't want to, but I'm here if you do. I may not know the right thing to say all the time, but I'll listen for as long as you need me to."

River's gaze met his, his eyes red-rimmed as he wiped at his cheeks. "Thank you. I'm doing better than I was a year ago. Therapy has helped and so has my aunt." His chest heaved. "You and her are the only ones who know besides my therapist." He took a deep breath and let it out, wiping more tears away. "My faith has helped, but it's still really hard sometimes." His chest heaved again and another tear slipped free.

"River, how can you believe in a God who would let something like that happen to you?" Skye blurted, then instantly regretted his words. That wasn't what River needed to hear right now, but he just didn't understand. "I just don't get it."

River only gave a soft smile. "It took a long time for me not to blame Him, not to feel like He had abandoned me. But I realized how much He hated what had happened to me, how much He grieved for me. How angry He was. Reading the Bible, seeing God's promises, His truths, that He was there for me, that's what kept me going. If it hadn't been for that I probably would have given up a long time ago.

"I know you've been hurt, Skye, and you have a right to feel the way you do. You've been mistreated your entire life by people who claim to love God, who claim that God is love, but then turn around and spew hate, who are trying to take away your right to exist, to have a family, a job, who call you terrible things, because of your sexuality, and there is nothing okay with that. People do shitty things in the name of religion and in God's name. But the religion itself isn't evil because some of the people in it are, and God isn't evil because some of his so-called followers are. I don't believe God makes mistakes. And you are not a mistake. You are good, and God loves you exactly as you are."

Skye bit his lip and nodded. He wasn't sure what he thought about River's words at the moment. But something else tugged on his mind, too. "What do you mean you probably would have given up a long time ago if it hadn't been for your faith? Is that what these are from?" He slid his fingers over the scars on River's forearms. River twitched slightly but didn't pull away. He nodded. "It's been a while, but yeah, I used to self-harm. It was the only way I knew how to cope before I got some help."

"And the nightmares?" River looked at Skye, his eyes wide behind his glasses.

"Am I waking you?" He looked mortified. "Crap, I'm so sorry. I told my therapist I should have a single room but she insisted I was doing better and that it would be a good idea for *me to have a roommate. That it was an important step to take and all that. She didn't want me being alone and never making friends..." He looked like he was starting to panic and Skye shook his head.*

"Hey, don't worry about it." He rested his hand on River's arm. "I'm not upset. I just figured if you wanted me to wake you next time it happens, I will." River nodded, relaxing at Skye's touch. And Skye couldn't help feeling a sense of pride, that River did, in fact, feel safe with him. He would always, always make sure of that.

"What do you say we take a break from homework and watch a movie?" Skye said, thinking it was time for a change of topic. "I'll pop us some popcorn."

River gave a soft smile. "Star Wars?"

"A New Hope? That way I can drool over Harrison Ford." Skye waggled his eyebrows and River laughed. It was the most beautiful sound in the world, and Skye wanted more of it.

"Deal," River said.

~

It was a few days later when Skye woke to the sound of muffled cries coming from River's bed. He scooted out from under his covers and slid under River's. "Riv, you okay?" River turned and buried his face in Skye's shoulder as he sobbed once again, and Skye held him.

"I wanted to save myself for my wife. I wanted to choose who I gave myself to. They took that, Skye. They took my choice."

"Riv, look at me," Skye instructed gently.

When River pulled away, Skye could see the torment etched on his features and his chest ached. Goddamn, those assholes. He wanted to take River in his arms and make everything better, take away all of his hurt and suffering. What the fuck was wrong with people? How could anyone be so fucking sick and twisted? He couldn't imagine going through what River had gone through, and not letting it destroy him. He was incredible. A survivor. And so damn brave. What kind of courage and strength would it take to move forward after something like that; to face it and heal from it? Skye was so amazed by River, by anyone who had been a victim of assault or abuse, and the strength it must take to live day to day.

"I know how important saving sex for marriage is for you, okay?" Skye said. "But you need to remember something. What you just said there, about not being able to choose who you give yourself to, that's wrong. You do get to choose. You didn't give yourself to them. They took it. What they did was cruel and despicable, and you didn't deserve that. No one does. But you still get to choose who you give yourself to now. So if saving sex for marriage is still important to you, then hold on to that. And if your future wife doesn't understand that, then she doesn't deserve you."

River sniffled and Skye handed him a tissue. He blew his nose and wiped his tears. "Stay with me?" Skye could tell his roommate was a little embarrassed by the request, but he didn't mind one bit.

"Always." River snuggled up next to him and Skye held him. It wasn't long before they were both drifting to sleep.

∾

PRESENT DAY

River rarely talked about what happened. Occasionally he would let Skye know he was having a rough day, or had scheduled an appointment with his therapist—who he was now seeing on an as-needed basis—because he was struggling, but he hadn't given Skye any more details since that night ten years ago, and Skye hadn't asked him to share more, either. But River knew if he wanted to talk, or just climb into Skye's bed and cuddle, or cry, Skye was there; would always be there if River needed him.

River sniffled and Skye wiped his tears and pressed a kiss to his hair. His sobs diminished but he didn't pull away. "You know you can stay," Skye told him. His friend let out a shaky breath and clung to him. Skye felt River's nose against his neck. He rested his cheek against River's head and held him tightly as they drifted back to sleep.

The following morning when Skye woke, River was still next to him, sound asleep. They had separated during the night but River had stayed in his bed.

He looked so peaceful, and Skye hoped his dreams had been happier after he came to join Skye in his bed.

He stroked a finger over River's lightly stubbled cheek. River twitched, his eyes fluttering open, and Skye found himself staring into those gorgeous blue orbs.

"Morning, handsome." Skye traced his thumb down River's jaw and over his chin, and River let him, the feel of River's stubble under his fingertips sending shivers down his spine. There weren't many people who River felt comfortable enough with to let them get this close to him. But Skye was lucky enough to be one of them. "You're gonna be okay." River nodded.

Skye couldn't imagine the kind of fortitude it took to deal with everything River had to deal with every day, doing his best to live and be happy despite his past, despite his scars. To know he was loved and worthy, and that life could still be good, but he was determined to keep reminding his friend how strong he was, and that when he couldn't be strong anymore, he could lean on Skye.

"What do you say we start the day with a delicious break-fast cooked by yours truly?"

River nodded again. "Bacon and eggs sound good? Maybe hashbrowns?" Another nod. "You wanna shower while I cook?"

River's eyes glinted mischievously. "Actually I was gonna go for a run, if you want to join me."

Skye pressed a soft kiss to River's forehead. "You're so sweet, angel. But I would rather have my wisdom teeth yanked out and put back in."

River laughed and slid out of bed. "Breakfast when I get back?"

Skye nodded, and River headed to his own room to change, Skye assumed. He could still smell River's scent on the side of the bed he'd slept on even after he was gone. Watermelon and coconut. The smell of River.

He found himself burying his face in the pillow River had used before he realized what he was doing. What the actual hell? He shook his head and climbed out of bed, making his way to his own bathroom. If River was going running first then Skye had time to shower before he started breakfast.

After he stepped out of the shower he tried to tame his blond waves, but it was no use. They'd always been unruly, so he just let them be and they fell over his forehead and almost into his light green eyes. Since it was the weekend he decided to forgo shaving until Monday.

When he emerged fifteen minutes later with a towel wrapped around his waist, River was gone. Skye sauntered back to his own room and dressed in jeans and a T-shirt before he made his way to the kitchen. He turned on the Keurig and made himself a cup of coffee. He didn't need to start breakfast until River was in the shower.

He heard the sound of the front door opening and closing a few minutes later and his roommate meandered into the kitchen wearing joggers and a tank top that showcased those luscious biceps. Sweat clung to his skin, shirt plastered onto his back and chest, hair damp. He looked beautiful. He looked happy.

River gulped down water and then headed to his room. Minutes later, Skye heard the sound of his shower running.

He pulled out the griddle, then grabbed the eggs and bacon out of the fridge, along with a couple of potatoes, and got to work.

When River emerged again he was dressed in jeans and a T-shirt. He sat down on a stool at the bar overlooking the sink, his dark hair still damp from the shower and tousled from being towel dried. It was adorable.

Skye reached over the sink and handed him a plate of freshly cooked bacon, eggs, and hashbrowns, like he'd promised. Then he set a cup of coffee with a little bit of cream and no sugar in front of River, just the way he liked it, and River gave him a soft smile.

"You work today?" Skye asked.

"Yeah, noon to four, and then I'm hanging out with Anna. You?" River took a sip of coffee before starting in on his breakfast. Anna was the girl River had been dating for the past several months. She was kind, caring, but didn't take shit from anyone. There was nothing wrong with her, honestly, but for some reason Skye felt himself bristling at the mention of her name. She had been spending more and more time at their condo lately, and the last time she was over Skye had hid away in his room after half an hour of watching her and River cuddling and kissing on the sofa. He just couldn't stomach it anymore. When he brought it up to Nick and Jenna, they told him he was jealous. What the fuck did they know? Skye wasn't jealous. Why would he be jealous? River was his best friend. He just didn't like to watch PDA, that was all.

"I think I better make a grocery run," he said. "Then I've got more papers to grade and lesson plans to make for next week. Thinking about hanging out with Jenna and Nick tonight. You and Anna could join us if you want."

"I'll see," River said, taking one more swig of his coffee. "I can go to the grocery store with you if you want. I need stuff too."

"Sure. Just let me pee first."

When he walked out of the bathroom, River was loading the dishwasher. He smiled at Skye and Skye swore butterflies filled his stomach. His friend seemed to be doing better.

"Almost done," River said. Skye grabbed his keys and wallet and slipped his shoes on as he waited for River to finish, then they were on their way out the door.

CHAPTER 3

Skye

"Good grief." Jenna rolled her eyes at Skye from where she was sitting next to Nick on the other side of the table. They were at *Jake's* and River and Anna had just gone up to the bar to get the group some more drinks. Anna had her hand on the small of River's back and he leaned over and whispered something in her ear, making her laugh. He looked genuinely happy.

Skye wanted to punch something.

"You're hopeless." Jenna took a sip of her soda and Skye glared at her.

Nick laughed. He was a big guy, six foot three, and all muscle, with short dark hair and hazel eyes. Very handsome. Despite his intimidating appearance though, he was a total teddy bear, reserved and quiet, like River, even more so, really, and wouldn't hurt a fly.

Jenna, on the other hand, was about as sassy and feisty as they came, and super outgoing. The four of them had met in college at one of the events for the Gay-Straight Alliance. Jenna was bi, Nick was straight. Skye loved them both to death but they drove him insane.

"Just what is that supposed to mean?" he said. They both laughed and Skye glared harder.

"You have been staring at him all night," Jenna said, leaning over the table and talking in a hushed voice, her cleavage showing under the v of her blouse. Heat radiated up Skye's neck and across his face.

"I have not." He totally had. And he was thinking that asking River and Anna to join them had been an incredibly stupid idea, because the more he had to watch them flirt and touch and be all...them, the more tense he got and the more his stomach knotted. What the fuck was that about? Since when had he been so fixated on River? And why couldn't he let him and Anna be without getting so...so...

"Jealous," Jenna said, and Skye flinched. Had he said that out loud?

"What?"

"You're jealous. Admit it."

"I am not. Why would I be jealous? It's River. He's my best friend."

Jenna exchanged a glance with Nick. Her dark hair was cut short and her green eyes sparkled. She had large hoop earrings in her ears that swayed when she turned her head. Or really, if she moved at all. Skye was pretty sure they were as big as her face. He was also pretty sure she was trying not to laugh again.

"You're totally jealous, bro," Nick said. "Just tell him how you feel and get it over with. Watching you is painful."

"There is nothing to tell," Skye hissed, as River and Anna made their way back to the table.

There wasn't. He swore to God there wasn't. River was his friend. That was all.

~

"Okay guys, time's up, pass your papers forward," Skye said on Monday morning, as he stood in front of the students' desks and motioned with his hands.

There were a few groans and some last minute scribbles

before the papers started coming forward, and he collected them.

"Are we going to have a pop quiz every week?" Amanda, a girl with short dark hair asked in dismay.

"If I tell you that it kind of defeats the purpose, don't you think?" Skye grinned at her but she just rolled her eyes.

Another girl raised her hand. She had short blonde hair, freckles and braces, and was one of the most hard working students in the class.

"Yes, Gwen?" he asked.

"Did you grade our papers yet?"

"I did. You'll get them back at the end of the period. Which reminds me, there are some of you who need to remember to write your names on your homework. I'm gonna start deducting points for it if it keeps being a problem. It takes me long enough to grade them without having to go through them all and figure out who they belong to. Got it?"

There were some nods and a few groans.

"Okay, open your books—" Skye was cut off by his phone buzzing in his pants pocket.

"Mr. Mckenzie, your ass is calling," Gwen said with a chuckle, and the students laughed as he reached for it and silenced it without bothering to check who it was. He didn't get calls during the day unless they were spam, because everyone knew he was at work. And if it was an emergency they would call back or call the front office.

Only seconds later his phone was buzzing again.

"Maybe you should answer it," another student, Kevin, said from the back row.

Skye held up a finger and checked the caller ID. When he saw that it was the same unknown number both times he started to worry.

"I'm gonna step into the hall for a second," he said. "You guys behave."

When he got out to the hall he swiped the phone to

answer it, his heart racing as he put it to his ear. "Hello?" His voice was not nearly as sturdy as he was trying to make it.

"Hello, is this Skyelar Mckenzie?" the female asked, and his heart rate picked up even more.

"Yes," he managed. "Who's this?"

"I'm calling from South Memorial Hospital. We have a River Dawson here and you are his emergency contact."

"Oh, God." His stomach roiled and his chest squeezed painfully. "What happened? Is he okay?" His hands were shaking and he felt like his knees were about to give out on him.

"I'm afraid there's been an accident. He's stable, and conscious. Are you able to come?" Skye's breath left him in a relieved puff of air and he ran his fingers through his hair. Fuck. *Breathe,* he told himself. *Breathe.* He's okay. He has to be okay.

"Yes, yes, of course," he said, trying to stop shaking. God, he didn't think he'd ever been more scared in his life.

"Good. Just ask for him when you get there."

"Okay." He hung up the phone and called the front office to explain the situation and see if someone could watch his classes for the rest of the day, and then he went back into his room with his best 'everything's fine' face on for his students and told them he would be taking the rest of the day off for personal reasons.

"Is everything okay?" Gwen asked, and he heard the genuine concern in her voice.

"It will be," he said, giving her a small smile. "I have a friend who was in an accident and I need to go see him. But yes, he's okay."

He saw lots of concerned looks on their faces but didn't take the time to explain anything more. Another staff member showed up shortly and Skye grabbed his jacket, keys and messenger bag, and headed out the door.

His hands were shaking as he drove to the hospital, and his heart pounded. *God, River, please be okay*, he pleaded.

∼

Skye was relieved to find that River was sitting up in his bed, reclined, sipping on water when he arrived. There were no doctors or nurses in the room at the time. He looked peaked, and a little shaken, a bandage on the side of his head and some mild cuts and bruises, but he seemed okay. Skye, however, was a different story. When he thought he might have lost River in the brief second on the phone before the nurse told him he was conscious, Skye couldn't breathe. He honestly didn't know what he would do if something happened to his best friend.

Seeing him now, Skye just wanted to rush over and take River in his arms, but he didn't. He knocked on the open door and River's head shot up, his Adam's apple bobbing as he swallowed his water. He pushed his glasses up on his nose with one finger. Skye was kind of surprised the glasses had made it through the accident unscathed.

"Skye," River said, his voice filled with surprise. "What are you doing here?"

Skye's eyebrows furrowed. "Are you fucking kidding me?" He walked over and set his things down on one of the chairs in the room. "You're in the hospital. They called me. They said you had an accident."

"Yeah, but I'm okay. You didn't have to come. You should be at work." He slowly reached over to set the cup of water on the tray next to his hospital bed, wincing as his face screwed up, and he rested a hand on his left side.

"Yeah, aces, I can tell," Skye said. "How are you really? And don't shit with me."

River sighed. "I'm pretty sure I have some broken ribs. Or at least cracked. It hurts just to breathe. And bending or twisting is even worse. I have the mother of all headaches and my ankle is throbbing."

"That's all?" Skye said. "Jesus, you don't even need to be here." River smirked at him.

"What happened? That phone call scared the hell out of me." For a brief moment he'd even wondered if River had tried to hurt himself, but looking at him now he was certain that wasn't the case. The woman on the phone had just said "accident", though. That could have meant anything, and River had been down lately. In all the time Skye had known River, his friend had never tried to hurt himself, so he knew it was unlikely, but still, not impossible, given his history. The thought had shaken him and he was still trying to calm his racing heart, and his nerves. River was here. He was safe.

River's eyes met his. "I'm fine." Skye's face must have been radiating concern because River reached over and squeezed his arm. "It was scary, but it could have been a lot worse. Someone tried to change lanes and didn't see me, so I got hit and ran into someone else, and we both swerved off the side of the road. I was unconscious when they found me, which was pretty scary because I don't remember hitting my head or anything, but they got me to wake up pretty quickly. I think my car looks worse than I do."

Fuck, that's scary. Skye could have lost him. River...he... fuck. Skye managed a small smile. He didn't want to panic and freak his friend out. He was okay. He was fine. A few cracked ribs was nothing compared to what it could have been. Jesus, why wouldn't his heart stop racing? "You sure you're okay?" he managed to ask, giving himself credit for how not freaked out he sounded. "I would be pretty shaken after something like that."

"I am shaken," River admitted. "Not sure I want to be behind the wheel of a car again any time soon."

"Have they done imaging and all that yet? Did they check for a concussion?"

"Yeah, I'm waiting on the results. I wouldn't be surprised if I have a concussion, and I'm pretty sure I have a broken ankle, too, with how much it's hurting."

"Right, I'll shut up. Just rest. But I'm staying until I talk to a doctor and find out what's going on with you and how long you'll be here," Skye insisted.

River nodded, lowering his head to the pillow and closing his eyes.

Skye sat in the remaining chair and pulled out the pop quizzes to grade, realizing as he did, that he never did give his students their papers back as he'd promised. Oh well. This was more important. River was always more important than anything else in his life, it seemed.

This gorgeous man with his sapphire eyes that make even the deepest blues of the ocean pale in comparison. Those thick, full lips, the light dusting of stubble along his face that hadn't been there when they met all those years ago, but made him even more handsome now, Skye thought. His long, dark eyelashes that fell just above his cheekbones now that his eyes were closed. The dark, almost raven hair. God, he was beautiful. River Dawson was the most breathtakingly beautiful man in the world, inside and out.

As Skye watched him, asleep in the hospital bed, River's chest rising and falling with every beautiful, perfect breath, he couldn't deny it any longer. Jenna and Nick were right. He was more than just attracted to River. He was falling in love with River. The realization hit him so hard it knocked the breath from his lungs. His chest ached and tears stung his eyes.

With every fiber of his being, he was falling in love with his best friend. With his compassion and kindness, with his humor, his gentleness and his strength, with his courage and resilience. He was falling in love with River's beautiful smile and his infectious laughter. If he had the balls to admit it to himself, he'd been falling in love with River for years, but trying so very hard not to, for two very good reasons.

First of all, River was religious. He believed in all that God and Jesus and praying stuff, doing Bible studies and going to church on Sunday mornings, and Skye didn't. He loved and respected River for his faith, and the fact that he was a Christian who loved God but also loved the LGBTQ community made Skye respect him even more, even if he didn't agree with his beliefs. He knew River accepted him for who he was and he had never asked Skye to change, but having a best friend who didn't share your faith was one thing. Having that person be your life partner was different, right? Surely someone who shared River's faith would be a better fit for him. And neither of them should have to compromise who they were for the sake of a relationship. If River ever developed feelings for Skye, could they make it work without giving up a part of themselves? He wanted to believe they could. But did it matter? Because the second reason, and the most blatantly obvious one, was the fact the River was straight.

But regardless of both of those things, Skye felt his resolve crumbling. That giant wall of ice he'd built in his head to protect himself from falling for River wasn't as strong as it had been ten years ago, or five years ago, or three. It was melting now, and he didn't know what to do to stop it.

I'm not falling in love with him. I'm not. I'm not. I...I can't.

Falling in love with River would only lead to heartache.

~

Skye was awoken by a knock on the door. He didn't even remember falling asleep, but the sound startled him and he jumped as a very undignified snort left him, all of his papers falling from his lap and onto the floor. He grabbed his neck, which was sore from sleeping in the chair, and groaned.

River was slower to regain consciousness, his eyes fluttering open. He looked a little dazed and pretty exhausted still.

Looking at the clock on the wall, Skye realized it'd been a couple of hours since he arrived.

"Hi, I'm Dr. Rosemary," a woman in a white coat said, reaching her hand out to Skye.

"Skye," he told her, shaking her hand, then proceeded to pick up the scattered papers.

"How are you feeling, Mr. Dawson?" Dr. Rosemary asked, turning to River, clipboard in hand.

"I've been better," River replied, groggily.

"Yeah, that's not surprising," Dr. Rosemary said. "Are you okay with Skye staying while I discuss your results?" River nodded and she continued.

"You have three cracked ribs, and a mild concussion, and your ankle is broken. Nothing too severe, so no surgery required, but still, lots of rest in your future. What do you do for work?"

"I'm a physical therapist," River said.

Dr. Rosemary grinned at him. "Well then, I guess I don't really need to tell you what to do to take care of yourself. But I will. Ice, rest, more ice, and more rest. Okay? We'll send you home with some breathing exercises to do for your ribs, every couple of hours. If it's painful you can put a pillow against your ribs to help. But it's important that you do them to reduce the risk of pneumonia or other complications. Don't push yourself. Start working on your ankle once it's ready, and not before. In the meantime we'll put it in a cast and give you some crutches to get around on for a while. Using the crutches with cracked ribs will be uncomfortable at best, so only move around if you need to. Do you have stairs in your house?"

"No, thankfully," River said.

"I can prescribe you some pain relievers," Dr. Rosemary said. "And of course, no driving until your ankle and ribs are better. I assume you're in good hands at home." She nodded at Skye.

"Oh, yeah, he'll be fine," Skye promised with a small smile. "How long before he can get back to work?"

"We'll be monitoring the ankle injury every few weeks or so to make sure it's healing properly, but the process itself could take up to 6 weeks before he's able to put any kind of weight back on it. In the meantime he can use crutches if he needs to, but it's best to keep the ankle elevated and be icing it as much as possible. Once he's able to put weight on it again he can move from crutches to a boot. It could take several months before he's fully functional again and he'll have to keep up with his PT at home, but he'll get there. I would recommend taking as much time off as possible to rest and heal. Talk to your employer and human resources where you work and see what their policies are and how much they are willing to work with you. But in your line of work and with the injuries you've sustained, I'd say four weeks minimum off work to recover. And of course I'll give you a note." She looked to River again and he nodded solemnly.

Skye knew this wouldn't be easy for River, being practically bed bound for weeks, not being able to work or go places with friends. Not being able to go to church or his weekly Bible study. Why did it seem like every shitty thing in the world happened to his best friend? And yet he had to remind himself that it could be worse. River could be dead right now, instead of sitting in the hospital bed next to him, looking forlorn.

"There was one other thing we saw on the x-rays we took," Dr. Rosemary continued. "We don't know if this is from the accident or from an earlier injury. Have you had any falls recently, Mr. Dawson?"

"Um, no, not recently," River said, the surprise evident in his voice. He pushed his glasses up his nose again even though they hadn't moved. He shifted slightly in his bed and then winced, grabbing his injured side. "I had a fall in college, about seven years ago," he grunted out.

"Can you expand on that?"

"It was winter, and I was walking down some icy steps. I slipped and landed pretty hard on my butt. It hurt like crap at the time for a solid thirty minutes or so and kinda knocked the wind out of me. I was sore for a while but I just kinda walked it off, and after that I was fine," River explained.

"Well, if it's not bothering you then it's really not a problem, but your tailbone is dislocated," the doctor said. She showed them the image. Sure enough, River's tailbone was deviated to the left a bit. "It's possible the accident just exacerbated the issue and it wasn't this bad before. Do you have any pain when you sit, either in the low back or coccyx, or any pain during intercourse?"

River flinched and flushed bright red. And when the doctor's eyes shifted to Skye and then back to River, Skye felt his cheeks heating, too.

"No!" Skye said at the same time as his roommate.

"No, he's not, I mean, we're not," River stammered, gesturing between them. He winced again, his face looking drawn and pale.

"We're not together," Skye said more calmly. "Just roommates."

"Oh, I'm so sorry." Dr. Rosemary blushed herself. "My mistake. Well, if it does become painful for whatever reason we've given you the information for an orthopedist with your discharge papers. We'll get those here soon and you should be ready to leave within the next couple of hours. Take care of yourself." She smiled at them and left.

"That was awkward," River said, his face flushed yet again. He didn't make eye contact with Skye as he bit his lip.

"Whatever," Skye shrugged, and River glanced at him. "She thought we were together. It's not a big deal. I didn't know you had that fall back in college, by the way. You never told me that."

River rested back against his pillows again. He spoke

softly. "Didn't really seem important. Besides, what was I supposed to say? 'Hey, Skye, guess what, I fell on my ass today on my way to class. Everyone saw me. It was super embarrassing and my bum hurt like hell the whole way there. By the way, how's your Philosophy class going?'"

Skye couldn't hold back his chuckle. "Smart ass." River gave him a small smile and his chest constricted. That smile made him weak in the knees and he didn't see it nearly enough.

"I texted everyone while you were asleep," Skye told his friend. "Nick and Jenna said there are easier ways to get out of our weekly game nights."

That made River laugh, but Skye immediately regretted it when his friend winced in pain. Shit.

"Sorry," he grimaced. "They also said to let them know if we need anything. I couldn't text Anna 'cause I don't have her number, so you probably want to do that."

River nodded and Skye handed him his phone. It took him longer than normal to send the text but he finally did and put his phone aside again, already looking peaked.

"Your Aunt Jodi offered to come too, but I told her she didn't need to make the drive until we knew what was happening."

There was a moment of silence before Skye spoke again. He looked down and fiddled with the pen in his hands. "Did it bother you?" he asked. He felt River's gaze on him and looked up.

"Did what bother me?" River's blue eyes were soft, searching his, those full lips puckered ever so slightly, just begging to be kissed. *Stop it*. Skye glanced down. *Ice wall. Ice wall. Very, very thick ice wall. With a couple of dinosaurs in front of it and a tank and some sumo wrestlers, too.*

He knew better than this. He knew better than to ask this question. Why was he stepping down this road? He knew it was dangerous. Still, he found himself saying, "Her, assuming we were together. Did it bother you?" he felt his throat closing tightly. The room suddenly got ten degrees colder. His heart rate spiked as he waited for what seemed like an eternity for River to answer.

"I don't know," River said, honestly, unable to meet Skye's gaze as if he were ashamed. "I don't know," he repeated. "I don't know what was going through my mind when I said 'no' to her question about intercourse. I don't know if it was because it was directed to you and me and I found it disturbing because we're friends and not lovers, or if I was just afraid of what *you* would think when she said that because I wanted to make it clear on your behalf we weren't together, because I didn't want to make *you* feel uncomfortable." He looked Skye in the eyes now. "Honestly, I think that just the *mention* of me having sex with another man is hard for me, after what happened to me in high school, and maybe that's what I reacted to most of all. Not you. Or us."

Jerk. Skye was a big fat jerk. Here he was, trying to size up their relationship, putting River under a spotlight, after he'd just been in an accident that had left him immobile for the next six weeks, and then he gets bombarded with memories of his past. Skye was such a jerk.

"River, I'm so sorry," he said. "That makes perfect sense, and I shouldn't have asked you that. It doesn't matter."

River tilted his head to the side in a way that Skye found so very endearing. "Of course it does." His voice was so sincere. "If I claim to love and advocate for the queer community I shouldn't be ashamed or disgusted to be counted as a part of it, whether on purpose or by accident. I don't blame you for asking."

Skye gave him a sideways grin. But he almost wished River hadn't said that, because now, one of the sumo wrestlers Skye had put in front of the ice wall was gone.

CHAPTER 4

River

"Stay here," Skye demanded, putting the car in park and turning to River. "I'll get the crutches out of the back seat and bring them to you.

"River, I mean it," he added, when River opened the passenger door and shoved it open even further with his foot, putting his good ankle on the ground. "You take one more step and I'm spitting in your dinner."

River sighed and rested his head against the back of the seat as Skye came around to the passenger side with the crutches. He set them against the car and wrapped his arm around River's torso. River could tell how careful Skye was being, trying not to touch his cracked ribs as he lifted him out of the car and then handed him the crutches. Using them was painful, just like the doctor said it would be, and River had to keep from grunting and hissing as he made his way up the pathway to the front door, Skye right beside him the entire time like he was afraid River would trip and faceplant. It was driving River nuts how much his roommate was fussing over him and how attentive he was being, but he knew it came from a place of love, so he didn't say anything.

Seriously, though, River was going to go crazy if Skye

hovered over him like this for the next six weeks. It was bad enough that he'd needed his help getting dressed before they left the hospital. Skye had taken it in stride but River knew it was awkward for him, too. He'd seen the blush creep up the other man's cheeks as he'd helped slide River's pants on, and River had been wondering if he could possibly get away with staying in the same clothes for the next six weeks to avoid that embarrassment all over again.

Skye unlocked the door and they stepped inside. "Let's get you comfortable and then I'm gonna make a run to the store for some ice packs and to pick up your meds."

River sighed. He hated the idea of Skye picking up anything for him. He hated feeling this helpless and needy. But what choice did he have? Gritting through the pain of using the crutches to get around was one thing, but he literally couldn't drive, so he had to depend on Skye, and he'd have to depend on him for a while.

Damn it.

"Where do you want to be? Couch? Bed?" Skye asked.

"Couch, I guess." River made his way over, very slowly, on his crutches. His ribs were throbbing with every movement but he tried not to show it. He didn't want Skye babying him any more than he already was.

He realized once he got to the couch that he wasn't sure where to put the crutches while he sat down, but Skye was right there and River reluctantly handed the crutches to him, then slowly settled onto the sofa. He sat on the left side and propped up his ankle using the recliner.

"If I put these on the coffee table does that work?" Skye asked, lowering the crutches as he did, and River nodded. "You need anything else before I go?"

River patted his pockets to make sure he had his phone and looked around to make sure the remote was within reaching distance. "I think I'm good."

"K. Text me if you think of anything else you need while

I'm out. If you want to, you can invite Anna over for dinner. She'd probably like to see you, know you're okay."

"Yeah," River said. "I'll call her." Honestly he wasn't up for a bunch of company. He felt like he'd been run over by a bulldozer, and he just wanted to eat something and then rest, but he knew Anna would want to see him after what happened, and it was really sweet of Skye to think of her.

"See you in a bit."

Skye was out of the room in a few strides. River heard the door closing behind him as he put the phone to his ear.

The phone rang twice before River heard the soft feminine voice of his girlfriend on the other end. "River? Are you home?"

"Hey. Yeah, just got settled on the sofa while Skye plays errand boy."

"Are you okay?" she asked. "You sound exhausted."

"I'm fine. Just tired, in pain, and hungry."

Anna lets out a soft chuckle. "Just that, huh?" He heard the genuine concern in her voice when she spoke again. "Gosh, River, getting that text from you really scared me. I'm glad Skye was there with you. And I'm glad you're okay."

He gave a soft smile, though she couldn't see it. "Skye wanted to see if you wanted to come for dinner tonight."

"Oh, that's really nice of him. I'd love to come if you're sure you are up for it."

"I think so, just a quick visit should be okay. I'd like to see you."

"Okay. I'll stop and get Chinese on the way so Skye doesn't have to cook. I'm sure he's tired, too."

"Yeah, sure." River rubbed a hand across his forehead. The headache he'd had in the hospital was starting to get worse and he needed his pain meds. "Thanks, Anna. See you in a bit, okay?"

"Okay, bye."

He hung up and set his phone down, resting his head

against the back of the couch, and then groaned when it started to ring. *Seriously?* But he smiled when he picked it up and saw that it was his aunt.

"Hi, Aunt Jodi," he answered.

"River," she said, sounding relieved. "It's so good to hear your voice, sweetheart. You about gave me a heart attack today." Then he was bombarded with all the questions. *How are you? Is Skye taking good care of you? How long until you can get back to work? Can I do anything?*

"I haven't really talked to Skye about anything yet," he admitted once he'd fielded all of the other questions. "We haven't really had the time. I know he can't take off weeks to take care of me, though, and I wouldn't want him to. I'll manage on my own."

"Uh, yeah, no," Aunt Jodi said on the other line. "Talk with Skye and see what he can swing and then call me and I'll see what I can do on my end. I'm two hours away, River. I can afford to take some time off. Not a lot, but some. I'm not leaving you there to fend for yourself with a broken ankle and three cracked ribs. You are like a son to me."

"I know," he said, smiling slightly.

"Then you also know that if I don't hear from you in the next couple of days about what the plan is, I'll be calling Skye or just showing up on your doorstep. So call me, okay?"

River smiled again. He hated inconveniencing anyone, but Aunt Jodi was not someone to be trifled with and if he was going to be cared for by anyone other than Skye, he would want it to be her.

"Okay."

"Okay," she said, sounding appeased. "I'll talk to you soon, kiddo. Say hi to Skye for me. Take care of yourself."

"Bye, Aunt Jodi." He hung up the phone for the second time as Skye walked in the door with bags labeled Walgreens.

"So I wasn't sure what kind of ice packs to get you, so I kind of just went nuts and got a couple of each," Skye said, giving him a dopey grin. "I figure you'll be using them for a while with your ankle and your ribs. They'll have to be in the freezer for a couple of hours before they are cold enough but I got a couple of the ones you can break and use instantly too. Want me to bring you one?"

"Can you bring two?" River asked, shifting himself on the couch slightly. He winced at the pain in his ribs. "And can you wrap them in towels?"

"Sure," Skye said. A minute later he was at River's side with the ice packs, pain meds, and a glass of water. River took the meds and chugged the water. Then he took the ice packs and attempted to reach down and rest one on his injured ankle. But when he cried out in pain and grabbed his side, Skye yanked the ice pack back and scowled at him. "Dumbass. I'm here to help you, Riv. You didn't have to hurt yourself. Just communicate, okay?"

River returned his friend's glare, then held the ice pack he still had against his ribs and rested back, frowning.

"Look, I know you don't like being taken care of, okay?" Skye said, his green eyes narrowed at River and his golden hair falling into his eyes, "but suck it up, buttercup. This is the way it's going to be for a while so you might as well get used to it. Now where do you want this?" He held up the ice pack he'd snatched from River.

"How about up your—"

"Riv," Skye cut him off. A small smile formed on his lips. "There's only a handful of things I'm willing to stick up there and none of them are shaped like this. And you might want to be nice to me because I am in charge of your pain meds." He smirked and River furrowed his eyebrows. "Now where do you want this? It's freezing my hand off."

"On my ankle," River huffed.

"Yeah, I got that much, Einstein. Where?" Skye snarked back. He placed the ice pack over River's ankle and looked back at him. "Communicate," he said again.

River glared at him. "A little lower," he mumbled, and Skye shifted the icepack a little.

"Better?"

"Yes."

"Did you call Anna?"

River nodded. "She's on her way with dinner."

"Oh, cool." Skye ran a hand through his waves and they flopped right back over his forehead and into his eyes. "You want a pillow for your ribs?" he asked. "For those breathing exercises they were talking about?"

"Yeah, I guess," River said. "And because my hand is freezing holding on to this ice pack."

Skye smiled at him, then left the room and returned a second later with a pillow, placing it on River's lap.

"Thanks," River said. He hated to admit it but it was definitely helping his fingers not go numb and the weight of it was perfect against his ribs. There was a moment of silence before he said, "Skye, my Aunt Jodi called, too. She wants to come help out."

"That's nice of her." Skye slumped down on the other side of the couch, head resting back, eyes closed, and he yawned. "I gotta call Mr. Richards and let him know what's going on and that I'll be out for the next few days." He pulled out his phone.

"Skye—"

"Shut up, Riv. I'm taking off work to take care of you, and that's that."

River sighed. He wanted to protest, but he knew he would lose and he felt too crappy to argue. He listened as Skye talked with his boss and then hung up the phone.

"Everything okay?" he asked, still feeling guilty that Skye was taking off work to look after him. With the pain he was in, though, he knew he needed help. He just didn't want to need it.

"No, they fired me," Skye said, looking down and frowning.

River gaped, his eyes wide, then glared the second he realized Skye was jerking his chain. "Dick."

Skye laughed. "They're giving me the rest of the week. Everything's fine. I just have to get plans ready for a sub before tomorrow morning." He rubbed his eyes with his hands and yawned again.

River frowned. Skye looked so exhausted and now he had more work to do thanks to him. "Skye, I'm sorry," he apologized.

"Yes, what were you thinking, getting in an accident and ending up in the hospital?" He chuckled and slapped River's thigh playfully. "Come on, Riv, don't worry about it, it's fine."

~

Skye

"Ahh, dinner," Skye said, his stomach growling when a knock sounded on the door. He stood and crossed the room, opening the door and inviting Anna inside. He thanked her for the food, taking the bags of Chinese from her and bringing them into the kitchen, and he didn't miss how quickly she hurried over to River.

He should have been smiling when he saw her plant a kiss on his roommate's forehead and sit just next to him, taking his hand in hers. It should have warmed his heart to see someone caring for him so much, making him happy. He should have been happy for River, so why was his jaw clenched, and why was he gripping the take out container so hard his knuckles were turning white.

What the fuck? She makes him happy. He deserves to be happy. If anyone deserves to be happy, he does. Get over yourself, you selfish dick.

"River, you look awful," Anna said as her gaze roamed over him, taking in his scrapes and bandages. "In the best way, I mean." She flushed and gave him a soft smile before leaning in and pecking him on the lips, and Skye had to look away.

She brushed her hand over River's forehead, coming into contact with the bandage that was still on the side of his head. "Does it hurt?"

He nodded. "I have a mild concussion." She frowned and then Skye heard her voice carrying across the open space as he finished unpacking the takeout and got plates from the cabinet.

"Thanks for being there for him, Skye," she said.

Skye wanted to snarl, but he didn't. "Yeah, no problem." *She's his girlfriend, you idiot, get over it.* But Skye couldn't get over it, couldn't get that tiny little kiss out of his mind, couldn't stop thinking about the fact that Anna got to kiss River whenever she wanted.

"Let me help you," Anna said, moving into the kitchen. She opened the different containers filled with rice, noodles, chicken and vegetables, and different sauces. It smelled amazing and Skye's stomach growled again.

Anna grabbed a plate. "River, what do you want?" she asked.

"Some of everything," he replied.

She nodded and filled his plate up before taking it over to the couch. Skye did the same with his, and although he felt a bit awkward about being the third wheel, took a seat across from River and Anna on the chair. They didn't seem to mind him being there and he relaxed. Anna even asked him about how work was going and seemed genuinely interested in his answer, which sucked because it just made it that much harder to dislike her.

"Guess we won't be seeing you at Bible study or church for a while, huh?" Anna said, sounding deflated as she addressed River.

"Yeah, guess not," River replied. "I'm gonna be a hermit for a while, it looks like. You'll come visit me though, right?"

Anna smiled at him. "Of course."

Skye felt like he was going crazy. This girl was perfect for River. She was kind, generous, and thoughtful. She obviously cared about River. They shared the same beliefs. So why was he so...so...

Jealous. Jenna's words came back to him, hitting him so hard he swallowed his food down the wrong pipe, and had to pat his chest to get it down.

"You okay?" River asked. Skye nodded and took a sip of his water. That wasn't embarrassing at all.

I am not fucking jealous, he had to keep himself from growling out loud as he tried to convince himself that his feelings for River were strictly platonic.

That he absolutely was not falling in love with his best friend.

CHAPTER 5

Skye

River seemed relieved when Anna left right after dinner. And if Skye was being honest, he was relieved, too. It had been a long ass day for both of them, and he could tell by looking at River that he was exhausted and in pain. He needed to get some sleep.

Skye's mattress called to him, too, but first, River. He would be sleeping sitting up on the couch for the next several weeks. It would make it easier on his ribs and help with his breathing.

"I'm gonna finish up in here, and then I'll go get your pillow and some blankets," he told River from the kitchen. River nodded from his spot on the sofa. He hadn't moved since they had gotten home.

Skye finished up with the dishes and dried his hands, then crossed through the living room and into River's bedroom. He came back with a pillow and two large blankets.

Just as Skye was about to drape the blankets over him, River said, "I need to use the bathroom, actually."

Skye smirked. "I'm not holding your dick for you, River, I have my limits."

River just rolled his eyes like he always did any time Skye

made a dick joke. "Just help me up and hand me my crutches, please?"

So Skye did. "Are you going to need help once you get in there?" he asked as River slowly made his way through his bedroom to the attached master bath, letting out little grunts of pain as he went.

"No," he growled.

Skye was grinning a second later when he heard River calling his name with a resigned sigh.

"Yes?" he said, peeking his head into the bathroom and grinning slightly at the sight of River standing in front of the toilet. He had one hand on the wall and the other braced on the counter. He'd managed to get his crutches up against the wall at least but not being able to put any weight on his ankle or bend at all without being in pain was causing him problems. He glared at the toilet, as though it was somehow to blame. "Do you need *help*?" Skye asked with a grin.

He couldn't help chortling when River gave him his best bitch face. "Shut up and get over here," he retorted, a flush creeping up his cheeks. "I need help with my pants. It hurts my ribs too much and I don't have enough balance." His cheeks were flaming now and Skye bit his lip. He did feel sorry for his friend, but the fact that he was so flustered was kind of endearing.

"I'm gonna need your help getting them back on, too," River told him. Skye tried to spare him some dignity, as much as one can when they're taking their friend's pants off so they can piss, and just did his best not to make a big deal out of it. He reached his hands around River's slender hips and tugged the pants down and off, until they slid down River's legs and were draped over his one broken ankle that was still suspended in the air, and his other ankle resting on the floor.

"I'll give you some privacy," Skye told him, and walked back into the bedroom, closing the door behind him.

"Okay," River called a moment later, and Skye poked his

head back in, before making his way over to him. He carefully pulled River's pants back up and then handed him his crutches.

"Thank you," River mumbled, not meeting Skye's gaze. A flush crept up his face yet again. "I think I should change into pants with an open fly so that you don't have to help me do that ever again."

Skye couldn't help laughing. "What if you have to take a shit?"

"I'll hold it."

"For six weeks?"

"Yep."

"You do that and we're gonna have a whole new set of problems."

"I'll figure it out."

Skye chuckled again. "Okay. Pajamas?"

River nodded.

"Which drawer?"

"Second."

"Do you care which ones?" he asked, rummaging through River's dresser as his roommate made his way back into the bedroom on his crutches.

"No." He winced, and Skye could tell it was taking every last ounce of his energy to stay upright. Moving around at all looked excruciating. Just bending over to use the crutches so he could keep the weight off of his ankle looked like it was making him miserable.

"Okay, let's get this done so you can get some sleep," he said, then pondered as he walked over to his friend. "How are we gonna do this if you can't put weight on your ankle?" He rested his hands on his hips and bit his lip. River just stood there, eyeing him.

"I have an idea. You're not going to like it, but roll with it."

"Okay," River said, skeptically, raising an eyebrow.

"Give me your crutches." Skye held out his hands.

"And what am I going to hold on to?" River asked, his eyebrow raising even further.

"Me," Skye told him. "Just for a second."

River hesitated, but then handed one crutch to Skye and steadied himself against the wall with one hand as Skye tossed the crutch onto the far end of the bed. Then Skye reached for the other crutch as he wrapped his arm around River's waist, supporting him.

"Skye, what the . . .?" River started.

"Just hang on." Skye tossed the other crutch aside, next to the first one, and then bending over, he scooped River into his arms. His roommate let out an astonished gasp, his eyes widening behind his glasses. Skye smiled. "Hey, there, gorgeous." He gave a playful wink as he carried River to the bed.

"Skye, what are you doing?" River's voice had risen considerably, that gorgeous flush returning to his handsome face.

"I'm putting you down on the bed, so you can keep the weight off your ankle and not hurt your ribs while I get your pants off." Skye gently lowered River onto the soft mattress and then started to undress him once again.

"Can you lift your hips at all?" he asked, gripping the waistband of River's athletic pants, making sure he had *just* his athletic pants and *not* his boxers as well. That would be all kinds of awkward.

"Not without it hurting a lot," River said. He gazed up at Skye with those beautiful sapphire eyes, and Skye's mouth went dry. He swallowed and cleared his throat.

"Okay, that's fine," he said. "I might just have to get more up close and personal then."

"Whatever," River sighed. "I don't think this could get any more awkward, Skye."

Skye started to pull River's pants down once again and felt

a shiver run down his spine when his fingers brushed against River's hips.

He's my friend.

And even along his butt cheek a little.

He's my friend.

And then along his thighs.

My very hot, very sweet, very injured, very straight, friend. God, what is wrong with me? Pull it together. Ice wall. Ice wall. Ice wall.

Until the pants were finally off far enough that he didn't have to worry about his hands coming in contact with River at all. "Skye?" he heard River say, snapping him out of his daze, and he only then realized that he was biting his lip and staring at his best friend.

"Hmm?"

"Pants?" River said. "I don't really want to lay here in my underwear, if you don't mind."

"Right." Skye flushed and then mentally slapped himself for being such an idiot, and getting so lost in thinking about River that he'd forgotten about him at the same time. He grabbed the pair of pajama pants he'd gotten out and tossed on the bed earlier. "We can do this one of two ways. You can stay laying down, but you'll have to lift your hips at least some, or you can sit for the first bit, and then stand for the second."

"Let's sit and then stand," River said. "I have to get up at some point anyway. You're gonna have to pick me up again, though. I can't sit up on my own."

Skye nodded, and felt the heat creeping up the back of his neck and shoulders. Now he was going to be holding River in his underwear. Perfect. But he bent down and scooped his roommate into his arms once again, and carried him just a few paces over to the foot of the bed before setting him down. His cheeks heated as he knelt in front of River and pulled his pajama pants on one foot, and then the other, and then slid them up his slender legs, and over his knees, just like they had done in the hospital earlier that day. Then he grabbed River's crutches for him so he would have support, and helped him get his pants the rest of the way up.

He was pretty sure there was an audible sigh on both their parts when the whole ordeal was finally over.

"Thank you," River said, crutches under his arms and his ankle raised again as he hobbled towards the door.

"You're welcome. Let's get you settled on the sofa."

River returned to his spot on the couch. Skye couldn't give him more meds yet but he set some by him on the side table. "You can have these in four hours. I'll leave my phone turned up so you can text if you need me."

He placed River's pillow behind his head. River rested back and Skye draped the blankets over him as the other man closed his eyes and sighed.

Skye bent down and pressed a chaste kiss to River's bandaged forehead. "Get some sleep, angel," he said softly. "Love you."

River didn't open his eyes but a smile played at the corners of his mouth. "Love you, too, Skye," he murmured. "Good night."

CHAPTER 6

Skye

They stayed in their pajamas for the entirety of the next day. Skye worked on lesson plans for the substitute teacher while River went back and forth between watching tv, doing his breathing exercises, and sleeping. Skye switched out River's ice packs for him, helped him get to the bathroom, and brought him his meals and his pain meds. River, thankfully, was getting better about letting Skye help him, about communicating his needs. Even though Skye knew it was hard for his roommate to accept the help, he really didn't mind at all. In fact, he was realizing that taking care of River made him happy.

When River's eyes started to drift closed, Skye got up and draped a blanket over him. Sliding his glasses off, he placed them on the coffee table. Then he reached up and ran his fingers through River's thick, dark hair.

River squinted, smiling up at him, before closing his eyes once again. But Skye's fingers and his heart told him that this was all wrong. That the touch lacked something. Something he craved. Something he needed. Something that he wanted more than anything in the world. Something he had wanted with River for far longer than he cared to admit.

Intimacy.

He sucked in a breath and stepped back.

Fuck.

No! Ice wall. Ice wall. Ice wall.

He watched as River dozed off, snoring softly, his chest rising and falling, Skye's chest constricting because River was just So. Damn. Beautiful.

Intimacy.

He sat back in his chair and buried his face in his hands. *I'm not falling in love with him. I'm not. I'm not. I'm not.*

He looked back up at River, biting his lip as the reality settled painfully in his chest. *Damn you,* he told his best friend. Because as much as he didn't want to admit it, the other sumo wrestler he'd put in front of the ice wall was gone. He knew better than to do this to himself, and yet he couldn't help it. He couldn't help that he was falling in love with his best friend. His very straight best friend who had just stated only yesterday that the idea of having sex with another man made him uncomfortable, scared, even, because of what had happened to him as a teenager. And Skye didn't blame him, not one bit, but he didn't need sex. He didn't need anything River wasn't willing and ready to give. If they were together, boyfriends, or even husbands, he would be happy with just cuddles and kisses. He would be happy with just sitting in the same room with River, knowing that he was his, and that River loved him. He would treasure every look, every smile, every touch no matter how small, for the gift that it was because it would be River, and even that would be far more than he ever thought possible.

He started to tremble, and it was only then that he realized his cheeks were streaked with tears. They continued to fall as he realized there was nothing he could do to stop it. He was going to continue to fall deeper and deeper in love with River, and River would never know. Could never know. The only thing Skye could do was be River's friend, as he'd always been, take care of him, be there for him. And he would continue to do that. Not just because he cared for him, but because River needed him, because even though he couldn't be his lover, he wanted to be his friend. He just had to come to terms with the fact that River would never be his, not in the way he wanted him to be.

He would have to accept the fact that the one thing he truly wanted was something he would never have.

~

Skye was standing in the kitchen scrambling eggs the next morning when River came out of his bedroom dressed in the T-shirt he'd worn for the past two days, and his black swimming trunks.

"Going swimming, Riv?" he asked, less amusement in his voice than he had intended. He'd been trying so hard not to give off the melancholy vibes that surrounded him. He'd held it together throughout the evening, after River had woken up from his nap and they'd had dinner together, and watched *The Avengers*, but then his sleep had been restless at best. He knew he had to do something to snap himself out of this funk, and sitting around moping and pining for his best friend was, he knew, a colossal waste of time.

River smirked. "Yes, I thought I'd take a dip in our pool that we don't have."

Skye returned that smirk with one of his own. The banter reminded him that they were in fact best friends, and whatever else happened, or didn't happen, he could hold onto that. They would always have each other. And that thought brightened his spirits a little bit.

"I was actually hoping you could help me take a bath after breakfast."

Skye sputtered and choked on his coffee. "What?" he managed as he grabbed a washcloth to wipe off his shirt and chin while River stared at him, his eyebrow raised. He set his crutches aside and sat down at the bar. Skye blinked, unable to believe what he'd just heard. River was still staring at him like he'd gone crazy. "What?" Skye repeated.

River laughed now, but it made him wince. "Don't worry. I don't want you to actually help me take the bath. I just need your help getting in and out. I can rest my ankle up on the edge of the tub to keep it elevated and out of the water. Better than a shower at this point. Hence the swim trunks. Didn't want you to get the full picture."

"Oh." Skye's cheeks heated and he hoped River didn't notice. "Right. Sure, I can do that. After breakfast?"

River nodded.

"How'd you get into those anyway?" Skye gestured towards the swim trunks.

"Slowly and painfully," River replied, making Skye laugh.

"You could have asked for help."

"I could have. And then we would have had to get a friend divorce. Kind of defeats the whole purpose of you not seeing me naked if you have to help me get into them in the first place, don't you think? Besides, I'm gonna have to figure out how to do these things by myself by the end of the week anyway. I'm definitely not going to have my aunt helping me change."

"Guess that makes sense," Skye said, taking another sip of his coffee. He certainly was not going to tell River that he wouldn't at all mind seeing him naked.

They finished eating and cleared up their dishes, then made their way into River's bedroom.

"How warm do you want it?" Skye asked, turning on the faucet and testing the water. He looked back at River who was sitting on his bed now and pulling the bandage off of his head. The scrapes and scabs were healing nicely and it looked like he could leave the bandage off now.

"Warm, but not super hot."

Skye waited a moment and put his hand under the water

again to check the temperature. Deciding it was good he leaned over and plugged the drain to let it fill up. When he heard River wince he looked over.

"You okay?" he asked.

"Can you help me with my shirt?" River said, looking a bit sheepish. "It's hurting my ribs to try and do it myself."

Jesus Christ, Skye's brain was on overdrive right now. First River wanted help taking a bath and now he was asking Skye to take his shirt off? For fuck's sake, what was he trying to do to him?

Nothing. He wasn't trying to do anything to Skye. This was not sensual in any way. This was his friend needing help from literally the only person who could give it to him, and Skye needed to get his act together.

"Please?" River said. He winced again and Skye hurried over to him. He couldn't help the blush that crept up his cheeks when River raised his arms and he bent down to lift the hem of his shirt, pulling it up and over his head, all the while thinking, *his body is not fucking gorgeous, and I do not want it, and I am not thinking of him that way, and he's my best friend.*

"Don't get too close, I smell terrible," River said, grinning at him.

"That's gonna be a little hard to do if I'm supposed to help you into the tub," Skye remarked.

River chuckled and Skye handed him his crutches, then followed him into the bathroom. River rested the crutches against the wall next to the tub while Skye reached over to turn off the faucet.

"Maybe we should have some sort of plastic bag around the cast just to make sure it doesn't get wet," Skye suggested. "I'll be right back." He left and returned a moment later with a garbage bag. After helping River sit down on the edge of the tub, he knelt in front of him, sliding the bag over his cast and then using a rubber band to cinch it at the top.

"Might be easiest to just turn around and slide in," Skye said, standing and backing away slightly.

"Worth a shot." River turned around and slowly lowered himself into the tub while Skye stood nearby just in case. Fortunately, River didn't seem to need the help. He kept his left foot elevated. It got a little damp as he submerged himself into the water, but since the bag was around it it stayed safe. He sighed as he propped his ankle up on the end of the tub and rested his head back, clearly relieved to finally be in the warm water.

"Can you get me some soap and a washcloth?" he asked.

"Yeah," Skye replied, trying not to think about how gloriously sexy River looked right now, head resting back, eyes closed, arms up on the side of the tub, his chest dripping wet.

Skye opened the bathroom drawer for a washcloth and stepped into the shower for the soap, then set them down next to River on the side of the tub, his heart beating erratically as he watched the other man gather more water onto his arms and chest.

God, he had to get out of there before he popped a boner. He was headed for the door again when River stopped him.

"You might as well stay, unless you have something to do," he said. "I'm gonna need your help again in about five minutes to get out."

Skye didn't say anything, just bit his lip and backed up to sit down on the toilet, bouncing his leg up and down and forcing himself to look anywhere but at River. He pulled his phone out of his pocket and scrolled through social media for a few minutes to distract himself, before River's voice broke the silence. The bathroom was getting warmer, steamier, and the scent of River's watermelon and coconut body wash wafted through the air. Damn, Skye loved that smell. It was the smell of River, but it had never made his dick twitch until now.

"Skye?" River said, "Can you help me?"

"Help you?" he asked, trying not to sound as nervous as he felt.

"Yeah, I can't reach my hair without it hurting."

"You want me to wash your hair?" Skye asked, and God his emotions were all over the place. Fuck, yeah, he wanted to get his fingers all up in those gorgeous dark locks. But, shit, that was dangerous territory. It will be torture. And being so close to River without letting his thoughts wander...

"Is that okay?" River asked, no doubt sensing his hesitation. A flush crept up his cheeks. "Or does that cross the friendship boundaries?"

"No, no, it's fine," Skye assured him. "I think we crossed those boundaries when I had to help you get dressed and pee, Riv," he added lightheartedly, and River's flush deepened, but he smiled. "Let me get a cup or something to scoop water with, and I'll be right back."

Skye left and returned with a large, blue plastic cup, and knelt next to the tub, and River. *Okay, I can do this, and I can do it without popping a boner. I hope.*

He reached over and slid River's glasses off, setting them behind him on the counter. River grinned at him, his cheeks still pink. He tilted his head back as Skye dipped the cup into the water and poured it over his hair several times, the water sliding down his neck, over his chest and back. And God it was tantalizing, watching the droplets skate over corded muscle. Skye wanted to lick off every last drop.

River's hair was soaked in no time. Skye squirted the shampoo onto his hands and scrubbed it through River's dark locks, trying not to relish the feel of River's wet hair under his fingertips, and then poured more water on his head, running his fingers through the thick strands again to help rinse it out. A shiver raced down his spine when he noticed the way River's shoulders and back muscles moved and flexed as he shifted, and his cock twitched again.

Goddammit.

He poured more water over River's back and shoulders to get rid of the soap suds there as well, and then pushed himself up to stand as he said, "Okay, I think that's it." His heart was pounding as he dried his hands off, but he gave himself a mental high five for being boner free. Thank God. "You ready to get out?"

River nodded.

"Okay, how are we doing this?" Skye asked. He couldn't help thinking about how adorable River looked, soaking wet and smiling up at him, his hair plastered to his face. And God damn, he smelled good. No one had the right to smell that fucking good.

"Unplug the drain first, probably?" River said. Skye did, then leaned against the counter waiting for the water to drain.

"Now what?" he asked once it was gone.

"I think if you grab my arms I can use my good foot to push myself up. As long as I don't slip."

"Okay." Skye stepped forward and took hold of River's upper arms, trying not to notice how strong and firm they felt under his grip, but also trying to make sure he didn't let go, since River was still quite wet.

River gripped Skye's arms in turn and Skye lifted him as River pushed up with his right foot and brought his left foot down as he stood, being careful to keep the weight off of it still.

"I think I'm gonna need you to put your arm around my shoulders to help me out," River said. "I can lift my bad ankle out first but I can't put it down, so I'll need your support while I get my other foot out."

Skye stepped as close to the side of the tub as he could and held his arm out for River. He wrapped his arm around River's shoulders and River lifted his bad ankle out of the tub first, holding it in the air, which put him awkwardly off kilter while he tried to get his right foot out of the tub, and as he did, he practically collapsed into Skye, wrapping both arms around him and staring him in the face, their chests pressed together.

Skye inhaled, stumbling backwards slightly as River fell into him, his arms coming around his friend. It had happened naturally when they collided, in order to steady themselves, but Skye swallowed hard now. River was pressed so close to him, eyes gazing into his, and Skye felt like he couldn't breathe. River's lips were only centimeters from his. But the space grew in a flash as River pushed away and supported himself on the counter.

"Sorry," he said, cheeks flushed. "That was a little more contact than I intended."

"No, it's fine," Skye assured him, still flustered, but pretending he wasn't as he cleared his throat. "What next?" He handed River his glasses and the other man slipped them on, his cheeks flushed once again.

"I think I'm gonna need you to dry me off."

Fucking fuck fuck fuck. Is he trying to tempt me? But he couldn't help the smile that tugged at his lips as River bit his lip. Damn, that was all kinds of adorable, and hot. Super hot. *Ice wall*, he reminded himself. *Ice Wall.*

He reached for a towel and stood in front of River as he began to dry him off, starting with his hair and working his way down. He dried off River's smooth chest, feeling his firm, toned body beneath his palms, unable to control the shiver that raced down his spine.

He moved to his strong arms, his slender abdomen, down to his knees, his legs, and down to his feet—well, foot—all the while telling himself, *Ice wall, Ice wall, Ice wall.*

He brought the towel up to the bottom of River's swim trunks and used it to squeeze out some of the excess water that was still dripping onto his feet, and the floor, and then he stood.

"Anything else?" he asked, his voice soft and a little huskier than normal, his face only inches from River's once again.

There was a pause before River spoke, his eyes locked with Skye's. "Just the crutches," he said, and Skye noticed that his voice was soft, too. Thoughtful, almost, and he inhaled. He couldn't remember River ever looking at him the way he was now. And when River spoke again it was in the same soft tone. "Thank you, Skye."

Skye's heart was pounding as River reached up and gently brushed the blond locks from his eyes and then threaded his fingers through the wavy strands for a brief moment.

"You're welcome, Riv." River smiled at him as he reached over and grabbed his crutches.

"You'll be okay changing on your own?" Skye asked, his mind racing, wondering what the hell had just happened there. The way River had looked at him, the way he'd held his gaze, the way he'd spoken to him, warm and soft, the way he'd touched him. He'd never touched Skye like that before. It was almost as if...no, he was being ridiculous. River was just being appreciative and friendly. He didn't have feelings for Skye. He had a girlfriend. And he was straight. It was just wishful thinking. God, he had to stop thinking about River like this. He was misinterpreting everything now.

"Um, could you get some underwear and pajamas out for me to change into and leave them on the bed? The rest I'll manage on my own," River said.

"Okay." He never thought he would be fishing through River's underwear drawer, but here he was. He pulled out a pair of boxers, figuring those will be easier than anything else his friend had in there to get over the cast, and then found a pair of pajama pants and a T-shirt and tossed them on the bed.

"Good?" he asked, and River nodded, so he left, shutting the door behind him.

CHAPTER 7

River

Before he knew it, Saturday evening had rolled around. River and Skye had spent the last five days together and Skye would be going back to work on Tuesday while River's aunt Jodi came to fill his place.

River couldn't help but notice that Skye had seemed a little off all week. He'd been a bit quiet, which wasn't like him, but the worst part was the sadness River had seen behind those gorgeous green eyes, and he wondered if maybe this week had been too much for his friend. If he missed his normal life, hanging out with Nick and Jenna, work, the night life he'd grown accustomed to, though he hadn't been going out to clubs nearly as much lately. River wondered what that was about.

Skye hadn't complained, not once, about being at home with him, taking care of him. But something was definitely bothering the other man and River couldn't figure out what it could be other than that he was bored, and maybe a bit restless and tired of having just River for company. They hadn't exactly been living it up the past few days. If he could give Skye a break from everything maybe that would help.

That gave him an idea. A way for him to get help and for Skye to get a break. He picked up his phone and called Anna.

~

"Hey, Skye." River grinned at his roommate when he walked through the door, having just returned from his grocery run. "I just talked to Anna and she's gonna come over tonight, so if you want to go out, you can."

"Oh," Skye said. "Okay, sure. How long do you want me to be gone?"

River blinked. "I don't *want* you to be gone. I just thought you could use a break. You've been cooped up here for days. And I haven't seen Anna in a while, so I thought it would be a win win. But you don't have to go. You're welcome to stay here and hang out with us."

Skye gave him a soft smile, but it was a sad one, the brightness in his eyes dimmed.

"No, that's okay, Riv, you guys don't need a babysitter." He unloaded the groceries in silence while River sat there, wondering what on earth just happened? Did he just make things worse by suggesting Skye go out?

"I'll see what Jenna and Nick are up to. It would be nice to get out." Skye gave him another smile but River still wasn't convinced. Something was definitely bothering him.

"Are you okay, Skye?" he asked. It was barely noticeable, but River saw the other man tense. The way his shoulders drew up ever so slightly, the muscles in his neck tightening.

"I'm fine, Riv." His tone was gentle, but River knew better.

"Skye, we've known each other long enough to tell when the other person is lying. Be honest with me. Has taking care of me this past week been stressing you out? Has it been hard on you?"

Skye shook his head. "No, Riv, really. I haven't minded. I

promise." He sighed and ran a hand through his hair. "I think I'm just restless, like you said," he added. "A night out will be good for me."

⁓

"I've missed you," Anna said, sitting next to River as she handed him an ice pack for his ribs. There was another one already resting on his ankle.

Her long red hair was up in a ponytail and her green eyes flitted over his face as she took him in.

River put the pillow against his ribs, and then turned to his girlfriend. "I missed you, too," he said, and then pressed his lips to hers in a soft kiss. But it was short because he came to find that the effort it took to kiss made his ribs hurt more. He pulled away, wincing.

"Sorry. It's painful. Just breathing is painful."

"It's okay," Anna assured him. "I understand." She shifted a little and sidled her small frame up next to him, sliding her arm under his and intertwining their fingers together. She smelled like peaches, and for some reason it made River smile. And yet, he found himself craving the smell of bourbon and oak that he'd become accustomed to over the past five days. The past several years, really.

Skye.

How did he miss him already? His scent, his company, his care, his laughter. The way he made River feel so seen and heard, and valued. Like there was nothing that mattered to him more than River did.

Anna's words pulled him from his thoughts. "I'm glad you asked me to come over. It's nice to have the place to ourselves. I think Skye felt a little bit like a third wheel the last time, poor guy." She stroked River's arm and rested her head on his shoulder. "You guys have known each other for a while, huh?" she said, thoughtfully.

"Mmm," he mumbled, resting his head on hers. "Ten years."

"I can tell he really cares about you. You guys have something special. I see that when you're together."

"Yeah, he's pretty great," River said with a slight smile.

"You ready for him to go back to work?"

"For his sake, yeah. He needs it. I think being stuck at home is depressing him. That's why I made him get out tonight. He's been acting weird all week. And I feel kind of bad. I think I've made him feel uncomfortable with some of the stuff he's had to do for me. Helping me change and go to the bathroom I think has put our friendship to the test." He chuckled and so did Anna.

"I doubt that," she said.

"Yeah, me, too. I think it would take more than that for Skye to abandon me. For my sake, I'm gonna miss him when he goes back to work. My aunt Jodi is coming, and she's great, but it won't be the same as having Skye. I just feel safe with him, you know? Comfortable. I always have. Like, I don't have to hide anything or be anything other than who I am. Like there's nothing he wouldn't do for me. And he puts up with me. Even when I'm stubborn and sarcastic. He'll call me out if it gets to be too much, but he also gives me space, and he's patient, too." He paused for a moment. "I just feel...I don't know..." he trailed off, lost in thought, stroking Anna's hand with his thumb.

Anna tilted her head and met his gaze. "Loved?" she asked.

River looked at her for a moment. "Yeah, I guess."

Anna just nodded and rested her head against his shoulder again.

"I mean, my aunt loves me too, I know, and I enjoy her company. She's amazing honestly, but Skye's . . ."

"Special," Anna finished for him.

"Yeah. I guess I've always had a connection with him. I don't know. Guess that's what makes us such good friends."

~

Skye

"Hey, what's up, man?" Nick asked, bringing Skye in for a side hug and ruffling his hair. "I haven't seen you in forever."

Skye pushed his friend away and smirked as he fixed his blond waves. "Dude, it's been a week."

Nick frowned. "Yeah, but that's like seven weeks in bro weeks."

Skye couldn't help laughing as they took seats at the bar and ordered beers. He was not going to get drunk no matter how much he wanted to, because then he wouldn't be able to take care of River, and how selfish would that be? But one or two beers wouldn't hurt.

"Where's Jenna?" he asked, looking around. He let out a very undignified shriek seconds later when he felt something wet on his ear, and nearly jumped out of his seat. When he turned, Jenna was behind him, doubled over in laughter. Nick's laughter joined hers, his big body shaking so hard Skye was surprised he didn't fall off of his stool.

"Very funny." Skye grabbed a napkin and wiped his ear where Jenna had licked it, then turned his attention to the beer he'd spilled on his button down shirt. "You guys are hilarious."

"We know," Jenna said, finally pulling herself together. She wiped at her eyes, before giving Nick a high five.

"Why don't we get a booth?" Skye suggested. The two hyenas agreed, and after ordering some burgers they headed over to the booth in the corner. The bar had an upbeat, relaxed atmosphere. Warm LED lanterns sat at all of the tables. The floors were a rich, dark wood, and the music was lively. Skye didn't miss how close Nick and Jenna sat next to each other as they took their seats.

Their meals came relatively quickly and they dug in.

"So, how is River?" Jenna asked, then took a sip of her coke, her red lipstick leaving a mark on the straw when she pulled away.

"He's okay. In a lot of pain still, but the meds and ice packs are helping. I think mostly he's pissed and bored. And it's only the first week, you know? He's got several more to go before he can get back to work. It's gonna drive him crazy. He's introverted but he still likes to be up doing things, feeling useful. Not being able to go to work sucks."

"That does suck," Nick said, taking a bite of his burger. "We should come over, if you think he's up for it. Maybe tomorrow afternoon?"

"Yeah, I think he would be. He can't visit for long periods of time because it hurts to talk, but I'm sure he'd love to see you guys for a short visit. Maybe do something that doesn't require a lot of talking."

They both raised their eyebrows at Skye and he rolled his eyes. "You guys are messed up. You know what I mean. Like watch a movie or something."

They chuckled and Nick spoke, his mouth half full of food and his cheek puffed out, making him look like a chipmunk. "I can kick his butt in *Super Smash Bros.*"

"How are you doing?" Jenna asked, nibbling on a fry now.

Skye looked up from his own plate and met her warm gaze. Jenna could be very playful and tease a lot, but she was also very sincere and heartfelt when she needed to be.

He swallowed. "I'm okay. Just tired, I think." But Jenna wasn't fooled. She never was. He could tell by the way she looked at him that she knew there was something more going on. Still, she didn't press him.

As they ate, and talked, and laughed, Skye found himself being very grateful that River had forced him out of the house. Sometimes he didn't realize what he needed until he was getting it.

He'd been in a rut for the past several days and being out was reminding him just how blessed he was.

Good food, good music, good friends.

He had a lot to be thankful for.

~

River

"Hi, Skye," River heard his aunt Jodi say from his permanent spot on the sofa. It was Monday evening and she'd just arrived from Cincinnati. Skye had gone to greet her at the door since River was immobilized.

Aunt Jodi loved Skye like a son, too. She'd always been fond of him, and he of her. She was a special person. Feisty, fun, incredibly thoughtful, full of laughter, and she radiated kindness. It was rare to see her not smiling. Given that she was a cop, River always found it even more compelling that she managed to maintain such a positive disposition with all the crap she'd had to deal with, but she'd always told him that life was what you made of it, and she had learned early on that when things got tough, there was no shame in asking for help.

She'd seen some ugly stuff but she'd had some great therapists and awesome friends to help her deal, too. And she knew all too well that if you didn't find a way to handle your demons, you ended up taking out your grief and anger on the people you loved, and that wasn't fair to them, so she'd always advocated for counseling and mental health awareness. In her words, "Only the strongest people ask for help." She'd been River's anchor ever since he'd lost his parents, and when he'd been assaulted she was his strength and support, and probably the main reason for him being able to cope with and overcome his trauma. When he'd chosen not to report his assault she hadn't pressured him. He had felt so much shame and embarrassment, so much humiliation and grief, and he just couldn't stomach the thought of reliving the incident over and over, or standing up in court and trying to prove that he had been assaulted with his perpetrators right there in the room. The thing he had wanted most was to never see them again.

It had been after Jodi had received a phone call about River not being in school that she'd finally talked with him about his strange behavior and how concerned she was for him, and he'd broken down and sobbed in her arms as he told her his story. He had switched schools and started seeing his therapist, and Jodi had been there through all of his tears and heartache in the months and years that followed. He didn't know what he would do without her.

He heard her voice echoing from the other room. "My nephew didn't give you too bad of a time this past week, did he?"

"He was as charming as always," Skye replied, his voice a mixture of sarcasm and fondness that sort of made River's chest ache.

"Oh, gosh, I'm sorry," she said, and they laughed.

"You know I can hear everything you're saying," River called as he gave up and pushed himself up on his crutches, making his way very slowly into the other room.

"He can hear everything we're saying," Jodi whispered loudly. "So let's not say anything embarrassing. Like the time he—"

"Very funny," River interrupted, entering the room. He smiled at his aunt and she gave him a hug even though he couldn't reciprocate it because of the crutches.

Skye glared at him. "You're supposed to be sitting down."

He stuck his tongue out at his roommate and Skye rolled his eyes. "Listen," he told Jodi, "we don't want you paying for a hotel for an entire week, so you can have my room. I sleep sitting up on the couch anyway because of my ribs, so it's really not a problem. You'll have your own bathroom and everything. Skye cleaned it for you even though he hates cleaning bathrooms." He smiled at his friend and was a little surprised when Skye flushed, then cleared his throat and ran his hand across the back of his neck.

"Well, thank you, Skye. I'm sorry you had to go through that," Jodi teased. "And thanks for taking care of River. I rested a lot easier knowing he had you here."

"Of course," Skye said, that flush still there. "I'll take your things to River's room." He reached behind Jodi and grabbed her suitcase and bag.

"You should sit, sweetheart," Jodi said, gesturing for River to move towards the sofa.

"Have you eaten dinner?" he asked as he made himself comfortable—well, as comfortable as he could be—on the couch. He winced slightly at the pain in his ribs.

"Want me to get you an ice pack?" Jodi asked.

"Sure." She entered the kitchen and came back with one, handing it to him.

"Dinner?" River asked again. "Skye's a great cook. I'm sure he could whip up something for you if you are hungry."

"I had fast food on the drive here," she said. "But thank you."

"'Kay, got you all set up in River's room," Skye announced, returning to the living room. "Clean sheets and everything."

Jodi smiled at him. "Thank you. Anything I should know before you go to work tomorrow?"

"I think you already know everything," Skye said. "As long as you know where his ice packs and pain meds are, you should be good. Hopefully you won't have too much trouble helping him get up and down. He's heavier than he looks."

"I'm still right here," River said, eyeing both of them as he gestured to himself. "Literally right here." They laughed and Skye winked at him.

"I'm gonna crash," Skye said. "If I don't see you in the

morning, which I probably won't, then I'll see you when I get home."

"And when is that?" Jodi asked.

"Five-ish, usually. As far as food goes, if you can find it you can eat it, just make yourself at home. I'll plan to make dinner. And if River says anything about me that makes me sound less than perfect, he's lying."

Jodi grinned. "Got it. Goodnight, Skye."

"Goodnight. Goodnight, Riv." His eyes met River's and there was a sadness behind them that seemed to be lingering, despite the smile.

"Night, Skye," River said, and his roommate disappeared down the hall.

Jodi watched him walk away, then turned to River. "That boy is pretty special. He really cares about you, you know?"

River nodded. He did know. But why did people keep telling him, like they thought he didn't?

Skye smiled when his fourth period class strode in the door the following afternoon. He probably shouldn't have favorites, but these sixth graders were his. And being back at work was a welcome and much needed distraction.

"We missed you!" one student said.

"You were gone forever!" another said.

"Please, don't ever leave us for that long again," Gwen pleaded. "It was horrible. And not just because we never got our papers back."

Skye smiled at her and held up said papers in his hand. "Here." He handed her hers and then began to pass the rest of the long overdue papers back.

He stopped short when one of his students, Ben, asked, "So how is your boyfriend?"

"Idiot, he's not his boyfriend," Kevin chimed in. He looked at Skye. "Is he?"

"No," Skye replied, his palms starting to sweat. *So much for the distraction.* "No, he's not my boyfriend. We're just roommates."

"Told you," Kevin said to Ben.

"It doesn't matter," Ben snapped. "The question is still the same. How is he?"

"He's recovering slowly. He'll be fine." He gave them all a small smile and finished handing back their papers, before going over a quick summary of the past week to make sure they had gone through what they were supposed to go through with the sub, just as he had done with his previous classes.

"All right then," he said, "and that brings us to the Civil War."

"What's civil about a war?" one student teased, and they all snickered.

"That's actually a good question," Skye said, smiling a little as he leaned against his desk, fiddling with a pencil. "Anyone want to guess what that means? Usually when we say civil we mean peaceable or quiet, but you're right, the Civil War was clearly anything but that."

"Was it because the war was being fought between citizens of the same country?" Gwen asked.

Skye nodded. "Very good."

Gwen beamed.

"And what was the reason for the Civil War?" he asked, looking around the room at the chairs full of students, and waiting. Kevin raised his hand and Skye nodded at him.

"Slavery, right? One side was for it the other side wasn't?"

"Yes, the South, and the North, also known as the Confederacy and the Union." He walked over to the whiteboard and picked up a marker, then started to scribble down terms and dates as the students took out their notebooks and pens. "This is all in your books, but it's a good idea to take notes, too," he said.

"Yeah, just in case there's another pop quiz," Gwen remarked, and they giggled.

"Can you guys think of any issues today that our country

faces that divide us, maybe not enough that they've caused a civil war, but are still pretty big?" he asked.

"Well, race is still something that divides us," Kevin said. "It shouldn't, but it does."

Skye nodded. "It's true, and even though the Civil War is long over and slavery has been abolished for a long time, our country still has a long way to go in regards to equality in that area. Anything else?" He looked around the room.

"Gay and trans rights," another girl, Claire, said, somewhat timidly, and he eyed her. She didn't speak up very often and it was good to hear her input, especially on something so important. From the look in her eyes Skye wondered if her words were personal.

"Yes, that's a really big one," he acknowledged. "Understanding and accepting your sexuality and gender identity is difficult, and it can be really scary. And living in a society that shames you and berates you for it makes it that much harder. A truly beautiful world would be one where our differences unite us rather than divide us. I think the best thing we can do for ourselves is to be authentic, and the best thing we can do for others is to be accepting."

He was looking at the whole classroom as he spoke, but his eyes landed on Claire when he was finished, and he noticed that she was shaking a little as she tucked her hands into the sleeves of her sweatshirt. She opened her mouth like she was about to ask something, but then closed it again.

"Claire, did you have a question?" he asked.

"Uh, no, it's, it's nothing," she stammered, looking down, her blonde hair falling in front of her face.

"You sure?"

She looked back up at him, and the words tumbled out of her mouth. "Are you gay?" She slapped a hand over her mouth, her eyes wide in horror, her cheeks turning bright red.

"Woah," Kevin said. "That happened."

Skye smiled a little, partly because of Claire's reaction, but partly because he really wasn't bothered by her question. She seemed so sincere, so earnest. And if his honesty could be of some help to her, then he was willing to give it. After all, that's why he was there, wasn't it? To help these kids? To make a difference? Although he would have preferred to have this conversation in a one on one setting, maybe this was easier for Claire, and it would help more students than just her for him to say it.

"Yes," he said. "I am." The way her eyes lit up, and the frown on her face turned into the faintest hint of a smile, made it one hundred percent worth it. "And if you, or anyone else wants to talk about it more, you can see me after class, okay?"

"Ha, see, so it could have been his boyfriend," Ben said. "I was so right." He turned to Kevin and pointed a finger at him.

"Yeah, but he isn't," Kevin argued.

"Well, do you have a boyfriend?" Gwen asked.

"We've gotten way off topic now, guys," he said.

The class just groaned and Skye smiled. He loved his job.

~

River

"Hey, Skye, how was your day?" River asked when his roommate walked in the door later that afternoon.

"Good," Skye said, beaming. His eyes were sparkling and his cheeks flushed.

A wide smile split across River's face. "It must have been. You look like you're on cloud nine. What happened?"

"I came out to one of my classes," he said, that huge smile still brimming on his cheeks as he sat in the chair across from River.

River's eyes widened. "Really?"

Skye laughed. "Well, it was part of the conversation. I didn't just come in and announce it out of the blue. But there's a student who I think it might have really helped. She asked me point blank if I was gay, so I told her, and you should have seen the way her face lit up, Riv. It was like she could breathe again. It made my day."

The joy radiating off of Skye made River smile even more. "Good for you. I'm glad you get to be back there. They need you."

Skye's eyes met his. "I'm glad to be back, too, angel, but I don't resent taking care of you. You know that, right? I was happy to do it, and I would have been happy to do it longer if you'd needed me to. I mean that."

The way Skye looked at him, and the sincerity in his voice had River's stomach doing weird flips. He found himself unable to look away from Skye, staring into those apple green eyes. He blinked and swallowed, his mouth dry all of a sudden.

"Where's Jodi?" Skye asked, looking around and bringing River out of his daze.

"Oh, uh, she's napping. I think she was pretty worn out from working all day yesterday and then making the drive. She's only been in there for a few minutes. I told her I would be fine til you got home."

"How was your day?" Skye asked, resting his head back on the chair and closing his eyes.

"It was good. We talked a lot and played some games. Watched some tv. She makes me laugh like crazy, which is kind of a bad thing right now 'cause it makes my ribs hurt more. And she seems to like you a lot, could't stop going on about how amazing you were, although I'm not sure why," River teased.

Skye opened one eye to look at him and raised his eyebrow. "I can still spit in your dinner," he said, and River grinned. "Besides, I'm adorable. What's not to like?"

River gazed at his roommate, his smile fading. Skye's eyes were closed again, arms folded across his chest, and River couldn't think of an answer.

CHAPTER 9

Skye

"So when are you going to ask Jenna out?" Skye asked. It was a couple of days later and he was sitting across from his friend at one of the high top tables at their go to bar. He watched with mirth as Nick choked on his beer and it dribbled down his chin, his eyes watering.

"What?" Nick croaked as he grabbed a napkin and wiped up the mess.

Skye chuckled. "You heard me. I've seen the way you look at her, man. The way you've *been* looking at her. For years. What's with you guys?"

Nick shook his head. "Hell, no. We aren't touching that with a ten foot pole until we talk about the obvious crush you have on a certain roommate of yours."

Skye's cheeks heated. Shit. He'd walked right into that one. "That's different," he said, twirling his straw around in his drink.

"Why?" Nick raised an eyebrow. "We're both crushing hard on our best friends. What's the difference?"

"Ha, so you admit it," Skye's gaze jerked up to meet Nick's as he pointed at his friend. "You do like her." He was beaming as Nick flushed brightly and his eyes widened.

"No, I...I mean, ah, fuck." He threw a french fry across the table, hitting Skye in the head.

Skye laughed. "Ask her out, man." He picked the fry up from his own plate where it had landed and plopped it into his mouth.

"I can't." Nick frowned, his broad shoulders slumped.

"Why not? At least your crush is an option. Mine is straight and in a relationship. I'm screwed."

Nick shook his head again. "She's out of my league, man, I can't expect her to date someone like me."

"What the hell does that mean?" Skye said, eyebrows furrowed. He couldn't imagine anyone not wanting to date Nick. He was the whole package. Gorgeous, sweet, fun, thoughtful.

"Jenna's special. Smart and classy. I'm not like her. I'm messy, and scatterbrained, and I work at a goddamn hardware store. That's not her. She needs to be with a banker, or a lawyer or something. Someone who can provide her with everything she needs and wants, and who dresses in suits and ties and can take her to the theater and spoil her. I can't do that. I live in a one bedroom apartment and I'm still working on paying off my student debt. I got a degree that I don't use. She doesn't want to be saddled with that. Being friends with me is one thing, but dating me is something completely different."

Skye sighed and shook his head now. He knew Nick was wrong, that Jenna had feelings for their friend. He'd noticed for a while now how they flirted with each other, looked at each other when they thought no one noticed. But he didn't feel like it was his place to say so. Still it bothered him to hear Nick talk down about himself like that. Sure he'd gotten a degree he wasn't using, but he loved his job and he worked hard. And the only reason he'd gotten a degree in psychology in the first place was because that's what his parents had wanted him to do. He'd hated it, so when he'd graduated he'd gone a different route. And Skye had been proud of him for doing what he wanted, even if it meant letting his parents be disappointed. He'd worked his way up at the hardware store and was now the manager, and he was happy there. He wasn't rolling in the money, but he was doing well enough.

"Enough about me," Nick said, interrupting his thoughts. "You sure you and River aren't gonna happen? I've seen the way he looks at you too, you know?"

Skye just laughed. "I think you've had a little too much to drink, my friend."

~

River

It had been six weeks since the accident, and River was finally back at work. He'd gotten his car back as well, though he wasn't driving it yet, so Skye had become his chauffeur. It was getting cooler now in Indiana as fall gave way to winter and there was a chill in the air, though no snow covered the ground just yet.

River's ribs were doing better. He had more range of motion now, and was finally able to sleep in his own bed.

Most of all he was just thankful to be off of the couch and out of the house, back to doing what he loved. His ankle wasn't completely healed yet, but he could finally put weight on it, so the doctors had moved him from a cast to a boot, so he wasn't completely immobilized, and he was making slow, steady progress. He was able to do things for himself now, which meant no more asking Skye for help getting in and out of the tub, or drying off, or getting up off of the couch to go to the bathroom, or awkwardly trying to figure out how to dress himself and asking for Skye's help when he failed.

He was back at church and his weekly Bible study, thanks

86

to Anna driving him back and forth, and, God, it felt good to be mostly him again.

Skye had taken him to additional doctor's appointments to check on his ribs and ankle and make sure that everything was healing properly over the last several weeks, and so far, so good. Hopefully in a few more weeks he'd be able to get the boot off, too, and then back to the things he really wanted to be doing again, like running, and rock climbing. He never did them with Skye because his roommate hated running and he was afraid of heights.

He smiled thinking of all the things that made him and Skye different, wondering how on earth they had ever become best friends. But he wouldn't trade it for the world. He loved Skye, more than anything. More than anyone. And just thinking that made his stomach do that weird flip thing again. Man, that was happening more and more lately whenever he thought about Skye. And he was smiling more and more whenever he thought about Skye, too. Even now he felt like he was missing him, which was ridiculous because they'd spent the entire weekend together. They lived together, for Pete's sake. *What is going on? Maybe it's just because he was so good about taking care of me over the past few weeks.*

His phone buzzed in his pocket and he took it out. It was Skye.

Hey, angel, I'm here. You ready?

River flushed at the endearment from his friend. Skye had been calling him that for years, and he'd always liked it. It lifted his spirits and made him feel special, but it had never made him react this way before. **Be out in a sec,** he replied. **Just finishing up with a patient. They're on ice. When they finish I'll be done for the day.**

You doing okay?

Mostly. My ribs and ankle are both a little sore but other than that I'm fine. I could use some ice of my own though.

I'll take care of you when we get home and you can rest, okay? I want you to heal.

Thanks. See you in a bit, River didn't even realize he had a huge smile spread across his face until he tucked his phone back in his pocket and his cheeks were a little sore.

However, he did notice the pain that made him hiss when he stood up. And it wasn't coming from his ankle this time, or his ribs. It was coming from his tailbone. *You've got to be kidding me. Now my ass is hurting too?* Then he remembered back to when Dr. Rosemary had shown him the x-ray at the hospital when he'd had his accident. *Crap. Seriously, I can't get over one thing before something else starts?*

Maybe it was just a one time thing. Maybe it was just the way he stood up, or maybe he'd been sitting down for too long. Maybe it was the chair. He knew in all practicality that it wasn't any of those things, because he had seen the x-ray. He knew his tailbone was dislocated. But why was it waiting until now to cause him problems? *Well, if it's just when I stand up after sitting down on a hard chair for a while, I'll manage.*

But it wasn't. Over the next couple of weeks the pain only intensified. Hard surfaces were the worst, and the longer he sat the more pain he was in when he stood–like someone was stabbing him in the rear end with a knife. It didn't last long, but it was uncomfortable to say the least.

Eventually it got to the point where no matter where he sat, no matter how cushioned the seat was, the pain was just as bad when he stood, and he had to keep himself from wincing.

After a month had gone by, it was to the point where it hurt to sit at all.

Skye

"Hey, did you get the text from Jenna?" Skye asked, walking out of his room and into the kitchen.

"Um, yeah, I don't think I can make it," River replied. He was standing at the bar shoveling scrambled eggs into his mouth.

"Why not? You have plans?" River hesitated but then shook his head.

"Okay, why don't you want to come? You never miss out on game night."

"I just don't feel up to it," River told him, and Skye eyed his friend. He'd been acting off lately and Skye didn't get it. He'd gotten his boot off last week and everything with his ankle was going well. His ribs were better. But he'd been avoiding going to church again and had opted to view it online instead. He'd been missing Bible study after only being back two times. He was being weird.

"Wanna tell me why?"

"Not really," River retorted, shoveling in another mouthful of food. Skye glared at him and he glared right back.

"Seriously, what the hell is going on with you?" Skye asked. "Now that you can finally get out and do stuff you don't want to? Come on, Riv, we want you there."

"Fuck off, Skye," River almost snarled, slamming his fork down on his plate. Skye's eyes widened in shock, his face heating. River had never spoken to him like that. And he couldn't remember him ever using the F bomb. He tolerated it when Skye used it but it just wasn't him. What the hell was going on? He was pissed, that much was obvious, but Skye didn't have any idea why. Did he do something wrong?

"Riv?" he asked as calmly as he could manage, "is everything okay?"

He was shocked to see a tear slide down River's cheek, his demeanor changing in an instant as a look of devastation washed over his features. He pushed his plate aside and rubbed his hands over his face. "I'm sorry," he said, sniffling. "I'm just at the end of myself. I didn't mean to be a jerk. My butt's been killing me for weeks now and I don't know what to do."

"What?" Skye replied, taken aback. "What do you mean?"

"I mean, it hurts to sit. And it hurts to stand back up. Sitting in the car, sitting on the couch, at the table, these stupid bar stools are the worst."

"Why didn't you say something?"

"I just did."

Skye held in a groan and scrubbed a hand over his face. "The doctor said this might happen. Did you call the orthopedist they referred you to? This is because of the dislocated tailbone thing, right?"

River sighed and looked up. "I think so, and no I didn't call anyone. I guess I just kept hoping it would go away. But it's not, Skye. It's getting worse. It hurts like hell." His voice was filled with dismay as he wiped away his tears.

"Have you iced it?" Skye asked, feeling like that maybe was a weird thing to ask about his best friend's ass.

"Yeah, it helps while I'm icing it, but that's it. As soon as I'm done it's hurting again. And it hurts like the dickens to stand back up when I'm done."

"Don't they sell seat cushions for people with sciatica and stuff? Maybe something like that would help."

"I guess I could try that. I'd feel ridiculous, though."

"Better than being in pain every time you sit down, isn't it?"

"Maybe," River moped.

Skye rolled his eyes and pulled out his phone, searching for *seat cushions for tailbone pain* online, then showed River his screen. "There. Find one and try it."

River smirked at him and took the phone.

"If this doesn't help, or it gets worse, you're seeing a doctor," Skye stated, emphatically.

"Yes, Mom," River snarked back, not looking up from Skye's phone.

"So, game night?" Skye said, ignoring his friend. "You coming?"

River bit his lip. "I want to. But I don't know how to play a game if I can't sit down. Plus the car ride there. I just don't think I can. You can go, though. No reason you should miss out on a good time."

"Come on, Riv, they want to see both of us. We're not going to leave you here alone. We'll just explain what's going on and see if they can come here instead of meeting at Jenna's."

River handed Skye his phone back but hesitated.

"What's wrong?" Skye asked, fingers poised on his keypad.

"I don't know if I want to announce that my butt is bothering me. It sounds ridiculous for one thing, and it's embarrassing for another."

"Well what do you want to do? Lie to them?"

"No," he grumbled. "Why don't we just tell them I'm not up for going out?"

"Of course you can, if that's what you want. But don't you think they'll wonder what's going on eventually if you are never sitting when they are around or coming up with excuses for not being able to go anywhere? Do you plan to avoid them forever?"

River let out a breath and ran his fingers through his hair. "God, this is so frustrating."

"Look, I'll tell them," Skye said. He typed a message in the group chat and showed it to River.

Hey, so remember when River had his accident? When they did the x-rays they found that his tailbone was dislocated. Sounds kind of crazy and it wasn't bothering him at the time but now it's acting up and he's been in a lot of pain, especially when he sits, so any chance we can hang out here to avoid a car ride? He might need to lie down or stand for the majority of the evening

"Can I send it?" he asked. River nodded reluctantly, so he hit the send button. "It's going to be okay, Riv. They're our friends. They care about you."

A minute later both of their phones pinged with a text alert. River picked his up and read the message from Nick at the same time as Skye read his.

Ouch. That sucks. I'll bring the beer and chips

I'll bring the dessert Jenna responded a second later. **I hope you get better soon, River. I'm sorry things have been so rough for you lately. Can't wait to see you! We'll play a game on the floor so you can lay down. It'll be fun** 🙂

"See, what did I tell you?" Skye said, smacking him gently on the shoulder, and River smiled, too.

~

River

River found a small amount of relief when he sat at the kitchen table with the seat cushion, but he'd had to give up on sitting at the bar all together now. It was just too painful. The couch only worked if he put the seat cushion down and an ice pack on top of it, and that only lasted for as long as he could keep the ice pack on, which was about twenty minutes, so he'd taken to lying on the couch instead, which meant that it was pretty much the only place in the living room he could be. Bending over had become painful as well, and even walking sometimes. He hated it. He hated what this pain was doing to him, the person it was turning him into. He was exhausted, cranky, and getting angrier and angrier. After finally getting his boot off and feeling like life was getting back to normal again, he was having issues somewhere else.

He'd put off going to see the doctor still because he knew what they would recommend. More physical therapy. Well, he'd been doing physical therapy for his ankle and his tailbone on his own and while his ankle was improving, he couldn't say the same thing for his tailbone.

He didn't even realize how overwhelmed and upset he was until he felt tears sliding down his cheeks as he lay on the couch one evening while Skye made dinner.

~

Skye

"Hey, angel, you—" Skye started, but then stopped short when he turned and saw that his best friend was wiping tears from his eyes. His chest constricted as he walked over to where River was lying on the couch, and knelt down next to him. He didn't even think, just started running his fingers through River's hair, trying to soothe him. It felt so natural, so perfect. Like this was what his fingers were meant to do. They were meant to care for River, to keep River safe, to love River.

"Hey, what's going on?" he asked gently.

"I'm just so angry," River replied. His chest heaved slightly as he wiped away more tears. "I feel like I've just traded one pain for another. I don't understand what's going on. I want my life back."

"I know, angel," Skye said as he moved his fingers to gently, very gently, stroke River's cheek. His roommate's breath hitched and Skye didn't know if it was because of his touch, or because he'd been crying, but either way, River didn't ask him to stop, or push him away. In fact, he seemed to relax, his breath slowing, his eyes closed.

Skye continued to stroke River's cheek softly, just below his ear. Pretty soon, River's chest was rising and falling gently, and though it was inevitable, he knew, the two dinosaurs that Skye had put in front of the ice wall were gone. And Skye wasn't even going to try and put them back.

CHAPTER 10

River

He couldn't do it anymore. It was what he kept telling himself after months of non-stop physical pain, frustrating limitations and feeling overwhelmed emotionally and mentally. He was frustrated, depressed, and honestly the most prevalent emotion was fear. Because he didn't know what to do, or why the pain was so strong. He didn't know why his body wasn't healing itself or if he would ever be back to the way he was before the accident. If he would ever be able to sit again without being in pain.

But the truth of it was, he could tell himself that a hundred times a day, and it didn't matter, because he didn't have a choice. Whether he felt like he could do it anymore or not, he had to.

He'd gone to see his orthopedist at Skye's insistence, and they'd given him pain meds to try which had given him horrible side effects, and hadn't worked, so next he had tried a cortisone injection in his tailbone, which had been painful as hell, and also hadn't helped. He'd gotten relief for all of two hours, and then the pain was back.

So now he was back to see his orthopedist for what felt like the millionth time, carrying his seat cushion with him, which had become his constant companion. At least at the orthopedist's office he didn't feel quite so awkward hauling it around, and wouldn't have to deal with people looking at him like he thought he was too good for normal seats, not realizing that he had a serious reason for actually needing it, and would do anything to be able to not have it.

"So we've tried PT, we've tried injections, and medication," the doctor said. "And nothing has helped?"

"Right." River felt kind of ridiculous being here, but he didn't know what else to do. He was in so much pain, he wasn't even sitting down to talk to the doctor. "Is there anything else? Is surgery an option? I know that seems drastic, but that's where I am right now. I can't sit, or bend over. It even hurts to walk some of the time. And I'm starting to have pain in my low back and hips, too." That had started a couple of weeks ago and was just the icing on the cake.

He wanted to keep going, tell the doctor everything else he couldn't do, hadn't been able to do for weeks, now, because of the pain. *It makes driving really painful so I can't travel far at all. It's making doing my job difficult, which I just finally got back to. I have to take up the entire couch at home. I can't have any sort of social life. No dates, no church. No movies or restaurants. I still can't run or go rock climbing.* But he didn't say any of that. Instead he just said, "I'm pretty extra desperate. I'd be okay at this point with just taking the thing out."

"That's rarely done," the doctor said. "None of the physicians here actually do tailbone removal surgery. It's a major operation. The recovery is long. And the scar tissue resulting can be just as painful if not more so. There's a risk of infection and damage to the colon. And it takes anywhere from 3 months to a year to even *start* feeling relief after the surgery. So it may or may not help."

"So, what do I do?" River asked, trying not to let his voice tremble as he spoke.

The doctor spoke with sympathy. "Keep up with the PT

and keep using the cushion. I'm afraid that's all you really can do."

When he got back out to the car he rested his head against the steering wheel, and sobbed once again.

~

Skye

"How did your appointment go?" Skye asked when River walked in the door a little after six that evening. He looked exhausted, crestfallen. His shoulders stooped and his eyes were glassy, like he was in a world far away. "River?" he repeated gently, putting his hand on his friend's arm to get his attention.

"Hmmm?" River mumbled, gazing up at him, his lips pursed.

"How was your appointment?"

"Not good," he said with a sigh. "I asked about surgery. He didn't flat out tell me no, but he said it was rare. He said they don't 'recommend it'." He put the phrase in finger quotes. "I don't know what else to do, Skye. I can't keep living like this. Not living. I'm scared." He bit his bottom lip as his eyes swam with unshed tears.

"Okay, well I was looking into it," Skye told him, "and I may have found something that can help you. But it sounds pretty unpleasant."

"What is it?" River asked, a spark returning to his sapphire eyes. He'd been through so much the past couple of months and had tried not to get hopeful over new things to try, because so far they hadn't proven effective. But Skye could see the hope in his gaze now.

"I'd never heard of it before, but you may have, in your line of work," he said. "Pelvic floor therapy?"

"I'm familiar with it," River said. "I know they can teach

you some stretches and do strengthening exercises and stuff, but that's usually used for women, especially after childbirth. That's not really my problem, Skye."

"No, but I was looking at their website and it looks like they can also move your tailbone back into position manually, which might help. I know the chiropractor didn't work but this is a little different 'cause they manipulate it from the inside. It's worth a shot, right?"

Skye watched as River's face went ashen and he swallowed. His chest started rising and falling as his breathing picked up. He recoiled and backed away from Skye, shaking his head. "No," he said, trembling. His voice was soft when he spoke, his lower lip quivering. "I can't do that." Then he walked into his room and shut the door.

~

When Skye knocked on River's door seconds later there was no answer, so he opened it slowly and walked in to see River lying on his side in bed, eyes closed, his legs drawn up and his arms crossed over his chest. He took deep breaths in and out, and Skye noticed that the bottle of anti-anxiety meds on his nightstand was open and he was gripping the ring on his middle finger, twisting it around, trying to ground himself.

Fuck, what had he done? He'd made River have an anxiety attack. He hadn't meant to. He had just wanted to help, and the pelvic floor therapy had sounded like a legitimate option. God, he was so stupid.

He made his way over and sat on the edge of the bed next to his friend, then began to rub his back. "You're okay, Riv," he told him gently. "You're okay."

River started to breathe more evenly as the tears descended once again. Skye never minded when River cried, except that it broke his heart every single time, and he was pretty sure he'd seen him crying more in the past month and a half than in the last ten years combined. And all because of his tailbone. It wasn't just that, though, Skye knew. Not just the physical pain, but the reality of what it meant. Of how limited he'd been, how much this injury was affecting his life.

Remarkable how such a small part of your body could cause so much pain by being dislocated, how it could inhibit so many aspects of your life that you would normally not even think about; how something so unremarkable as sitting was something he was now realizing he'd taken for granted over the past twenty eight years. How he could sit down without thinking twice about it, without having to carry a seat cushion everywhere he went in order to take the edge off of the pain. How he could travel, or ride a bike, or go to a theme park, and how River couldn't do any of those things now. God, he never thought he would see being able to sit down as a blessing. And he hated this for River. He doesn't deserve it. And he would give anything to make it better.

River sniffled and removed his glasses before wiping his eyes and nose. "I'm sorry, Skye," he murmured finally, his breath still shaky. "But I don't think I can do that. Even if it means living with the pain. I'm sorry you did all that work for nothing."

"Fuck the work, River, I don't care about that," Skye said. He rubbed River's back a little while longer before he asked, "Is it because of what happened to you?"

River nodded and sniffled again, then wiped his eyes once more.

"River, you don't have to do it, okay? You don't have to do anything you don't want to do. It was just an idea. And I didn't think of how it would trigger things for you. I'm sorry. I should have thought of that."

"It's okay." River gave him a soft smile.

"Hey. I do have something else that might help you. I'll be right back." Skye left and came back a minute later with a rather large box. River propped himself up on his elbow, looking at him curiously as he unpackaged it and pulled out a giant wedge pillow.

"I thought this might make it easier for you to recline in bed," Skye said, hefting it over.

River moved aside as Skye set it down behind him. He waited for Skye to lay his pillow on top of it, and then he rested back against it to try it out. Skye's chest expanded and his heart leapt when River smiled. Then more tears slid down River's cheeks.

"Are those good tears or bad tears?" Skye let out a breath when River smiled again.

"Good," he said. "It's helping. I can actually sit for the first time in months without being in horrible pain. This is amazing, thank you. I can't believe I didn't think of it." He could sense the relief, appreciation and gratitude in his friend's voice and the way he was looking at Skye with those beautiful blue eyes. "How did you find out about this?"

Skye shrugged and flushed. "I researched."

"You did all of this just for me? On your own time, without me asking or anything?" River was looking at him in the way that made his heart beat faster and his stomach fill with butterflies, his eyes so warm and tender.

"I, uh," he stumbled over his words, blushing. "Yeah, I guess." He reached up and rubbed the back of his neck with his hand, gaze darting to the floor. "You want some dinner?" he asked, "I can bring it in here."

"That would be nice. Thank you." There was that smile again. The one that made him weak in the knees. The one that sucked the air right out of his lungs until he felt like he couldn't breathe.

He might just as well chuck the tank he had in front of the ice wall now, too, 'cause that whole damn wall was melting right in front of him.

CHAPTER 11
River

River lay on his side on the couch, hands tucked under his head. Anna sat at the other end of the couch with his feet in her lap. She'd been asking about River for a while, wanting to see him, telling him she missed him, letting him know she was thinking of him. She'd been around at least twice a week in the evenings since he'd had his accident and they'd watched movies and had dinner together on the sofa as he iced his ankle and ribs, but ever since his tailbone injury he'd been more hesitant to have her around.

He didn't know how to tell her that he couldn't go out because his butt hurt. And he was humiliated at the idea of having her over to his house and having to take up the entire couch to watch a movie because it hurt too much to sit. It sounded absolutely ridiculous. What if she didn't believe him? What if she just thought it was some lame excuse for not spending time with her? But Skye had once again convinced him to be honest with her, and he had been, and she'd been just as gracious and understanding as Nick and Jenna had been. He still felt like a complete idiot but at least she was here, and they were spending time together. Even if she wasn't sitting next to him like she normally would be, holding his hand or cuddling close.

He felt her small fingers starting to massage his feet and he let out a soft moan. "You don't have to do that."

She smiled at him. "I don't mind. You've had it rough lately. You could use some pampering."

"It feels good," he said, and wiggled his toes. "I won't stop you." The movie continued to play and she continued to massage his feet. And God, it felt so good. Her hands were small, but they were warm, and soft, applying just the right amount of pressure. "You're good at that," he said, after a while, his voice relaxed and a bit rougher than normal. She smiled and planted a kiss on his foot, making him flush.

"I used to give my mom massages. She has fibromyalgia and it really helped her. I'm pretty familiar with chronic health issues."

He nodded, then reached over and squeezed her arm. "Thank you. For being so patient with me. I know these last several weeks I've been kind of MIA. I just, I didn't know how to tell you what was going on. I was scared you wouldn't understand. It's kind of weird, you know? And I'm not sure how much longer it's going to be an issue even, and I hate that I have to be laying here, taking up the entire sofa. I want to be better, and I want to be the boyfriend who's taking you out and going to church with you."

Anna scooted out from under his feet and leaned over, planting a kiss on his lips. He drank her in, placing a hand on her cheek and kissing her back. "God, I missed this." He looked into her green eyes as she pulled back and smiled.

"Me, too. I get it, though, us not spending as much time together with everything that's been going on." She took his hand and squeezed it. "But I don't mind being here, if this is where you have to be, River. As long as we're together. I know you're struggling right now, but please don't push me away. And please don't ignore me."

He nodded, so thankful that she understood, that she was so quick to forgive him. That she was trying to make this work. She moved back to her spot by his feet. "More?" she asked, grinning at him.

"Please?" He smiled back.

A moment later Skye came in the front door carrying bags of groceries. He unloaded them and then made his way into his bedroom before coming back out in his pajamas a while later.

"You guys having fun?"

"Yeah, we're just finishing up our movie," River replied.

"Okay, well, I'm gonna hang out in my room for a bit and then head to bed." Skye bent over and placed a chaste kiss on River's head. "Night, angel."

"Night, Skye," River replied, unable to keep the smile from splitting his face.

"Night, Anna," Skye said, waving at her. She waved back, but River saw her biting her lip as Skye exited the room.

"You okay?" he asked.

"Yeah, of course." She gave him a small smile. "I'm fine."

River's breath caught in his throat when he pulled up to their condo a couple of days later. Christmas lights adorned the bushes in front of their small window, and ran across the roof. In the middle of the yard was a single tree, its trunk wrapped in the same sparkling white lights. A sleigh and reindeer decorated the front lawn, and a giant red mailbox sat on the front porch that read, "Letters to Santa."

He'd been so focused on his pain and how miserable he was, on how he knew there was no way he would be able to make the drive to see his aunt Jodi this year. Normally, he would be the one to put up the Christmas decorations because of Skye's fear of heights, but he'd been so worn out from dealing with everything that he just couldn't. He hadn't even mentioned it to Skye.

But there they were. And they brightened up the whole neighborhood, and his heart. And they made him smile.

Skye made him smile.

Suddenly he couldn't wait to get inside and see his roommate.

It was two weeks until Christmas, and snow covered the ground. He was bundled in his gray wool coat, black gloves and a turquoise scarf when he stepped out of the car, wincing at the pain in his tailbone. He trudged through the snow and up the front walk, making sure to get rid of as much snow as he could before he stepped inside.

When he opened the door to the condo and saw the beautifully decorated Christmas tree with blue and gold ornaments, the white sparkling lights that adorned it, lighting up the dimly lit living room, giving it a warm ambiance, the gold ribbon on the tree for garland, and a twinkling star on top, he almost cried.

"Skye?" he called as he slipped off his shoes, then unwrapped his scarf and removed his gloves. He shoved the gloves in his coat pocket and hung the scarf over the hook by the front door, all the while staring at the tree. It was absolutely breathtaking.

"Hey, handsome," Skye said, entering from the kitchen with a smile as River took off his coat. "You like it?"

River met his gaze, Skye's green eyes warm and sparkling under the glow of the lights. He must have sensed how emotional this was making River because he looked down, shoving his hands into his pockets, blushing.

"You did all of this when you got home?" River asked. "After a full day's work? In this freezing weather? It's beautiful. And you even went up on a ladder? You don't do ladders, Skye. What's up with you, lately? You're being extra sweet."

"I just wanted to cheer you up," Skye said, shrugging his shoulders.

"Well, it worked."

Skye looked up, cheeks still flushed, and a timid smile on his handsome face. His gaze locked with River's, and River found himself swallowing, his chest tightening. What was happening to him? He was staring into Skye's eyes, and looking at his plump lips, and...what the heck? He swallowed again and glanced away.

"Dinner's ready," Skye said, clearing his throat as he motioned for River to follow him. "You want it in bed?"

"I can stand," River said, joining him at the bar. Skye had cooked a delicious meal of salmon, roasted asparagus and mashed potatoes, and it was making River's mouth water.

"You ready for a break?" he asked as they dug in. He had to stop himself from moaning around his mouthful as the flavor exploded on his tongue. Butter, garlic, and parmesan cheese. River loved Skye's cooking.

"Yeah, I'm excited to see my family," Skye said. "Heading to Mom's place in Kansas and Jaden and Chloe are gonna meet us there. I would have asked you to come, but I know you can't travel."

"No, it's fine. When I told Aunt Jodi what was going on she said she would come to me."

Skye smiled and nodded.

"Skye, I've been thinking," River said, after a moment of silence. He picked at his food, moving it around on his plate but never actually gathering it on his fork.

"About what?" Skye swallowed his mouthful of food.

"About that manual therapy you were talking about. I don't know. Maybe I should try it."

Skye blinked. "You sure?"

"No, I'm not *sure*. But I feel like I can't keep dealing with the level of pain I'm in, and I can't keep complaining about it if I'm not willing to try everything available to me to help me get better. It scares me, but I feel like, if it might help get me some sense of normalcy back, I need to give it a chance."

Skye's eyes were soft and compassionate as he gazed at River. Then he rested his hand on River's shoulder. "I'll support you, whatever you want to do. You know I'm here for you."

His eyes widened and he stammered when River asked, "Would you come with me?"

"Uh," he swallowed his food and covered his mouth with his hand.

"You don't have to." River looked back at his plate and bit his lip. "I get that it's kind of weird."

"No, I don't mind," Skye replied, quickly. "I'm just kind of surprised you want me there. I thought that would make you *more* uncomfortable."

"Yeah, I get that. But for some reason, the idea of having you there makes me less upset and anxious about the whole ordeal. And if I do start having flashbacks or a panic attack, I'm pretty sure you're the only one who's going to be able to help me work through it."

River heard his intake of breath, and then Skye swallowed. His response was barely audible, "Okay, I'll come."

∾

Skye

"You okay, Riv?' Skye asked as they sat in the car on the way back from seeing the pelvic floor therapist.

1.5 HOURS EARLIER

Skye couldn't be more proud of River. He'd talked with the therapist about his concerns, about his history, and why he was hesitant about the therapy, and she had assured him that he was in good hands, that he was safe, and that they dealt with many patients in their line of work who had a history of sexual assault and the traumatic memories and associations that went hand in hand with it, and were hesitant to go forward with this kind of therapy for the same reasons. She told him that if at any moment he felt uncomfortable or changed his mind, she would be done, he just had to say so. He nodded and Skye and the therapist left to let River get undressed from the waist down.

When they came back in, River was lying on his side, covered with a sheet, his hands under his head. "I'm going to put a glove on, and some lubricant," the therapist told him. "Are you okay so far?"

River took a deep breath and let it out, then nodded.

"Okay, I need you to relax, and just breathe," the therapist instructed. "Then bear down like you're having a bowel movement. That will actually make it easier for me to get in and less uncomfortable for you. It shouldn't hurt, but if it does, let me know. It'll feel cold, and you'll feel my finger sliding in, okay? If at any point you need me to stop, just say so."

"Can I stand by him?" Skye asked, feeling a desperate need to be by his friend's side.

"Of course." She smiled at him and he moved over to the other side of the table so he could see River. His eyes closed as he breathed in again, and Skye reached out and took his hand. River's gaze met his as he breathed out.

"You got this," Skye told him. "You're safe. I'm here." *I love you. You're so strong. And so beautiful. And you've never let your scars define you. I am so proud of you.*

River's grip on his hand tightened as he breathed out again, then shifted ever so slightly as the therapist's finger slid inside him.

"You've got a lot of scar tissue in here," she stated, matter of factly, "which could be causing a lot of the problem if the adhesions formed on the surrounding muscles and tendons are pulling on your tailbone. And your tailbone is definitely dislocated. It's deviated to the left like the x-ray showed and it's also tucked under. So I can move your tailbone back into place, but then we're gonna have to work on doing some pelvic floor exercises to relax those muscles and give you more room so your tailbone can stay in place. We'll also tape it on the outside so that it stays in place. But the exercises are going to be essential. And then I would recommend that you come back as often as possible to do some myofascial release and work on breaking up the scar tissue that's built up in here because that will help too. You doing okay so far?"

River nodded even as his gaze stayed locked with Skye's. His hand hadn't moved from Skye's, and Skye gave it a gentle squeeze.

"I'm fine," River said.

"Okay, I've reached your tailbone. You're going to feel a tugging sensation, and maybe a sharp pain."

River grunted and winced.

"You okay?" she asked again.

He nodded.

"Okay, I'm going to come out slowly now," she told him. "Just keep breathing in and out." River did. "Okay, one long exhale," she instructed, and then she was sliding out and standing up, removing her gloves and tossing them in the trash. Then she turned back to River with a warm smile.

"You did great. Now we'll get you taped up, and I'll show you those exercises. I would like to see you once a week for the next few months, just to get rid of some of that scar tissue and do the myofascial release I talked about. It'll be really similar to what we did today but it will take a little longer, and we'll do internal and external work around your tailbone. If you want to take some time to think about it you can. I totally understand. But I do think it would really help your physical health improve and help you get back some quality of life. Let me know what you decide. I'll be back with the tape and the copies of those stretches."

River sat up. "Can I ask you something?" he said, somewhat hesitantly.

"Of course," she answered.

"The scar tissue you're talking about, is there any way to tell what caused that? I mean, was it from the assault?"

"It's quite possible. I'm afraid that's often the case for victims of sexual assault. But I'm afraid there's really no way to know for sure in your particular case," she said. "You said you also had a bad fall several years back, and a car accident not too long ago, correct?"

River nodded.

"So any one of those things or a combination of the three could have caused it. But we're going to do our best to help you get better, okay? Just hang in there."

River nodded, biting his lip. "Thank you."

～

Skye's breath hitched when River reached over and took his hand, pulling it away from the steering wheel and interlocking their fingers together. His heart started beating rapidly as River's warm skin pressed against his, and focusing on driving became increasingly difficult.

"River?" he said, swallowing hard. He'd held River's hand before, especially lately, but not like this. River's thumb skated over his hand and Skye sucked in another breath. It felt different. Tender, and, dare he say...intimate. Breathing was becoming more and more difficult, and Skye's brain was malfunctioning.

His dick twitched. Fuck. He didn't want to take his hand away from River's but he felt like if he didn't they would end up in a wreck. He couldn't think straight with River touching him like this. And he didn't even know what River meant by it. Was it intimate? How could it be? River still had a girlfriend. And he'd never shown any kind of sexual attraction for Skye. What was he supposed to do with this?

"I'm okay, Skye," River said, softly. Then he reached over with his other hand, and took their linked hands into his, before placing them on his lap. He began to stroke over the top of Skye's hand repeatedly. Skye's cock twitched again and started to thicken in his jeans. If River didn't stop soon Skye was going to have a very visible boner. "And I don't know if I would have been without you. Thank you for being there."

Skye swallowed hard again. Okay, seriously what the hell was River doing? "Sure," he said, trying to stay calm and collected, as his body heated up and his skin prickled. He began to slowly remove his hand from River's and put it back on the steering wheel. Then he spent the rest of the drive home trying not to read too much into what the hell had just happened.

CHAPTER 12

River

River had a bit more pep in his step a week later. His tailbone wasn't giving him as much grief as it had been. He'd been doing his stretches, even though it made him feel ridiculous. He'd reapplied the tape like they had told him to when necessary, he'd even gone back in to see the therapist for another session and to have more internal work done, breaking up the scar tissue like she'd recommended. And he could feel some relief now. Not a lot, but some.

He was proud of himself for taking that step, as hard as it had been for him emotionally, to do what he needed to do physically. To take control of his health, of his life, to not let his past stand in the way of having a healthy present or a healthy future. He'd learned that these walls were going to keep coming up, and he would keep knocking them down, pushing forward, and becoming the best version of himself he could possibly be. He was worthy of healing. And that's what he told himself at every appointment. When he felt that pressure inside of him, when he felt his anxiety spike, he remembered that he was in control, and that he was safe. But he also knew that he could never have made it as far as he had without Skye. Without his loyalty, compassion, kindness, and support.

He pushed River to be better every single day, and to live the life that he deserved. River couldn't ask for a better friend.

He pulled into the parking lot of the coffee shop where Anna had asked him to meet her, and climbed out of his car. He was looking forward to seeing her. It'd been a tough couple of months for her, he knew, with them not being able to go places like they used to. He hated that. Honestly, he was a little surprised she hadn't broken up with him because of it. But she hadn't. She was still here, checking in on him, asking how he was doing. Visiting with him at his condo when she could. They had managed one date recently where River had taken her on a tour of Christmas lights, and they'd sipped on hot chocolate while they walked around, admiring the different displays, until they had gotten too cold and returned to the condo to watch a movie, with River lying on the sofa yet again.

He had told her that he'd started some new therapy but hadn't gone into detail about it. He wasn't really comfortable with that yet. But now that he could see a light at the end of the tunnel again he was hoping Anna and he could start to see more of each other, get things back on track. She'd been very patient, and he was hopeful that if he could start sitting for longer periods of time he could actually take her to a movie or dinner again. In the meantime maybe they could try bowling, or indoor mini golf, now that he didn't have as much pain when he bent over.

He'd decided he wanted to try and be more active again in general. It'd been months since he'd done something that truly made him happy. Unfortunately his ankle wasn't healed to the point where he could go running or rock climbing yet, but he was hopeful that in the next month or so it would be.

"Hey," he said with a smile when he saw her sitting at a small two person table in the corner of the cafe. Her red hair was down, falling over her shoulders, and she wore a black sweater with dark jeans and black boots. She had one leg crossed over the other and was playing with one of her earrings as she sipped on her coffee.

"Hi," she said, giving him a small smile in return.

He set his seat cushion down and sat on top of it. "We'll see how long this lasts. I haven't been anywhere but a doctor's office in a while and I'm only starting to feel some improvement."

"That's okay," she said, glancing down. "This won't take long." Her gaze met his and there was genuine sadness in her eyes.

River flushed and his heart stopped. "What do you mean?" His eyes danced over her face. "Are...are you breaking up with me?" He barely choked out the words. And when Anna's eyes started to fill with tears and she reached over to take his hand, he jerked it away, tears filling his eyes now, too. He pressed his lips together and looked away.

"Just listen, River," she pleaded gently. "Please. Before you go jumping to conclusions and assuming this is about your health issues, or us not spending as much time together as I'd like, because it's not. I like you, a lot. A lot, a lot. And I know you've been through a ton of crap the last few months that's not in your control, and you're doing the best you can to deal with it. You've been super honest about your past and your mental health struggles, and I respect that so much. In fact, it makes me love you more."

River looked at Anna and blinked, his chest constricting as he spoke through tears. "Wait, you..." he swallowed. "You love me?"

Anna nodded. "I think I do," she said, wiping away the tear that slid down her cheek.

River's head was spinning. "Then why are you breaking up with me?"

She reached for his hand once again and this time he let her take it. Looking into his eyes, both of them crying, she said, "Because, River, you don't love me, and you never will."

He gaped, eyes widening. "What? How can you know that?"

She gave a sad smile. "I just do," she said, squeezing his hand. "Your heart belongs to someone else. But I'll always be here, if you need someone to talk to." She stood up and kissed him lightly on the forehead, then walked away.

River sat there, stunned, confused, and heartbroken.

~

Skye

"Hey, you're back early," Skye said when he came out of the bedroom and saw River lying on the couch. "Does that mean your tailbone was hurting too much? I thought the therapy was helping." He made his way into the kitchen and started to make dinner.

"It is," River said softly, not looking at him. "My tailbone is okay, Skye."

"Oh, good. Guess I'll cook for two then. What do you want?"

"I'm not really hungry." River's gaze still didn't meet his as he played with the creases on the sofa.

"What's wrong? Is everything okay with you and Anna?"

River's chest heaved and then his eyes finally met Skye's. It was only then that Skye saw they were red and puffy behind his glasses.

"She broke up with me." He sniffled. "She told me she loved me, and then she broke up with me." His chest heaved once more as he removed his glasses and held them in one hand, wiping at his eyes with the other.

"What? Why would she do that?" Anna was crazy about River. Skye knew she was. He never thought she would be the one to break up with him. Not in a million years. Shit. He just couldn't catch a break.

River sniffled. "I don't know. She said something about my heart belonging to someone else."

A loud banging noise reverberated throughout the condo when the pan Skye had been holding hit the kitchen floor, his breath leaving his body at the same moment. He stood in the kitchen, unable to move, stunned, his heart pounding.

"Skye?" River said, jerking up from the couch at the noise. "What was that? Are you okay?"

Skye snapped out of his daze. "Yeah," he said, bending over to pick up the pan. "Just clumsy. Sorry. Are you okay?" He was ten different kinds of flustered right now and his brain was only functioning at about ten percent capacity, and for some reason he couldn't figure out where to set the stupid pan down. But his hand was shaking, so eventually he settled on the stove and took a deep breath, trying to calm his racing heart. Did Anna mean him? Who else could she have meant? But he couldn't allow himself to think that River could have feelings for him, because if he was wrong, there would be no coming back from that. Loving River, and not telling him was one thing. But believing River loved him back, and then having that stripped away, was a pain he couldn't live through.

River wiped his eyes and stood, making his way over to the bar as he slid his glasses back on. He rested his forearms on the counter as Skye washed his hands in the sink across from him. "I'm not so good right now," he said, "but I will be, I guess. I kind of have to be." He shrugged. "As much as it hurts, and as much as I know I cared about her and enjoyed being with her, I have to admit I wasn't in love with her. And maybe she's right. Maybe I never would have been. So maybe it's for the best. She deserves someone who will love her back. And I don't think that's me."

"You'll find the right person some day, Riv."

"So will you, Skye." River gave him a small smile.

I found you ten years ago, River.

CHAPTER 13

Skye

Skye gave his brother the biggest hug ever when Jaden and Chloe showed up at Grace Mckenzie's place in Kansas the following week for Christmas. He gave almost as big of a hug to Chloe.

"It's good to see you, too, Skye," Chloe said, trying to catch her breath. Her dark hair was up in a ponytail and it swished as Skye put her back on her feet again, her brown eyes full of warmth.

"Man, I missed you guys," Skye said, beaming at them.

"Where's Mom?" Jaden asked.

"Be there in a minute!" Grace called from the kitchen. "Busy burning a pie!"

They all laughed and Chloe hurried off to help Grace in the kitchen.

"How's work?" Jaden asked as he and Skye settled in the living room.

"Good," Skye said. "How's school?"

"Good. Busy, and insane, but good. I actually had to bring some stuff with me but I'm hoping it won't take up too much of my time." Jaden was getting his Masters degree in anthropology.

"So, when are you two gonna tie the knot?" Skye asked, lifting a bottle of beer to his lips and grinning at his brother.

"As soon as I'm out of school, hopefully," Jaden said. "We've talked about it. Trust me, it's happening."

"It better. If you don't marry her, I will." Skye winked at his brother and Jaden chuckled.

"Since we're on the topic," Jaden said, giving Skye *that* look. "You seeing anyone?"

Shaking his head, Skye swallowed another sip of beer.

"Well, is there anyone you are interested in?"

Skye glanced away as a flush crept up his cheeks.

"Ahh, I knew it." Jaden scooted closer to the edge of the couch in anticipation. "Come on, spill. Who is it?"

Skye didn't say anything, just took another sip of beer.

"Skye?" his brother prodded. "Who is he? Where does he work? How do you know him? And if you are interested in him, why the hell haven't you done anything about it?"

Setting his drink on the coffee table, Skye grimaced as he turned to his brother. "'Cause it's River," he admitted, his face heating even more as he bit his lip.

Jaden's eyes were wide. "River?" he said. "River, River? Like, college roommate, guy you've lived with for ten years, best friend, River. That River?"

Skye nodded. "Yeah, look, I know it's ridiculous, Jay. There's no way things could ever work out between us. And I've been doing my damnedest to keep it from happening, but..." He buried his face in his hands and groaned.

"You're in love with him."

The groan was louder as Skye nodded. "That damn ice wall is a fucking puddle now," he mumbled, then took another sip of beer, leaning back in his seat on the sofa.

"What?" Jaden raised an eyebrow.

"It's nothing," Skye sighed, running his fingers through his blond waves. "It's an image I had in my head of a giant ice wall that I kept up, kind of like a barricade of all of the reasons that kept me from falling in love with River over the last ten years, and in my mind I had all this stuff in front of it, but they're gone now, and so is the wall, and—"

"Wait a second." Jaden held up a hand. "What do you need some metaphorical wall for, anyway? Why can't you be in love with River?"

"Well, for starters, he doesn't exactly bat for my team. And for another thing, he's religious. I just, I don't know. I'm sure he wants to be with someone who will go to church with him and read the Bible, and pray, and all that stuff, right? But that's just not for me. I can't make myself believe what he does, no matter how much I love him. And I would never ask him to stop believing in what he does for my sake."

"Why would either of you have to do that?" Jaden asked. "Skye, even if your relationship changed, why would either of you have to change what you believe or who you are to make that happen? You've made it work so far. You think River would expect you to become a Christian if you guys started having sex?"

"River won't have sex before marriage," Skye said. "Religious thing."

"Right, okay, so if you guys started dating, do you think he'd expect you to suddenly change who you are, or what you believe? 'Cause that doesn't sound like River to me. He's never forced anything about his faith on you. He's always loved you and accepted you for who you are. And you've done the same for him. That's part of what makes your friendship so special. You guys see that you don't have to agree on everything to get along and care for each other. You don't have to believe the same things to build a life together. And I think you both could respect those differences just like you do now, if anything were to happen between you."

Skye bit his lip, mulling over his brother's words before he said, "Well, there's still the whole River not being gay thing."

Jaden shrugged. "Yeah, maybe."

"What does that mean?"

"I'm just saying, I've seen the way you guys interact with each other, and I'm not entirely sure that's true."

"Are you kidding? Jaden, I'm the gay one. Don't you think I would notice if River was flirting with me?"

"Not if River doesn't even know it himself. I think River might not be aware of that part of himself yet. Sometimes it takes people longer than others, for whatever reason. Maybe it's something he still needs to figure out. I'm just saying, don't give up on him yet. Give him time. You might be surprised."

Skye took another long swig of beer. *I think I need to get drunk.*

CHAPTER 14

Skye

"Hey, Riv, how was your Christmas?" Skye asked a week later when River stumbled out of his room around nine-thirty in the morning. His dark hair was tousled and he wore a gray T-shirt and plaid flannel pajama pants. Skye couldn't help smiling at how adorably rumpled River looked as he blinked behind his black frames. He took his glasses off and wiped them on the hem of his shirt, lifting it just enough to give Skye a peek of his flat, toned stomach and the trail of dark hair leading down to the waistband of his pants and disappearing underneath. His mouth watered and his dick twitched but he managed to hold in his groan.

River slid his glasses back on and yawned, with no fucking clue how completely captivated Skye was by him. How much he turned Skye on. How fucking beautiful he was. How much Skye ached to touch him, kiss him, make love to him. How desperately he wanted River to be his. How Skye would feel complete if he could just spend the rest of his life taking care of River, and loving him to the best of his ability, knowing that River loved him back.

"It was fine," River said, then ran his fingers through his mussed hair. "Sometimes I wish I had more family to celebrate with, but at least I have my aunt. I told her about Anna and I breaking up. She said she was sorry, but she didn't seem surprised." He shrugged. "She slept in your bed. I hope that's okay. I changed the sheets and stuff."

"Of course," Skye told him. "Not a problem."

"How's your tailbone?" he asked as he handed River his coffee and watched him smile. "Doing any better?"

"It's a little better. Still having trouble sitting for long periods of time, though, or without my seat cushion at all. I don't think I'm ever getting rid of that thing. I'm still doing therapy for it. Getting rid of the scar tissue seems to be helping but it's not a cure all, unfortunately, and I've had to have my tailbone re-positioned multiple times because it doesn't want to stay in place."

Skye smiled softly at him. "You know that ring on your finger, Riv?"

River looked at it. The one that said, 'Rise'. "What about it?"

"You live up to that, every single day. You're amazing, and strong. And I'm so proud of you."

River gave a soft smile and his cheeks pinkened. "Thank you."

River's phone rang just then and he walked into his room to answer it.

Skye heard him say a hello, and then something muffled, followed by several minutes of silence. When River walked back out of the room with the phone in his hand, he looked dazed, shell-shocked, and a bit unsteady. Like he wasn't quite sure he believed whatever he'd just heard on the phone.

"River?" Skye said, moving closer to him. "Is everything okay?"

But River was still in a daze and now tears were starting to form in his eyes. His knees gave out and he collapsed, his breath coming in short gasps, as he let out a broken, choked sob. Skye knelt next to him as he shook and wept, gathering him in his arms. "My aunt..." River choked out between sobs, "there was an accident." Then he was pressing closer as Skye's arms enveloped him, his hands rubbing up and down River's back and arm, Skye's forehead pressed to River's temple. River turned, burying his head in Skye's neck, his body shaking as he wept, his arms wrapping around Skye's shoulders, and Skye hugged him tighter, his arms sliding around River's waist as he pulled his friend close. River was practically in his lap now. "She's dead," he wailed. The anguish poured off of him in waves, and Skye couldn't help the tears that filled his eyes now, too.

Fuck. No. Not this. River doesn't need any more shit to deal with. Not this. Not Jodi. Fuck. Fuck. Fuck.

As tears fell from Skye's eyes he held River close and let him weep. This beautiful warrior who never seems to be done fighting, losing, enduring. "I'm so sorry, River," he whispered. He kept one arm around his friend's waist and the other moved to the back of River's neck. He stroked the short hairs there, and River folded into him even more.

Skye promised himself that he wouldn't let go until River did.

~

"Riv, can I do anything for you?" Skye asked later that day after River had called his boss to talk about taking some time off for bereavement and a trip to Cincinnati for Jodi's funeral.

"I think I'm gonna go lay down," his friend said. "I'm feeling pretty drained. Thank you, Skye." His eyes were red and puffy from all of the crying he'd already done, and he looked exhausted in every sense of the word. And Skye knew this was only the beginning.

River puttered off to his room and shut the door, and didn't come back out for hours.

Around five o'clock, Skye decided to check on him and see

if he was awake and wanted to eat something, so he knocked on the door softly.

"Come in," he heard River say. When he opened the door, River was wiping tears from his eyes and sniffling.

"Hey, came to see if you're hungry. Can I bring you anything?"

"I don't really feel like eating," River said, sitting up. "But I probably should."

"Soup sound okay?"

River nodded and Skye headed to the kitchen to start on his spinach and tortellini soup. It was one of River's favorites and Skye was hoping it would help comfort him, even a little. When it was ready he brought it to River's room, and his heart shattered when he saw River sitting in bed, against his wedge pillow that Skye had bought him, staring into the distance as silent tears spilled down his cheeks.

"Hey." Skye sat on the side of the bed next to him. "It's ready. Try to eat something." He handed the bowl and spoon to River and brushed his thumbs over his friend's cheeks, wiping away his tears.

River took the bowl but didn't touch the spoon for the longest time. Finally he looked up at Skye and said, "Would you stay with me?" His voice was so broken, just a shell, and Skye nodded.

"Of course." He ran his fingers through River's hair and pressed a kiss to his forehead, his heart lifting at the thought that just his presence might be a comfort to River right now. He sat on the bed next to his friend, pillows propped up behind himself, and he smiled when River started eating. He smiled even more when River finished in only a few minutes. Then Skye took their dishes and brought them out to the kitchen before coming back to check on River and deliver a glass of water.

River took the glass gratefully and drank it down. "Do you still want me with you?" Skye asked.

River's cheeks reddened a little and he nodded. "If that's okay." He rubbed his arm with his hand. "I don't want to be alone right now. And my bed is more comfortable than the couch."

"It's always okay," Skye said, climbing back onto the bed. "Do you want me to set up the laptop so we can watch something?"

"Sure," River shrugged. "You can turn on anything. I don't really care."

So Skye set the laptop up on the bed and turned on Disney's *Up*.

River raised an eyebrow at him. "Really?"

"What?" Skye said. "It's cute. I like Dug."

River smiled ever so faintly, and that made Skye's heart soar. Being able to put a smile on his face in the midst of such a difficult time was priceless.

Half way through the movie River removed his wedge and replaced it with his regular pillow so he could lay down. Skye decided to join him.

"Skye?" River said, a moment later, his voice filled with exhaustion and defeat.

"Ready for bed?" Skye asked, looking over at him.

River nodded.

Skye sat up and closed the laptop, then stood and moved it off the bed. He was heading towards the door with it in his arms when River said, "You could sleep in here."

Skye smiled. "I will. Just let me put the laptop away and change, and I'll be right back." He could tell River didn't want him gone for even that amount of time, but his friend nodded.

Skye returned a few minutes later after changing into pajama pants and a T-shirt. He had also brushed his teeth and used the bathroom. He slipped under the covers once again and turned off the bedside lamp.

River was pressed up against him moments later, his warm body clinging to Skye as if for dear life, and Skye heard his sniffles again. He took River in his arms and held him close, rubbing his hand up and down his friend's back and arm, pressing a kiss to his hair as he shook softly and cried.

And Skye almost cried, too, but for a different reason. *I love you, and I only wish I could tell you.* He pressed another kiss to River's hair, lingering a little longer than necessary, and drinking in the smell of his watermelon and coconut body wash as he drifted to sleep.

~

"Hey," Skye said, smiling slightly at River when he felt him rousing the next morning. The sunlight was peeking through the curtains, casting a warm light over the navy blue comforter. River shifted against him and then yawned. Skye expected him to move away, but instead he snuggled closer, his head resting on Skye's chest, his dark hair tickling Skye's chin.

"Thank you," River murmured into his chest, his eyes still closed.

"For what?" Skye ran his fingers through River's hair and heard him let out a sigh.

"Staying with me," his friend said. "I'm sure I slept better than I would have if you weren't here." He tilted his face now and looked up at Skye with those gorgeous sapphire eyes. Still red, still puffy. But still beautiful. River had always been so beautiful despite his pain and heartache. So strong, so brave, so resilient, and so fiercely determined to make the best life he could for himself even after everything he'd been through. To be happy, despite everything. These last few months had been hell for him, though, and Skye had a feeling his resolve was wearing thin. He hated that for him. He hated that he couldn't seem to catch a break lately. He would do anything, be anything, say anything, to make it all okay again.

He realized that he was just staring at River, now, and that River was staring back at him. Maybe they should be moving, getting up, getting started on their day, but he couldn't seem to force himself to care about anything but the feel of River in his arms. Warm and rumpled, safe and his. He felt so perfect here, so right nestled into Skye's side as he held him close. "How are you feeling?" he asked, starting to stroke River's hair.

"Sad," River replied. "Still processing everything, honestly. I have a feeling I'll be doing a lot more crying today."

"Cry as much as you need to," Skye told him. "I'm not going anywhere." River blinked, his gaze never leaving Skye's. His hand reached up and he started to stroke Skye's cheek gently, making his breath hitch. He'd never touched Skye this way before. *Please tell me what's going on*, Skye wanted to beg. His heart felt like it was on a roller coaster with all of the signals River had been giving him lately. He didn't know if his friend was seeking comfort, or if he really was falling in love with him, too, and discovering his sexuality like Jaden thought he might be. But the way he touched Skye now, once again, just like the time in the car when River had taken his hand, felt so...*intimate*.

River's gaze stayed locked on Skye's when he spoke. "You have beautiful eyes, Skye."

Skye swallowed and butterflies swarmed in his stomach, threatening to burst out. "You're just now noticing that?" Skye asked, his voice barely a whisper.

"No," River said. "I'm just now saying it." It was so sincere, Skye felt like someone had just punched him in the sternum. He wanted so badly to tell River how he felt, to figure out what all of this was that was going on between them.

But instead, he reached up and took River's hand away from his cheek, smiling at him. "I think I need some coffee," he said. "And I have to pee."

River nodded and moved away to let Skye get up. They

both used the bathroom and brushed their teeth, but didn't bother getting changed just yet.

Skye made waffles for breakfast, complete with strawberries and whipped cream, and to his delight River ate every last bite.

After breakfast they showered, changed, and then headed to the grocery store. Skye offered to do it alone but River told him he could use the distraction.

He was, however, crying again on the way home.

"Go rest," Skye told his friend when they got inside the condo. "I'll put away the groceries."

River didn't argue with him, just took off his coat, scarf, and gloves and kicked off his shoes before sauntering to his room.

When Skye peeked his head in the room a few minutes later he was lying down in bed. "Anything I can get you?" he asked.

River shook his head, then turned to look at Skye and wiped tears from his eyes. "I'll come out if I need anything."

Skye nodded and left the room, closing the door behind him.

The next morning, Skye peeked his head into River's room. His roommate had his suitcase splayed out across the bed, barely anything in it. He shuffled through his dresser, not grabbing anything, and Skye was pretty sure he was trembling. He didn't blame his friend one bit. He was overwhelmed, that much was clear. He'd already had to deal with all of the funeral arrangements by himself, and that had been difficult enough for him. He'd been crying on and off, and getting very little sleep even when he did try to rest. He'd talked some, expressing how he wasn't sure what he was going to do now that he didn't have any family left, while Skye held him and tried to soothe him as best he could. And now Skye watched as River shoved about a dozen pairs of socks and underwear into his suitcase haphazardly, tears sliding down his cheeks and his chest heaving. He looked utterly wrecked and exhausted.

When Skye stepped further into the room and pulled River into a hug, his friend melted against him. And when Skye pulled away and pushed his own loaded suitcase towards the bed, River just blinked, bewildered.

"What's that?" he asked, sniffling and wiping tears from his cheeks.

"My suitcase," Skye told him, sitting down on the foot of the bed, sideways.

River stared at him and sat partially on the bed beside Skye, his leg tucked under him and his other foot on the floor. "Your what?" He looked from Skye to the suitcase and then back again, as if needing proof that they were actually a package deal, and that Skye wasn't pulling his leg.

"My suitcase," Skye repeated, with a slight chuckle at River's reaction. "I can't let you go on this trip alone, Riv. You're my best friend. I know how close you were to Jodi. And she meant something to me, too. I want to be there, for you and for her."

River's lips were on his. River's *lips* were on *his*. And his hands were on Skye's face. *Holy fucking shit*. His brain was short circuiting. River was *kissing* him. Hard. And it took the breath out of him. He sucked air in through his nose and grunted. His eyes were still open. He was stunned. River's thick, beautiful, perfect lips were on his. He wanted to kiss River back, to close his eyes and take this incredible moment in, but he was too slow, too slow to respond. And he didn't know where to put his hands, and he was caught so off guard.

As soon as he closed his eyes, River's hands were gone, and his lips were gone, and the heat from his body being so very close to Skye's was gone. The perfect, beautiful moment Skye had envisioned in his head for months, for years, was gone.

And when he opened his eyes again, River was standing several feet away, his eyes wide, breathing heavily. He looked absolutely terrified.

"I...I didn't." His voice trembled. "I'm sorry," he said, then walked past Skye and out of the room.

~

River

River couldn't get out of the condo fast enough. He threw his coat and shoes on and headed out the front door before Skye had a chance to come after him. He didn't know where he was going but he didn't care. He just started walking.

It was bone chillingly cold, especially without his scarf and gloves, or a hat, all of which he'd forgotten in his haste to leave, but at least that made it easier to think. And what exactly had he been thinking when he'd *kissed* Skye just now?

I love you. That's what he'd been thinking when he grabbed Skye's cheeks and pressed his lips to his. *I love you.* He'd always loved Skye. But this, this feeling that has been stirring inside of him for the past few months, that made him want to touch Skye, and look at Skye, and be with Skye, and have Skye close to him, that feeling that made his stomach do those weird somersaults, that had his heart beating a little faster when Skye did those super sweet things for him, was a different kind of love than what he'd felt for Skye most of his life.

Your heart belongs to someone else, River.

He stopped walking as his breath caught in his throat and the cold air bit at his skin. She knew. Anna knew this whole time how River felt for Skye. That's why she had broken up with him. But that thought terrified River. What if Skye didn't feel the same way about him? He could have just ruined a life-long friendship with one stupid kiss. God, what was he

128

thinking? There were so many things that could go wrong with this. He knew Skye found him attractive, but that wasn't the same as being in love with him. Even if he did reciprocate River's feelings, he knew Skye's penchant for sex, and he didn't know how he was going to navigate a sexual relationship with another man, even if he did love him and find him attractive.

Even with Anna, and the level of intimacy they had shared, River rarely got an erection. And they had never had sex. But sex with a man was a whole new concept for him, one that he had never really considered, because he didn't think it was even in the realm of possibility. He was only ever interested in girls, until now.

And maybe that's why he'd resisted kissing Skye and touching him, and looking at him in the ways that he truly wanted to for as long as he had. Because underneath it all, he was scared that he couldn't give Skye the sexual intimacy he knew his friend needed and deserved.

River hardly ever cursed but this seemed like an appropriate moment for it. "Fuck," he whispered to himself, rubbing his hands over his face. *I'm bisexual, or gay, I don't know. Bisexual, I think. I mean, I still find girls attractive. Whatever I am, I'm definitely not straight. I'm in love with Skye. I'm in love with my best friend.*

His ears, nose, and fingers were turning numb now, and as much as he hated the idea of facing Skye, he knew he couldn't avoid him forever, so he turned and started making his way back home.

They had a lot to talk about.

CHAPTER 15

Skye

"River?" Skye called when he heard the front door open and close, then footsteps a moment later. He'd been pacing back and forth for what seemed like an eternity waiting for his roommate to come home, and to say he was freaking out was an understatement.

His palms were sweaty, his heart was racing, and he'd been pausing every once in a while to try and take deep breaths. He didn't think he'd ever been more nervous or panicky in his life. And it wasn't because River had kissed him. That part had been fucking amazing. But he had no idea what was going to happen now. Would River want to pretend it never happened? Would he be so freaked out he'd want to leave for good? Would he chalk it up to being exhausted and emotional? Would this ruin their friendship? God, he couldn't stand the thought of losing River.

He swallowed nervously as River shuffled into the room, hands shoved in his pockets, his gaze not meeting Skye's. "Where were you?" Skye asked.

"Just walking." He murmured it so softly Skye could barely hear him. He still didn't make eye contact.

Skye sifted his fingers through his hair. "Can we talk?"

River wrapped his arms around himself and nodded. Skye saw him swallow and it was clear as day how anxious he was over the situation. God, Skye hoped he didn't regret it.

"Skye, I..." River started quietly, but didn't finish. He was trembling slightly as he finally made eye contact with Skye and a single tear slid down his cheek. "I'm so sorry."

Skye stepped closer immediately so River didn't have the chance to spiral because of this. He wouldn't let him think that that kiss was anything but perfect and beautiful and the best thing that had ever happened to him.

"Hey, none of that," he said, gripping River's face ever so gently in his hands. "It's okay, angel." He wiped the tear away with his thumb and smiled.

River's eyes widened slightly. "It is?" Skye nodded. He couldn't help but smile even more at the way River blushed and bit his lip, the way his sapphire eyes danced with...hope? And the way his body relaxed under Skye's touch.

"Yeah, Riv, it's more than okay." Skye's gaze fell to River's mouth and he noticed his friend's breath was picking up. River's hands reached out to grip Skye's hips and it felt amazing.

His grip tightened as he said, "I've never kissed a guy before."

Skye smiled softly and stepped just a bit closer, their chests almost touching now. "Did you like it?" He stroked River's cheek again and his friend shivered, leaning into his touch and closing his eyes, letting out a soft breath as he reached up and placed his hand over Skye's. Skye inhaled, his heart clenching in the most beautiful way. *Please say you liked it.*

River's long eyelashes fluttered from behind his glasses as he opened his eyes, gazing into Skye's. Then he bit his lip and nodded. Skye's heart leapt in his chest. "I liked that it was you," River said, flushing as he looked down. His bashfulness was so fucking endearing. "I...I think I would have liked it better if you had kissed me back, though." His gaze met Skye's again, before darting to his lips. Skye couldn't help but notice the way his friend's chest rose and fell as his hand slid around and gripped the back of River's neck. Couldn't help noticing the way his pupils dilated and the way he sucked in a breath as Skye wrapped an arm around his waist.

"Can I kiss you back now?" he asked, his gaze falling to River's full lips once more, voice low. He felt the shiver that ran down River's spine and his cock twitched, but he told it to calm the fuck down. They were taking things slow. This was just a kiss.

A flush crept up River's neck and cheeks, tinting his ears. He swallowed again and then nodded.

Slowly, so slowly, Skye lowered his mouth to River's, and pressed their lips together. There was no tongue. Just the feel of River's slightly chilled but so very soft lips on his. He felt a breath leave River, and his friend tightened his grip on Skye's hips. Skye kissed him again. It was slow and gentle as he took his time, drinking River in, memorizing him, breathing in his scent mixed with the winter chill that still clung to him. He basked in the feel of his lips, their fullness, the way his bottom lip was slightly more plump than the top, and the way they fit so perfectly with Skye's. The way Skye was holding him, touching him, tasting him, as River kissed him back. He angled River's head slightly, the kiss intensifying. His cock jerked when River moaned, his arms sliding around Skye, drawing him closer, their bodies pressed together now.

He was fully hard. How could he not be with River this close to him, making those glorious sounds? Little moans and whimpers escaping him as Skye cradled his lightly stubbled cheeks in his palms. Like Skye was kissing him the way he'd been waiting to be kissed his entire life. Like he craved Skye.

Skye pulled back, not wanting to rush things, or scare River. The last thing he wanted was to ruin this before it even started.

River blinked, his glasses slightly askew and fogged up, his face flushed and his lips swollen from their kisses. Skye didn't think he'd ever loved anything more. "Why did you stop?" River whispered.

"I didn't know how far you wanted to go," Skye told him honestly, stroking his cheek again. "I was, uh, getting a little excited." He smiled, flushing, and glanced down at his crotch, his erection still very prominent and noticeable in his jeans, and River's gaze followed.

"Oh, um, well, I would like to keep kissing you," Skye was relieved to hear him say. "Can we stick to that?" Skye nodded, and their lips found each other's again, but Skye didn't press as close to him this time to keep things more chaste. It was still incredible, just this. It was more than he ever dreamed he would have.

They kissed for several more moments, and even without the closeness of their bodies, Skye's cock was so hard it hurt, precum leaking out and leaving a wet spot on his underwear, but he didn't press closer, he didn't touch himself, and he didn't touch River, other than his hands on his face and neck and his lips on his.

"Fuck," River breathed when they finally parted for the second time. His hands gripped Skye's biceps as he rested his forehead against Skye's, closing his eyes, his chest rising and falling.

Skye chuckled. "You never swear."

River laughed. "I never get kissed like that, either." Skye couldn't help the grin that took up his entire face. And he knew he couldn't keep it in any longer. "I love you, Riv," he said.

River looked up, and met his gaze. "Really?"

Skye almost laughed again at the disbelief in his voice. "Yeah, really. I've loved you for a while now." He reached up and adjusted River's glasses. River bit his lip and Skye saw the anxiety written on his face, felt it in the way his friend tensed in his arms. Shit. Did he mess up? Should he not have said anything? Was he putting too much pressure on River? He just wanted to assure him that this was real for him, not a game, or an experiment. Not a trial. He wanted River. Only him. Always.

"Shit. I shouldn't have said anything," he backpedaled. "I didn't mean to scare you or make you uncomfortable—"

River shook his head. "No, no, it's not that. God, it's not that. I...I love you, too." Skye's breath almost left him, but then River said, "I just don't know how to make this work." His eyes were so earnest when he looked at Skye, but there was something else there, too...sadness, pain even.

Skye's heart thrashed wildly. "What do you mean?" He swallowed. "If this is about me not being a Christian—" he stopped when River shook his head again, adamantly. Then it dawned on him. This was about the sex. River was afraid. He didn't think he could give Skye what he wanted. But he would give up sex for the rest of his life if it meant having River. If it meant kissing River, and holdling River, and falling asleep and waking up next to River, growing old with River. He might struggle some, sure, but he would never ask him to give more than he was comfortable with, and he would find joy in the knowledge that River was his, finally his, wholly and completely. He was about to tell him this when River spoke.

"You deserve someone who can give you everything you want and need sexually, Skye. And I just don't know that I can be that person. Kissing you and touching you is one thing. And I want that. I want it desperately. But, I don't know if I can be sexually intimate with you. I don't even think I can get an erection. No matter how much I love you or how attracted I am to you it just won't work. Even if we got married and were allowed to have sex, psychologically my body just won't let me get aroused by you, and...I still want you, but, it's not fair to you. You deserve better. I can't do that to you. I can't make you deal with all of that shit."

Skye gripped River's face in his hands tighter and stared

into his eyes. "Listen to me," he told him, his voice firm but gentle. "I am the one who gets to decide what I deserve, and what I need. I don't need sex, I don't need anything you aren't comfortable giving me. I just need you. Only you. *I. Love. You.*" He enunciated each word trying to get them to sink in. "I will never pressure you for sex. I will never make you feel guilty or ashamed. You make me so happy. I know you're scared, but you are safe with me.

"I can be patient, and we can take things as slowly as we need to, and we'll see what your body does over time, okay? If you decide that sex is something you want, we'll figure it out together. If not, we won't have it. I will be perfectly happy loving you and showering you with kisses, cuddling you on the couch, and holding you in my arms while we sleep at night.

"This is all brand new. Maybe you'll be surprised. Maybe your body and your mind will know that you're safe with me and loved by me, and it will work out on its own. You're in charge, River. You make the calls. But whatever happens, we'll figure it out together. Because your shit *is* my shit. Because I am *not* letting you go. There is no one better for me than you, angel."

Tears filled River's eyes as he looked at Skye. "I'm not worth all of this, Skye," he whispered.

"You are to me." Skye stepped closer and covered River's mouth with his once more, feeling River's salty tears against his lips and hearing him suck in a breath, a whimper leaving him that sent a bolt of pleasure down Skye's spine and straight to his cock. "I told you, Riv," he said, pulling away, "I love you. I want you. *All* of you. All of your hurt and scars, all of your grief and pain. All of your heartache and struggles. I'm not afraid to love you."

River's chest heaved and he sniffled. Then he stepped forward and embraced Skye tightly. "You wanna be my boyfriend?" he asked, his chin resting against Skye's shoulder.

Skye wrapped his arms around River, feeling the fabric of

his soft, black sweater, inhaling that watermelon and coconut scent, soaking in the feel of his warm body pressed against his, and he had tears forming in his eyes now, too. Tears of utter and complete joy. He nodded, his face brushing against the skin at the back of River's neck. "God, yes," he said as the tears fell down his cheeks. "Please."

River laughed slightly and nuzzled his nose into the side of Skye's neck. "Hey, Skye?" he said, "I don't think I'm straight."

Skye was laughing now. "Thank God," he said, and gripped River tighter. "Remind me to send Anna a fruit basket, by the way."

River chuckled and tightened his grip, too. "I love you, Skye," he whispered, his lips brushing the skin of Skye's neck and sending another shiver down his spine.

"I love you too, angel," Skye whispered back.

CHAPTER 16

Skye

Skye couldn't help feeling conflicted as he drove the Newport to Cincinnati with River in the passenger seat next to him. They were on their way to a funeral for someone that they truly cared about, the person who had been most important in River's life since he was a child, and he knew he should be feeling sad, but he couldn't keep the smile from his face. And yeah, that made him feel a bit guilty. But when he looked over to see that River was smiling, too, some of that guilt dissipated.

"It's okay to be happy, Skye," River told him, blushing. "I'm happy, too."

Skye's smile widened as he reached over to take River's hand. And when their fingers intertwined this time, he wasn't confused, just breathless at how wonderful it felt to have River's soft, strong hand in his, right where it belonged. "I feel like we shouldn't be going to a funeral with smiles on our faces."

"Yeah." River squeezed his hand, and almost as if on cue, his smile faltered. "Honestly, I can't stop thinking about how much Aunt Jodi would have loved to see us together, and she'll never get to now." He sighed and turned his gaze towards the window. Through the reflection Skye could see a tear slide down his cheek. "I miss her, Skye. I miss her so much it hurts to breathe sometimes."

"I know, Riv," Skye said, softly, squeezing his hand again. "Me, too. She was an incredible woman." Skye wished he could say more, do more. He knew River would be hurting for a long time, even if he wasn't showing it. Losing Jodi was devastating, but what did you say when your best friend lost the only family they had left? There were no words that would make it better, easier. Just love and support. That's all he had to offer, and he hoped it would be enough to help River through the grieving process, however long that took.

River looked back at him. "I'm really glad you're here, though. Making this drive by myself, honestly I don't know how I would have done it. Thank you for coming."

"Of course." Skye wished he could reach over and plant a kiss on River's forehead, but that would have to wait. Honestly he was still reeling from the fact that River was his boyfriend now. His *boyfriend*. How on earth did that happen? How did he get so lucky? River actually liked him back. River *loved* him back. For real. This was real. They were together. Part of him was convinced it was all a dream.

He knew he needed to focus on the funeral right now, and on River, and helping him grieve, but at least now he knew where he stood. At least he could support him as a boyfriend now, and not just as a friend. He knew he could hold River, and kiss River, and take River's hand in his, and know that it wasn't platonic, and that River *wanted* him to do those things, just as much as Skye wanted to do them. Well, he was pretty sure at least.

"Hey, Riv," he asked, clearing his throat.

"Hmm?" River turned to look at him again. Skye kept his gaze on the road but continued to hold River's hand.

"I don't know if this is the right time to bring this up, so if it's not, just tell me, but, as far as physical boundaries go, I mean...I know sex is off the table for a couple of reasons, and that's fine. I get that, and I respect it, but...I uh..." he slid his hand out of River's now and used it to rub the back of his neck. This felt awkward as hell, but he knew he needed to say it. "I mean, is there anything else that you don't want me to do, or..." he glanced over at River, who was biting his bottom lip in that way that made Skye want to pull it free and nibble on it, his blue eyes dancing with humor, and Skye relaxed.

"I'm fine with mostly everything. As long as you aren't touching my crotch, or trying to take my pants off, we're good."

"Can I touch your ass?" he asked, just to make sure. River flushed and nodded, and Skye grinned. "Okay, I think I can manage that. Let me know if anything changes." He reached over and took River's hand again, planting a kiss on it before resting both of their hands against the seat once more.

"Speaking of my ass," River said, the word sounding strange on his lips, "it's kind of hurting. And by kind of, I mean a lot. Can we stop somewhere soon so I can get up and walk around for a bit?"

"Sure, angel." Skye kissed his hand again.

River flushed. "You've been calling me that for years. Why?"

"Don't like it?" Skye glanced at him.

"No. I do like it. I like it a lot, actually." He shrugged. "Just not sure I deserve it."

"People don't *deserve* pet names, Riv. I call you angel because you are the best person I know," Skye told him. "You're my angel. And you gotta stop thinking you don't deserve shit. Or that you aren't worthy of good things. Cause you are. Sure you're a mess, but so is everyone. I know what those bastards did to you in high school made you think less of yourself, made you feel like you aren't good enough, but I'm telling you you are, okay? What they did is a reflection on them, not you. You are not less worthy or less loveable, or less anything because of your past. And you don't have to be perfect or have it all together to be worthy of love. I'm no scholar but isn't that what the Bible teaches? Isn't that what you told me our freshman year? That we're all created in God's image? Fearfully and wonderfully made exactly as we are? Not perfect, but good. So how can you view yourself as less worthy or deserving than anyone else? As far as I'm concerned you are the most worthy person in the world."

River stared at him for a moment before he wiped his eyes. "Can't believe you are the one giving me Bible lessons."

Skye grinned. "I do overhear some of those sermons you've been listening to online. And I have read the Bible on occasion."

"Was that because you had a crush on me, or because you were genuinely curious?" River smirked at him, and his eyes twinkled.

It was Skye's turn to smirk as he pulled into the gas station and parked the car. "A little bit of both. I wanted to understand why it was so important to you, because you are important to me." He turned off the car. "And it wasn't a crush. Crushes are for high schoolers. I was and am, head over heels in love with you."

River smiled and unbuckled his seat belt. But instead of getting out of the Newport like Skye expected, he scooted across the center seat and pressed his lips to Skye's. River kissed him hard and long, pushing himself up on his knees, his hands on either side of Skye's face. Tilting Skye's head just right, he deepened the kiss, and Skye felt River's warm, wet tongue sliding along his lower lip. He moaned and opened for his boyfriend. River slid inside, slowly, hesitantly at first, but then he was kissing Skye harder, sucking on his tongue. Heat flooded Skye's body, causing his cock to throb in his jeans and press painfully against his zipper. River tasted like peppermint, and mocha, and Skye couldn't get enough. His hands gripped River's waist as their tongues danced, and he felt his boyfriend's fingers running through his hair briefly, before he pulled away, both of them flushed and breathing heavily. River smiled dreamily at him, his eyes hooded.

"Wow." Skye closed his eyes and let out a deep breath, resting his forehead against River's. "If I keep reading the Bible will you keep kissing me like that?" He rubbed his hands up and down River's sides, smiling. His cock was still throbbing, but he ignored it, elated that they had this. Because this, right here, River's hands gripping him tightly, River's full, warm lips on his, was everything.

River chuckled. "Worth a try, right?"

Skye chuckled, too, and placed a kiss on his forehead.

"I need you to know something," River said, gazing into Skye's eyes with the utmost sincerity. His fingers played with the blond waves falling over Skye's forehead.

"What's that?" Skye asked, his voice barely a whisper.

"You don't need to change anything about yourself for me. Not now, not ever. No matter what we call each other, I will never ask you to be someone you are not for me."

Skye swallowed and tears stung his eyes. God he loved this man. "Thank you." River gripped his face and kissed him again, long and hard, stealing Skye's breath away before pulling back.

"Same goes for me, you know. I'd never ask you to give up your faith because we were together."

River smiled. "Ready to go?"

"Um, give me a minute?" Skye said, gesturing to his obviously tented jeans, and River looked down, then bit that full bottom lip again and blushed. "Oh," he said, "sorry."

Skye couldn't help the laugh that escaped him. "Sorry? Don't ever apologize for turning me on, Riv. You just gave me the best kiss of my life. I just need a second to cool off, that's all."

River blushed again and smiled, as Skye adjusted himself

in his pants, glancing at River. "Stop looking at me, it's not helping," he said with a smile.

"Why don't I get out? Then you won't have me here tempting you and I'll have more time to move around."

"Good idea," Skye said. He rested his head back against the seat once River was gone, pressing a hand against his aching cock and using his other hand to run his fingers through his hair. God, that was one amazing kiss. If it had lasted much longer he might not have been able to stop himself from coming in his pants like a fucking teenager.

The winter air bit at his skin as Skye headed inside a minute later, and he shivered. He caught up with River and they browsed around a little bit to give him a break from sitting. He grabbed a coffee to take on the road and then they got back in the car.

But as soon as River sat down again he winced, and even though he didn't say anything, Skye could tell by the way he kept adjusting his seat cushion that he was having trouble getting comfortable.

"You okay?"

"No," River admitted. "I haven't had to sit for this long since my tailbone started hurting and it's not happy with me. And we've still got an hour left to drive."

Skye chewed on the inside of his cheek and glanced behind him. "What if you laid down in the back?"

"What?" River sounded startled.

"You could lay down and take the pressure off your tailbone."

River looked behind him now, and there was that lip biting again. He hesitated before saying, "Okay. That does sound better. But I feel like an idiot, having you chauffeur me to my aunt's funeral while I lay in the back seat 'cause my butt hurts."

Skye grinned. "I don't mind. Except that I don't get to hold your hand."

River blushed again and this time Skye called him on it. "You're cute when you blush." He reached over and stroked River's cheek, which just made his boyfriend flush an even brighter shade of red as his eyelashes fluttered and he glanced down. "God, you're gorgeous." Skye couldn't help it. He slid across the seat just as River had done earlier, lifting his boyfriend's face and pressing his lips to his. And this time, he heard River moan as he slid his tongue into his mouth, tasting, licking, sucking. His cock was getting hard again and he knew driving with a hard on wouldn't be fun, but he didn't care. He couldn't get enough of River. God, he felt so good. Those luscious lips, that stubble under his palms, the feel of River's wool coat grazing his wrists as their tongues tangled and their knees knocked together in the confined space.

"Fuck," he said, pulling away and gazing into River's eyes. They were lust blown, his lips swollen and wet and his face flushed yet again. He looked wrecked. And insanely hot. "So fucking gorgeous," Skye said again, his voice raspy. "I could do this all day."

"Damn," River whispered, his breathing labored. "And I thought the last kiss was incredible."

Skye smiled widely. "There's plenty more where that came from, angel." He pressed his lips to River's again and this time River moved back to his knees, hovering over him, taking Skye's face in his hands and dominating the kiss. Skye's hands were on his waist, and they were both moaning now, River's fingers running through his hair as they sucked and nibbled and licked on each other's tongues and lips and jaws.

"Shit," River gasped, and Skye chuckled because his friend was cursing more and more and it was strange, but kind of awesome at the same time. "We have to go. This is so not cool, Skye. We're on our way to a funeral, and we can't be late because we're making out in the car. And we definitely can't show up with hickeys."

Skye chuckled. "Sorry. You're right. I'll behave. You get in the back seat and it'll be easier."

River smiled and gave him one last peck on the lips before climbing out of the front seat and into the back. He took his coat off to use as a pillow, and lay down across the back seat.

"Good?" Skye asked, looking in the rearview mirror. He couldn't help smiling. He hated that River was in pain, of course, but he did look pretty stinkin' adorable curled up in the back seat of the Newport. And Skye found that he, once again, felt right at home taking care of River.

"Mmmm," his boyfriend murmured, which Skye took as a yes, and pulled out of the parking spot and back onto the road.

A moment later he heard soft snoring coming from the back seat and his chest filled with warmth.

"River," he said, as he reached over the seat and nudged his friend awake an hour later. "Wake up, sleepyhead. We're here."

River moaned and rubbed his eyes. "Already?" he said with a yawn.

"It goes by a lot slower when you're driving," Skye said with a smirk. "Come on." He reached for his door handle and climbed out, and River reached forward over the seat and grabbed his seat cushion before joining Skye outside.

"Wow," River said, looking around at the full parking lot. "I knew she was active in the church and the community, but I didn't know there would be this many people here. There must be fifty cars, Skye, and I don't recognize most of them." Tears filled his eyes again and slid down his cheeks. Skye reached an arm around River's shoulders, pulling him close and planting a kiss on his temple.

"She meant a lot to a lot of people, it looks like," he said. And then his eyes caught sight of something on the church lawn, and it almost took his breath away.

"Wow." He let his arm fall to his side once again as River wiped away his tears. "I don't think I've ever seen that before." Across the lawn of the church were doors, all painted a different color, but together they made a rainbow, and across them were the words *All Are Welcome Here.* "Guess I don't have to worry about whether or not they'll accept our relationship," he said, a sense of peace washing over him. He'd never felt so unafraid, so free to be himself in a religious setting, and it was overwhelming for him to feel that kind of acceptance.

River smiled softly and took his hand. "This is the church I grew up in, Skye. They and Aunt Jodi taught me that no one has to choose between their faith and their sexuality. We are who God created us to be. Fully loved, and fully accepted. And as long as we honor and respect each other, I believe our relationship is honoring to Him, too."

Skye turned to him and squeezed his hand. "Let's go pay our respects to Aunt Jodi," he said. Then he placed a chaste kiss on River's temple and they walked into the church hand in hand.

CHAPTER 17

River

2 WEEKS LATER

"Hey, angel, you feel up to going out with Jenna and Nick?" Skye asked as soon as River got home from work. Then he was taking River's face in his hands and pressing a heated kiss to his lips before he could answer. It took River a moment to come back to reality once Skye pulled away. He blinked and smiled lazily, and Skye grinned.

"Sure," he said. "Guess I won't take my coat off, then."

"Your tailbone will be okay?"

"Yeah, it's getting better. It still hurts but I can manage." River knew he needed to get out of the house. Even if his bum was sore as a result. He hadn't done much of anything since Jodi had passed away and he needed to see his friends. Nick and Jenna always had a way of helping him feel better.

"You look good," he said, smiling and raking his gaze over his boyfriend. He really did look incredible. Skye had changed out of his dress clothes into dark wash jeans and a gray sweater, and was looking cozy, and very handsome. Those jeans fit him perfectly, hugging his rear and showing off his long, slender legs, and the sweater made his green eyes pop.

Skye looked down at what he was wearing, then back up at River with a gorgeous smile on his handsome face. "Thanks."

He leaned in and kissed River again. "Dinner," he said, pulling away. "They'll be waiting on us." He stepped past River and grabbed his coat, sliding it on.

"Hey, if your tailbone is getting better, maybe you can start going back to church," he said, and River's heart melted at how sincere and hopeful he sounded. In all the years they had known each other Skye had never once been to church with him. River had never asked him again after that first time in college. But that hadn't kept Skye from supporting River in his faith, encouraging him in it, even. He'd actually gotten River a really nice study Bible one year as a birthday present, and River loved it. And while Skye didn't believe in God, he knew River loved him, and that River believed God did, too.

"Hey, there's the cutest couple in the world," Jenna said with a beaming smile as Skye and River took their seats in the booth across from her and Nick. "Told you it would happen sooner rather than later." She nudged Nick with her elbow.

"Yeah, all right, you win," he grumbled, pulling his wallet out of his pocket and sifting through it.

"What's going on?" Skye asked.

"He's giving me the money he owes me." Jenna beamed and held out her hand, palm up. "Hurry up, slow poke." She poked Nick in the ribs. "I got things I want to do with that money." Her eyes twinkled and she winked at the couple as Nick slapped a wad of cash into her hand. She did a little happy dance in her seat as she tucked the cash into her purse. Skye and River laughed as Nick rolled his eyes.

"Wait a second, you guys were betting on us?" Skye asked.

"Not on whether you would end up together," Jenna said, "just on how long it would take. Before or after Valentine's Day."

"You couldn't have waited one more month?" Nick

pouted. He looked at the two men like they had genuinely betrayed him by falling in love without consulting him on the timing. River just rolled his eyes as Skye leaned over and kissed his temple, making him blush and smile like an idiot.

"Awww." Jenna grinned from ear to ear. Then she slid her arm through Nick's and pressed a kiss to his cheek, and it was River's turn to look at him in betrayal as his cheeks turned crimson.

"What the hell was that?" Skye said, echoing River's thoughts.

"Nothing," Nick said.

"Bullshit," Skye replied. Both men eyed him. Jenna was grinning and Nick was so red you could mistake him for a tomato. "Are you two together?"

They nodded and River's mouth gaped. "Since when?"

"A few weeks," Jenna said. She glanced at Nick who was clearly flustered, but so happy he could burst. "It happened right before Christmas, and we were going to tell you but then River's Aunt Jodi passed away and we didn't want to sound like assholes by announcing we were together right after hearing that news. We also just wanted some time to figure things out."

"I understand wanting time," River said, "but you definitely could have said something. I could have used the good news."

"I'm sorry," Jenna apologized, and River shook his head.

"Don't be sorry, just give us details," he told her. She laughed and Nick flushed all over again.

"There's not much to tell," Jenna said. "We were out one night together, got drunk and ended up in bed. When we woke up the next morning we weren't freaking out, and Nick told me he had feelings for me, and I said the same. After talking for a bit, we decided we didn't want it to be a one time thing. We wanted to see where things could go." She pressed another kiss to Nick's flushed face. He turned and buried his face in her hair. It was utterly adorable.

"Well, we're happy for you," Skye said, and River nodded.

"Thank you." Jenna smiled widely. Then she turned to Nick and whispered loud enough that Skye and River could hear. "I'll make sure that money goes towards a good cause." She nibbled on his ear and he turned bright red again.

They all laughed.

"You guys suck," Nick grumbled.

They laughed harder and Jenna gave him a third kiss on the cheek. River's chest warmed at the affection they obviously felt for each other, and he felt Skye's hand sliding into his and squeezing it.

"Bathroom break," River said, part-way through the meal. His tailbone was starting to throb and he needed a break from sitting. The seat was acutely uncomfortable even with his seat cushion, so he figured a trip to the bathroom was as good of an excuse as any. Plus, he actually did have to pee.

But as soon as he stood, his head started to swim. His vision grew dark, and his heart raced.

The last thing he remembered as his knees gave out from under him, was Skye's voice saying his name.

CHAPTER 18

River

When River woke up he was on his back, his legs propped up, surrounded by paramedics. Jenna and Nick were standing over him with worried looks on their faces and Skye was kneeling next to him, holding his face in his hands. He looked like he was about to cry.

"River?" Skye said, his voice sick with worry. "Oh my God, you scared the hell out of me, out of all of us. What the hell was that?"

River just blinked and shook his head.

He took some deep breaths and waited a few more minutes, Skye kneeling next to him the entire time.

"Can you tell us what happened?" one of the paramedics asked.

River blinked again. He felt weak and tired. He really had no idea what had *actually* happened. Only what he'd *felt*. And he was not ready for it to happen again. "I uh, my heart, it started beating super fast, and I got lightheaded, and I just passed out." He saw the way Skye's eyes widened and he closed his eyes again and took in a breath.

"We'd like to take you to the hospital and make sure it's

nothing serious. With heart issues you really don't want to take a chance," the paramedic said.

"Can I ride with him?" Skye asked, still gripping River's hand tightly.

"Of course."

River swallowed and Skye squeezed his hand before they loaded him on the stretcher.

Skye said goodbye to Jenna and Nick, promising to call them when they knew anything, and climbed into the back of the ambulance with River.

"How are you feeling?" Skye asked, his green eyes filled with concern as they waited in the hospital room, River in the bed with a blood pressure cuff around his upper arm and a pulse oximeter on his finger. God, he was getting far too familiar with this place. They both were.

River shrugged. "I feel fine, now. More anxious than anything."

"Your heart was beating super fast?" Skye said, the growing concern evident in his voice. "Like actually beating super fast?"

"Yeah, like it was painful. And scary, if I'm being honest." He put his hand to his chest and let out a breath.

"God, River, what the hell?" Skye ran his fingers through his hair, his anxiety palpable.

It was several hours later when they arrived back home after having tests run, blood drawn, an EKG, and an echocardiogram done, along with a chest x-ray, and being told that the doctors couldn't find any issues with River's heart, and his blood work was fine, but that they recommended he follow up with a cardiologist as soon as possible.

River knew they were right. But he was So. Sick. Of. Doctors.

~

"I wish you would let me come with you to your appointment," Skye said, as he slid his coat on, frowning.

River gave him a small smile. "I know. But it's a short trip, and I'm just getting hooked up to a monitor. You don't need to be there." He'd done a stress test, and passed that with flying colors. He'd done another EKG, and another ultrasound, and more blood work. Now he was going back in to get a heart monitor that he would wear for a few days and would give the cardiologist real time information about his heart, and hopefully give them some answers, because so far they had none. Everything else had come back normal. But there was nothing normal about this, and they both knew it.

He hadn't passed out again yet, but he had had several more episodes of his heart rate spiking, and feeling simultaneously lightheaded, seemingly for no reason. The doctor had asked him if it happened more when he was active, which it didn't. It actually happened when he was sedentary, and had even woken him up a few times in the middle of the night. It was scaring him, and Skye, but he'd found a way to manage it somewhat, too. If he wasn't already laying down, he did that as fast as he could when it started so he wouldn't pass out. And then he took a deep breath, and held it for a second or two, and his heart would calm down and go back to its normal rate. Sometimes it worked the first time and other times he would have to do it three or four times before it stopped racing, and the longer it raced, the more painful it got, sometimes causing pain in his jaw and even in his temples. The episodes could last anywhere from a couple of seconds to a couple of minutes, and those were the worst.

"I just don't like the idea of you driving yourself," Skye said, concern in his eyes as he rubbed his hands up and down River's arms. "What if it happens while you are on the road?"

"Then I pull over and wait for it to stop," River said. He knew it wasn't ideal but Skye couldn't be taking off all of the time to drive him to all of his appointments. This had been the fourth one in three weeks. And the Uber rides were getting expensive.

"Let me know how it goes," Skye said, leaning in and giving him a kiss on the forehead. "I love you. Be safe."

"I love you, too," River said, and watched his boyfriend walk out the door.

~

"So, how was it?" Skye asked when River got home that evening. He kissed him at the door.

"It was fine. I've got a bunch of electrodes and wires hooked up to me, and a device sitting in the middle of my chest in this little pouch. The fun part is going to be taking it off and putting it back on every time I shower, 'cause I have to wear it for three days."

"Can I see it?"

River raised an eyebrow and smirked. "Is this just an excuse to get me to take my shirt off?"

"What if it is?" Skye's eyes twinkled as he stepped closer to River.

River grinned. He unbuttoned his coat and took it off, and then lifted his T-shirt so Skye could see the device strapped over his shoulders, the electrodes stuck to different areas of his chest and the rectangular device in the center.

Skye reached out and ran his fingers over it. "Looks fun."

"Well, if that's all," River said, and began to lower his shirt.

"Not so fast." Skye reached over and grabbed the hem of River's shirt as River grinned at him knowingly. Skye's pupils were blown wide and his voice was low and husky.

"You're so predictable," River said, low and soft, stepping closer and allowing Skye to pull the shirt up and over his head. The shirt fell to the floor, and then Skye had one hand on the back of River's neck and the other around his bare waist and was kissing him fervently.

River felt his back pressing up against the cold door and grunted. Then moaned as he felt his boyfriend's tongue sliding into his mouth, claiming him. He returned the kiss, running his fingers through Skye's hair and sliding his other hand around, pressing it against the small of Skye's back.

Then Skye was gripping River's thighs and pulling him up and River went willingly, wrapping his legs around Skye's waist as he slid his tongue into Skye's mouth, deepening the kiss. Moans escaped them as their tongues tangled and their hands roamed, feeling along each other's arms and chests, and cheeks, and running through each other's hair.

"Crap," River said, suddenly breaking away, his breathing heavy. He looked at Skye, his boyfriend's face flushed, his blond waves a mess, green eyes blown wide with desire and affection. He didn't think Skye had ever looked sexier.

"What?" Skye asked, breathing heavily. Then a frown appeared on his handsome face and his eyes widened. He loosened his grip. "Shit, did I overstep?"

"No, no, you're fine," River assured him. But he removed his legs from around Skye's waist and slid out of his grip. "I just realized we can't really do that while I have this thing on."

"Oh." Skye looked down at where the heart monitor was on River's chest. "Why not?"

"'Cause they're recording my heart rate in real time, and I have to log when it starts to act up, and what I was doing at the time. So if we start making out and that makes my heart go crazy for some reason..." he bit his lip. "I don't really want to be recording that."

Skye smirked at him. "No making out for three days, is what you're telling me?"

River blushed. "I'm sorry. I'm probably being ridiculous. I just...I mean, we can still kiss, just not hot and heavy make out sessions."

Skye pecked him on the lips. "Fine. But as soon as that thing comes off, you're mine."

River blushed again and then grabbed his shirt off the floor and slipped it back on, before following Skye into the kitchen.

"Hey, Riv, can I ask you something?" Skye said, hesitantly as he set the timer for the oven.

"Okay," River nodded, his anxiety spiking a little as he shoved his hands in his pockets.

Skye turned to face him and bit the inside of his cheek. "I was just wondering...I mean, we've been together for a few weeks now, and we've been making out quite a bit." He stepped closer to River and rested his hands on his arms. He stroked them gently and peered into his eyes. "Have you...been aroused yet, at all?"

River flushed and tensed slightly. "I guess that depends on what you mean." His gaze darted to the floor. "I get aroused," he said, more softly. "I just..."

"Can't get an erection," Skye finished for him, his voice gentle.

River nodded, shame and embarrassment seeping through him. He started to step away, but Skye pulled him back.

"Hey, don't do that." His voice was gentle once again as he lifted River's face to look at him. "I'm just asking, angel. There's no judgment. I want it for your sake, just as much as mine. But it's not your fault. I know that. And I love you. The last thing I ever want is for you to feel embarrassed or guilty. There's no shame here. I want you to feel safe with me, always."

River nodded, and then Skye was pressing his nose against his, and River was smiling, before they kissed softly once again.

"Can I ask you something?" River said once they pulled away.

"Shoot."

"How long has it been since you had sex?"

Skye blinked at him, then gave a soft smile. "It doesn't matter." He pressed his lips to River's forehead.

"Skye," River said. "How long?"

Skye kissed him again. "A while."

"How long is a while?"

"River, I don't want to tell you this if it's just going to make you feel guilty. 'Cause it shouldn't. It should make you feel loved. And I'm really not trying to push you into anything. It was my choice, okay? I didn't have sex because I realized I didn't want anyone but you."

"But...but you couldn't have me, Skye."

"And I was okay with that. I still am. I'm so happy with what we have. And even if it never changes, even if we never have sex, I'm happier with you than I could ever be with anyone else. All the sex in the world can't compare to being with you. You are what I want."

River felt tears forming in his eyes again and wiped them away before they slid down his cheeks.

"Okay, I won't feel guilty," he promised. "But I'd still like to know. How long?"

Skye grinned and flushed. "Eight months."

River's mouth dropped open. "Holy shit."

Skye laughed and kissed him again. "And I'll go eight more if I have to. I'll go eight years, River, a lifetime. 'Cause you are it for me."

CHAPTER 19

Skye

Skye was lying on the couch with River snuggled up next to him, freshly showered after having gotten his heart monitor off. It would be another few days before they got the results, and they were both a little nervous. Maybe that was why Skye was having trouble following through on his promise. Part of him was also scared that if things did get heated it would cause River's heart to act up, and every time that happened it made Skye panic a little. The way River held his hand over his heart and rushed to lay down so he wouldn't pass out. The look of immediate exhaustion and pain that would cloud his features. River seemed to have it pretty well under control but Skye was never sure when River might pass out again, or if there really was something wrong with his heart that was potentially life threatening. And that thought made him pull River a little closer and hold him a little tighter. He kissed the top of his head.

"Hey, how's your tailbone been doing?" he asked. He'd been so focused on everything going on with River's heart that he'd kind of forgotten about the other chronic issue River dealt with on a daily basis.

"It's okay." River took Skye's hand in his and interlocked

their fingers together. "I'm doing the myofascial release once a month now just for maintenance to keep it from getting worse, but it's still not completely better. They said it should be better than it is by now. They are surprised I'm still in as much pain as I'm in and that I still have to use my seat cushion so much. I've done all the work. I mean, it is feeling better than it was months ago, but I don't think it's ever going to be all the way better. They tell me I'm complicated. Yay."

Skye chuckled slightly. "What about church?" he asked, pressing a kiss to River's hair. "You were kind of counting on it being better so you could get back." He ran his fingers along River's upper arm now as he spoke.

River pushed away and looked at him. "I was," he sighed. "But I still can't sit in church long enough to make it through a sermon."

"What about biking, and rock climbing?"

River nodded. "I'm hoping if we get some good news about my heart that I can get back to rock climbing. Biking doesn't work anymore. Sitting on that seat is impossible with my tailbone, but I'm running again, and that helps. Anything with fresh air and sunshine is good for me." He gave a soft smile, but it was a sad one.

"I'm sorry, Riv. I wish there was something else we could think of to help you. I can't imagine not being able to do so many of the things you want to do. Just being in pain every time you sit must suck."

"It does," River said, sighing, and resting his head back on Skye's chest. "Sometimes I feel like I'm learning to live with it, and other times it makes me incredibly angry. Like, I can't travel, Skye. That trip to Cincinnati for my Aunt Jodi's funeral was brutal for me and that was only two hours. That means I can't fly, or drive long distances, which means no road trips. No more vacations with you over the summer to visit Jaden and Chloe. No amusement parks, because I can't handle the rides. No plays, no concerts. Nothing that requires sitting for more than an hour, and even that's pushing it." *No honey-moon if we ever do get married.* "Even the meal the other night with Nick and Jenna was hard on me. I'm glad I went, and I enjoyed myself, but I was in pain about twenty minutes in and had to ice my tailbone when I got home. I am really tired of being so limited in what I can do. And the pain in my hips and low back is getting worse. And the heart palpitations are making me exhausted, waking me up in the middle of the night. I'm struggling at work because I'm so tired, and it's definitely not helping with my depression and anxiety."

Skye pressed another kiss to River's hair and held him tightly. He hoped that they would get some good news at the follow up with the cardiologist, and that maybe then River could get back to doing a few of the things he'd been missing out on for so long.

Skye was at work a little over a week later, and his heart was a little lighter. They'd gotten River's results back from his heart monitor and the doctor had said that while his palpitations, as he called them, were scary and inconvenient, they were not life threatening, and were not doing any damage to River's heart. It was just something, like all the other things, going on with River, that he would have to learn to adjust to and live with. As if saying that made it easier to do, somehow. The doctor had put River on a beta blocker that he said could help, and encouraged him to drink lots of water and increase his salt intake, and that was it. Skye was relieved, but he wasn't sure he was satisfied. He still got nervous every time River got behind a wheel that he would have an episode, and not be able to pull off to the side of the road in time and end up in another wreck. He had been begging River to let him drive him to work for the past several weeks but River insisted that he was fine, and Skye didn't want to take one more thing away from him, so he let it go. And maybe with this new medication River was on, he could rest a little easier.

There was a knock on the door that startled him, pulling him away from his thoughts, and every head in the room turned towards the door. Skye's eyes widened, and then he blushed and smiled widely as he took in the sight before him. River was standing there, in his dark gray woolen coat, his black gloves, dark hair covered in freshly fallen snow, a sapphire scarf tucked into his coat and poking out at the top, covering his neck and making his eyes pop behind those sexy as fuck glasses. He looked absolutely breathtaking.

And by looking at him you would never know that he dealt with so many health issues, so much trauma. You would never know by the smile that lit up his face that he had been sexually assaulted as a teenager, or that he dealt with anxiety and depression, or that he had dealt with chronic pain for the past several months. Just by looking at him you would never know his story; his anguish, his grief, and hardship. You would assume that he was healthy, well adjusted, and happy. And while River was really none of those things, he was still beautiful. And Skye loved him.

Skye blushed at the flowers River held in his hands, and his heart fluttered at the beautiful smile on River's face, knowing it was for him, and that River had driven here on his lunch break, across town, despite the pain it would cause him.

Standing from his chair, he walked over to the door.

"I'll be right back," he said to the class, and heard their murmurs as he stepped out into the hall.

"Are those for me?" he asked, nodding at the flowers in River's hand. They were a beautiful combination of roses, carnations, and lilies interspersed with baby's breath, and they were almost as stunning as the man holding them.

River's smile grew wider as he handed them to Skye. "Happy Valentine's Day," he said, and Skye's eyes grew wide.

"Oh, shit. I totally forgot. I didn't get you anything," he grimaced.

River smiled. "If it makes you feel any better I picked those up on the way here, and it was kind of a last minute decision 'cause I forgot, too. I guess neither of us is really used to celebrating Valentine's Day."

Skye smiled again. "That does make me feel a little bit better. Thank you." He gestured to the flowers he was holding now. "They're beautiful. And coming all the way over here was really sweet of you."

River stepped closer and placed a chaste kiss on Skye's cheek. "I'll see you tonight," he said. "I love you."

"I love you too," Skye said, and squeezed his boyfriend's hand before he walked away.

The questions that inundated him when he opened the door again were overwhelming, and he couldn't keep the smile off of his face for the rest of the day.

CHAPTER 20

River

When River got home from work that day, the condo was dimly lit and there was soft music playing. The table had been set for two with candles in the center and wine glasses at each place. Artificial rose petals lay scattered across the tablecloth. A smile formed on his face as his cheeks heated.

Wow. Skye was really going all out for their first Valentine's Day together. Warmth settled in his chest as he slipped off his winter gear and went to find his boyfriend in the kitchen.

Skye stood in front of the stove, and when River reached him he slid his arms around his waist, nuzzling his neck. "Hey, handsome," he cooed.

Skye smiled and flushed. "Hey, angel." He turned slightly and gave River a kiss on the cheek. "Dinner's almost ready. I set up the table but we can eat in your room, if that's more comfortable."

"No, I want to sit at the table. It looks so beautiful. I think I'll be okay with my seat cushion." River placed a kiss on Skye's lips. "I noticed you changed." He let his gaze roam over Skye in his dark wash jeans and the gray sweater that he loved so much, and he smiled.

"I remembered you liking it," Skye said with a blush and a smile of his own. "Besides, it's comfortable."

"You do look cute." River gave Skye another kiss, this time a little bit longer.

"I should get back to the food before it burns," Skye murmured, once they pulled away. He had one hand on the spoon he was using, still in the pan on the stove and the other hand wrapped around River's waist, their foreheads pressed together.

"Okay." River grinned. "I'm gonna go change, too." He slipped away from Skye and disappeared into his bedroom, and Skye laughed when he came back in pajama pants and a T-shirt.

"No need to get all dressed up on my account, angel," Skye chuckled.

River laughed, too. "This is more comfortable for me. Jeans are tighter. They put more pressure on my tailbone when I sit."

"It's okay, Riv, really. It's cute," Skye said. "Come on, dinner's ready."

They made their way over to the table and Skye dished their pasta onto their plates as River sat down with his cushion underneath him.

"Skye, you know I can't have alcohol," River said, gesturing to the wine glasses.

"I know," Skye said. "I wanted to use them anyway." He winked and then went into the kitchen, returning shortly with sparkling grape juice, chilled from the refrigerator. River smiled as Skye filled their glasses, then lit the two candles, the flames casting shadows over his handsome face. God, he really was beautiful.

"Thank you for doing all of this," River said, reaching across the table to take Skye's hand. "It's incredible."

Skye squeezed his hand back. "You're incredible, angel," he said sincerely.

River kissed him, and they ate their dinner mostly in silence, speaking now and again about each other's work. When they had finished eating, River stood up from his seat, blew out the candles, and took Skye's hand. Skye stood and let River lead him over to the sofa where River gestured for him to sit.

$$\sim$$

Skye

Skye sat, somewhat confused when River didn't sit down next to him, his eyes widening when River lowered himself onto Skye's lap, straddling him. River's eyes met his, and he was lost again in their blue beauty, his heart thundering. When River's lips met his, and he felt his soft, strong fingers running through his hair, he slid his arms around River and kissed him back. The heat went straight to his groin, and his heart rate skyrocketed. This was as intimate as they had ever been. River in his lap, their hands discovering and exploring each other. Their mouths moving together in perfect synchronicity. He pressed his hands against River's back and drew him closer, and River pushed himself up slightly to get a better grip on Skye's mouth, angling his head and sliding his tongue inside, letting Skye bite at his lower lip.

Skye heard the moan that escaped River's lips and he found himself reaching to slide his hands under River's shirt when his boyfriend pulled back suddenly, his breathing heavy as his gaze fell towards his lap. His cheeks flushed and tears filled his eyes as he started to shake, sitting back on Skye's lap.

Skye's gaze followed River's and his breath caught. Because there, clearly visible underneath River's pajama pants, was a partial erection.

"Holy shit," Skye breathed.

"Kiss me." River's voice was earnest, and he pressed his lips to Skye's once more, feverishly. Moments later Skye felt something twitching against his stomach and it was him that pulled back this time. They glanced down again and River had tears sliding down his cheeks at the sight of himself, now fully hard. Skye gripped River's cheeks in his hands and looked into his eyes, even as tears filled his own. "Are you okay?" he asked. River was flushed, but was smiling as wide as Skye had ever seen. Fuck it was beautiful.

River nodded, resting his forehead against Skye's as the tears continued to fall. "Surprised," he said, "and a little overwhelmed, maybe, but..." he cried harder now, clinging to Skye.

"I just didn't know...I never thought that...if I would ever be able to..." and he cried even more tears of joy, and even laughed. "God, I love you so much, Skye. I'm so crazy about you, and now my body is actually allowing me to show it. And it feels so good. I just hope it keeps doing it."

Skye looked down and smiled. "So far so good," he said, and River laughed again.

"I meant in the future, idiot."

"I know," Skye said, smiling. "But we have this, River. This moment. This victory." And he looked at it again because he couldn't believe that he'd finally gotten his boyfriend to this point, after everything they'd been through, everything River had been through. This was so huge. And seeing his body on display like this, it wasn't erotic in the sense that it normally would be, it was just fucking beautiful.

"Skye, you're staring," River said, with a smile, and another laugh.

Skye blushed. "Sorry." He looked back up at his boyfriend. "It's just so perfect." He rested his hand on the back of River's neck and brought him in for another kiss, and another, and another. They continued to kiss until their lips were sore and swollen, and their hands were tired from running them along each other's arms and down each other's chests, and through each other's hair, and they both had marks on their necks from where the other had kissed and sucked, and they would glance down every once in a while, and smile because River's erection hadn't gone anywhere.

CHAPTER 21

River

"River?" Skye said when River stumbled in the door from work the next day and immediately started turning off lights. "What's going on?"

River was holding his hand to his head and feeling along the wall with his other hand, trying to make his way into the kitchen for some Tylenol. Being on his anti-anxiety meds also meant he couldn't take ibuprofen or aspirin and his head was throbbing. It had started at work a few hours ago and had only gotten worse throughout the day and the drive home. Nausea coiled in his stomach and his head spun. The only thing he wanted was to take some medicine and lie down.

"River, you look awful," Skye said, appearing at his side. "What do you need?"

"Tylenol," River said, barely managing to get the words out, his eyes squinting as he gestured towards the kitchen cabinet.

"Go lay down," Skye said. "I'll bring it to you."

River didn't argue. He made his way to his room and collapsed onto the bed in the dark. He'd never had a headache of this magnitude before. The pain was so intense it was overwhelming. His whole head felt hot. The top of his head and his temples were throbbing, stabbing, like they were aching to get out. It felt like his skull was being crushed. He was having shooting pain in his ears, and his eyes were hurting. He was hoping that if he took some medicine and got some sleep this would all be over in the morning, nothing but a bad dream.

But when the alarm clock went off the next morning, the splitting migraine was still there, pounding against his skull again as soon as he was conscious. He tried to get up and get ready for work, hoping it would go away, but it didn't, and he decided he had better call in sick because there was no way he could make it through the day like this, let alone drive. He took more Tylenol and went back to bed, this time with an ice pack over his head to try and dull the pain that was radiating throughout his skull, setting it on fire.

When he awoke several hours later, the pain was still there, a pounding force against his head, like something living inside was screaming to get out. At this point he was wondering if he should be going to the ER, or Urgent Care at least, but he didn't feel well enough to get there and he certainly wasn't going to call Skye and ask him to come home from work for this. So he got up to use the bathroom, and then went back to bed, grabbing another ice pack, because that seemed to be the only thing providing him with any relief. The Tylenol wasn't helping at all, he was realizing. He was tempted to take ibuprofen. He'd done it before when he was desperate, feeling like the risk wasn't all that great and chances are he'd be fine, but Skye didn't approve and he hated to let him down. He knew he was only thinking of River's well being and safety when he asked him not to mix the meds.

He was feeling nauseous and hot and cold all at once as he lay there with his eyes closed, trying to block out every sound, the curtains in the bedroom drawn tight to keep the sun out. His eyes were hurting, his ears were throbbing, his head was pounding, and he realized he hadn't had anything to eat or drink all day other than the water he'd used to take his Tylenol, so that forced him to push himself up and out of bed, because maybe, just maybe being more hydrated would help.

He managed to get two full glasses of water down and then collapsed into bed once again, resting on his back, one ice pack at the base of his skull and the other draped over the front of his head, trying to get some relief from whatever this was. And he managed to doze off again.

He woke briefly at one point to gentle fingers stroking his jaw and a strong arm around his waist. "Skye," he murmured, nestling into the warm body behind him and dozing off again.

River almost cried when the morning came and his headache was still in full force. It hadn't started out that way. He'd felt like it was getting better as he'd gotten out of bed and started to get ready for work, but the more he moved around, the quicker it found its way back.

"River, are you okay?" Skye asked, noticing his boyfriend's distress as they ate their breakfast.

"No," River said in dismay. "I can't get rid of this damn headache, Skye. I don't know what's going on. I've never had a migraine like this in my life."

"Do you need me to take you to the doctor?" Skye asked.

"I don't know," River said, honestly. "I don't know what they would do for me. And I really don't want to waste the money. So, I guess not. Can you take me to work, though?"

"River, you can't be serious, you look like shit."

"I already called in sick yesterday. I can't take two days off in a row," River insisted. "Maybe it'll get better throughout the day. I have to try. Please?"

Skye sighed. "Okay."

But when he dropped River off at work thirty minutes later, River felt even worse, and when Skye texted him around four o'clock asking how he was doing, River replied, **Not good :(,** which was an understatement, because when Skye arrived at six o'clock to pick River up he practically had to carry him to the car. And when they got home ten minutes later River was shaking as they walked inside, holding onto Skye's arm to try and support himself because his eyes were hurting so badly he couldn't keep them open, and it felt like someone was stabbing knives into the sides of his head and squeezing it in a vice all at the same time. He felt nauseated again, and his body was aching. And to top things off, his damn tailbone was hurting too.

River stood in the entryway, delirious, as Skye unbuttoned his coast and slid it off for him, taking his scarf and his gloves as well, and then in a moment, he was in Skye's arms, being carried to his bedroom and placed gently on the bed, as Skye slid his shoes off.

"Do you want dinner?" he heard his boyfriend ask.

"If I'm awake, maybe," he mumbled. "Ice pack?"

"What?" Skye asked, leaning closer.

"Ice pack," River repeated, pointing to his head. "For my head. Please. And, Skye, I'd like to try some ibuprofen. I can't do this anymore. I'd like to see if it will help."

"Okay," Skye said, reluctantly. He returned a moment later with the ice pack and the ibuprofen, along with a glass of water. He waited for River to swallow the medicine, then pressed a kiss to his hair and left the room.

CHAPTER 22

Skye

The ibuprofen did not help, and neither did the Excedrin, or the Aleve, or alternating between Tylenol and ibuprofen, or drinking more water, and River's migraine had lasted days now. He'd made it through the end of the work week, but was in bed all weekend, absolutely miserable. He'd tried going to Urgent Care just to see if there was any sort of infection that might be causing it, but they couldn't find anything and didn't have any answers for him other than to follow up with his primary care doctor. So that's what he did the following Monday. Skye drove him because his head was still pounding and his eyes were still burning and he could barely see straight half of the time.

They suggested doing lab work, and an MRI and MRA just to make sure it was nothing serious. So, once again they were back, doing tests, waiting on results, scared and nervous, not knowing what was going on, or why.

Why River? Skye thought. *Why him? Why the man I love? Why does he have to be the one in pain? Why do we have to be the ones going through this, over and over again? Is this going to be our lives? Doctors and questions and endless struggles?* He found himself sitting in the waiting room where River was currently having his MRI done on a Saturday morning, and he let his head fall into his hands, letting out a deep breath. Every time they caught a break, it seemed, something else happened. Every time they took a step forward they would take two steps back. And he was sick of seeing his boyfriend hurting. Especially when he felt like there was nothing he could do to help. *He's twenty-eight, for Christ's sake,* but health issues, and chronic pain, and trauma, Skye was realizing more and more, didn't care how old you were. They didn't discriminate. And the person who looked the healthiest on the outside, could be the one suffering the most on the inside.

He wasn't sure if he was relieved or not when the results of the MRI and MRA both came back normal, and so did the blood work. Sure that meant there was nothing serious, which was great, but then why was River still in so much pain? It had been two weeks now, and his migraine only ever let up when he was asleep. So if he wasn't at work, that's what he was doing. Skye didn't blame him a bit, but he missed him terribly. He just wanted his boyfriend to find some relief. They did get a referral for a neurologist that the doctor recommended they see, so River scheduled an appointment with them, but it would be another month before he could get in to see them.

River

Finally, after another week straight of endless migraines, River woke up and found himself migraine free. He was confused more than anything, because he hadn't done anything differently, but he wasn't going to complain, because the pain was gone, and it felt like he could breathe again.

He rolled over to see that Skye was already out of bed, and climbed out of bed himself. He brushed his teeth and made his way into the kitchen, taking the cup of coffee out of Skye's hand and setting it aside, then placed both hands on his boyfriend's cheeks and kissed him tenderly.

"Wow," Skye said, when River pulled away. He slid his arms around his waist and smiled. "What was that for? You feeling better?"

"Yeah, I have no idea how, or why, but I am," River said, beaming. "And it's Saturday, so let's do something. I've missed you." He started to place sweet kisses all over Skye's neck and jawline.

Skye smiled and squirmed a little, sliding his hands up River's back. "I've missed you too," he said. He nudged the side of River's face with his nose, causing River to look at his boyfriend and give him another kiss. "I have an idea." River rested his hands on Skye's chest as Skye held him close.

"What?" he said, staring into those gorgeous green eyes. He knew he probably looked like a lovesick puppy the way he was gazing at his boyfriend with so much fondness, but he couldn't help it.

"I found a movie theater with reclining seats, so maybe that means you could sit without it hurting your tailbone," Skye said, hopefully.

River's face lit up at the idea. "Really?"

"But, it's a twenty-five minute drive to get there," Skye said, grimacing slightly. "Can you handle that?"

"I think so. I'd like to try."

"Or we could try to do something that doesn't require sitting, but if your heart acts up..." Skye said.

"I like the movie idea, Skye," River interrupted, smiling. "If it doesn't pan out we can just go for a walk somewhere and get some lunch. Also, my heart's doing okay. I haven't had an episode in a while."

"Okay," Skye said, smiling. They kissed once more and then pulled apart to shower and get ready.

～

"Have we ever actually been on a date?" Skye said as they drove to the movie theater.

River was holding Skye's hand and beaming, despite the discomfort to his tailbone. It was tolerable, and he was just happy to be migraine free and out of the house with Skye, enjoying the sunshine and fresh air. "No," he said. "I don't think we have. Unless you call our Valentine's dinner a date."

"Not technically, since we weren't out, but still probably the best memory ever," Skye said, and they both smiled and blushed. "Have you had an erection since then?"

River shook his head, frowning slightly. "No, I haven't. But we haven't exactly had the opportunity, either, my migraines were so bad."

"I'm happy to try again." Skye grinned. "Practice makes perfect, you know."

River blushed. He raised Skye's hand to his lips and kissed it, then brushed it along the stubble of his jawline, closing his eyes.

"Okay, stop it," Skye said, "'Cause now I've got one, and I can't walk into the theater like that." He shifted in his seat.

River smiled. He kissed Skye's hand once more and then let go.

His hand was back in Skye's as they walked inside. Neither one of them really remembered much about the movie because they spent most of it with their faces angled towards each other and their lips pressed together. When they weren't kissing, River was resting his head on Skye's shoulder, sighing contentedly, because this did seem to work, this reclining seat thing, which meant they could keep doing this, having dates here, and because once again, he was hard, and it was because of Skye.

CHAPTER 23

Skye

THREE WEEKS LATER

Overwhelmed didn't even begin to cover how Skye was feeling. The worry, grief and confusion. River had had a week of relief from his migraines, but they had been back in full force for several more weeks, now, with no explanation. He'd taken two days off of work to start out with, but when the pain hadn't subsided he'd struggled through the remaining weeks again. He'd seen a chiropractor to see if that would help, but it hadn't. He'd tried acupuncture and even botox injections. Neither one was covered by insurance and both had been in vain.

"I can't keep doing this, Skye," River cried as they lay in bed one evening. He was hugging Skye and Skye was rubbing circles on his back.

"I know, River," Skye said. "I'm so sorry. I wish I could fix it."

River sniffled. "I'm having a hard time," he said after a moment of silence. He pulled away, his breath hitching.

"I know," Skye said, rubbing River's arm with his hand.

River shook his head. "Not with the health stuff," he said.

"I mean, yes, with the health stuff, but I mean with my faith. With everything that's been going on lately, with all of my health issues, I'm really having a hard time believing." He wiped tears from his eyes and sniffled again.

"Believing what?" Skye asked.

"That God cares about me," River said, his pain filled gaze meeting Skye's. Tears slid down his cheeks again. "That He loves me, that He's good...that He even exists," he said with a final breath. And he was sobbing now. "I feel like I'm losing my faith, and God, it fucking hurts. It's been everything to me for so long, and now it's just...it's fading, and I hate that. I just don't understand."

Skye didn't know what to say. He didn't know how to encourage River in this way, since his faith wasn't something they shared. But he did know he loved him, and he hated for River to lose something that had been so central to his life for so long, and had grounded him and helped him through some really difficult times in the past. So he took his boyfriend into his arms once again and held him as he sobbed.

"Don't give up, angel," he encouraged. "If there's one thing you've taught me through the years it's that just because your circumstances change it doesn't mean that God does, right? I don't get it either. It makes me angry, too. And confused. But maybe your story, your pain, can be used to encourage or help someone else? Maybe there's a bigger picture here that we can't see. And, I don't know. Maybe it's about faith and trust, not having all of the answers. Not saying it's not okay to be angry, 'cause it is. And if you need to be angry or cry, I'm here for you. Just don't give up on your faith, River. It's brought you through so much. I'd hate to see you lose it now."

～

River

When they finally got in to see the neurologist, River was actually migraine free again. But he was not so ignorant this time as to assume they would stay away. The neurologist gave him a prescription to try for when the migraine started again and told him to take it as soon as he felt it coming on, and that if he didn't get relief in half an hour he could take another one.

River found out a week later that that didn't work either. And he was miserable for another three weeks until he could get back in to see the neurologist for a follow up to try something else. His migraines seemed to have a pattern of two to three weeks on, one week off, and they had gotten so bad this last time that he'd had to take several days off of work. He was running out of sick days and personal time off. If this kept up he'd have to take unpaid medical leave, and he didn't think he could afford that with all of the bills he had piling up from all of the doctor's visits and tests and lab work he'd had done in the last several months, not to mention the fact that he was still paying off his student loans from the seven years he'd been in school. This was starting to become the longest and worst year of his life.

Except for Skye. Skye was the one bright spot in all of his darkness. And for that, he was immeasurably thankful. Honestly, with everything River had going on, he wasn't one hundred percent sure why Skye still stuck around, why he still cared for him and loved him so fiercely. But he did. He kept sticking around, kept loving him, kept holding him, taking care of him, supporting him. And River couldn't believe that he was loved so deeply. And if there was any proof of God, that God still loved him, it was that he had Skye in his life to love him and walk through all of this with him.

When he finally got back to the neurologist, they offered him another medication to try. This one was a new one that they gave to patients who didn't respond to traditional migraine meds, and it was an injection that he would have shipped to his house and would have to administer to himself once a month. He was fine with that, and luckily didn't have an aversion to needles like Skye did, because this method never would have worked for him if he'd been the one with the debilitating migraines. The thought kind of made him smile until the doctor told him how much it would cost, and his heart fell into his stomach, because he wasn't sure he could afford it.

"Let me know if you want me to send the script over or not," the neurologist said. "I know it's costly but I think it's probably the best option for you."

River sighed as he stood and picked up his seat cushion, which he still got weird looks for, and left the doctor's office.

"Hey, River, how was it?" Skye asked, when River walked in the door of their condo after work. Fortunately today was one of his few non migraine days, so he wasn't as miserable as usual, but he was exhausted and stressed. He'd been trying to figure out all day what to do about the medication the doctor wanted to put him on. He desperately needed relief and at this point he was willing to try anything, but if he couldn't afford it, that was it. He needed to take a look at his finances, closely, and before another migraine hit.

"I don't know," he mumbled, slipping his shoes off.

"What do you mean?" Skye asked, looking at him warily.

River rubbed his eyes with his hands. "I just need to figure out some stuff," he said.

"What stuff? What did the doctor say?" Skye prodded.

River sighed. "She wants to put me on a new medication, but it's expensive. I have to figure out if I can afford it. I've had so many medical bills lately, and I'm still paying off my school debt." He sat on the couch and sighed. "I'm just stressed."

His gaze shot back up to Skye's when he heard him say, "I could help."

"What?"

"I could help," Skye repeated. He bit his lip, his hands in his pockets. "With the cost. If you can't afford it."

River blinked. "That's really sweet of you, Skye, but it's okay. These are my bills and my meds, and my debt. It's my responsibility. I'll figure something out." He rubbed a hand over his forehead and stood up, letting out a breath, but Skye's next words had him right back on the couch, stunned speechless.

"You could marry me."

River's mouth gaped. The wheels in his head were spinning so fast. "What?" he asked eventually, when he could finally bring himself to form words.

"Marry me," Skye said again, earnestly this time. He sat down next to River and took his hand. "Then you won't feel bad about letting me help you pay for it. It won't be your debt or your bills anymore. They'll be *our* bills and *our* debt." His eyes danced over River's face. "Marry me," he said. "Please."

River swallowed hard. He opened his mouth but nothing came out for quite a while. "I...I," he started. "Skye, I don't..."

"River, I love you," Skye said. "I know this isn't the world's most romantic proposal, but it's the most sincere. I *want* to be married to you. Not just so you won't feel bad about taking my money. But because I want to spend the rest of my life with you. Whatever you face I want to face it with you." He reached up and placed his hand on River's cheek, stroking it with his thumb. River swallowed again, but then he relaxed and leaned into the touch, even closing his eyes.

"Skye," he said softly, placing his hand on top of Skye's. The mood in the room had changed drastically in the last two minutes, from talking about bills to talking about marriage. And when he opened his eyes, and saw those beautiful emerald ones staring back at him, and felt the fluttering in his chest, he knew that this was what he wanted for the rest of his life too.

"Okay," he said, a smile spreading across his face. Then Skye's lips were on his, and they kissed hard and long.

"You're serious?" Skye said, pulling away eventually and pressing his forehead to River's, his breaths ragged.

"If you're sure you really want me."

Skye smiled. "I'm sure," he said, as tears fell down his cheeks. "God, River, I've never been so sure of anything in my life."

River smiled, too, but it quickly turned to a frown, causing Skye to pull away.

"What is it?" he asked, clasping River's hand in his.

River looked down, biting his lip. "Skye, you know I may not be ready for sex still, on our wedding night. I mean, I always thought I would be, back when I thought I would be marrying a woman, but now..." he trailed off, looking back up at Skye. "It might still take some time before I'm ready for that, and...that's not the reason for your proposal is it? Because if it is...I'm afraid you might be disappointed. Stuck with a chronically ill husband and lots of bills, and no sex. I mean, I'll try, and I'll work on it. I'll see a counselor for it if I need to. I will, Skye, cause I'd do anything for you, but, I just want you to understand that it might be a while..."

"River," Skye said, scooting closer to him again, their legs touching. "You don't have to be ready for anything on our wedding night, okay? You don't have to be ready for sex ever, if it's not something you want. That's not why I'm proposing. I do want you. Of course I do. I always have, but I think being married, knowing we don't have those boundaries anymore, might help you. Knowing you don't have to guard yourself, and you can look, and touch, and enjoy me freely, if you want to, uninhibited. Maybe you'll realize more of what you want, and if you really are scared or if you are just holding back because you feel like you have to. It's worth a shot, right? Either way, I want to be married to you." He planted a sweet kiss on River's temple, and then another one on his cheek, and then his nose.

River closed his eyes again as Skye's lips brushed against his face, and he could feel himself getting hard all over again, and he knew what his body wanted, what his heart wanted. He just wasn't sure his mind would cooperate. But being married would give him the opportunity to find that out. It scared him a little bit, but it also excited him, the idea of being able to explore all that marriage had to offer with Skye. And knowing that Skye truly would be patient with him, and love him, and guide him through it.

"When should we get married?" Skye asked, pressing soft, addictive kisses to River's neck and jaw, making him harder still. He could hear Skye breathing in his scent and feel his nose against his bare skin even as Skye's lips brushed the short stubble on his face. He gasped and his dick twitched. God, he hoped being married to Skye would give him the courage to try being intimate. He wanted this man so much.

He was so gone on how Skye was making him feel that he almost didn't comprehend the question.

"Riv?" Skye said.

"Hmm?" he asked, and he heard Skye chuckle, his warm breath ghosting over River's neck, sending a shiver down his spine.

"When do you want to marry me, beautiful?"

River tried to catch his breath. "Um, tomorrow sounds good," he muttered, his heart racing and his cock throbbing now, as Skye pressed his palm to River's cheek and continued to lavish him with warm, soft kisses, even nibbling on his ear. It felt incredible. He didn't think he'd ever been so turned on in his life. Skye made him feel things, want things he'd never wanted before. He never thought another man would be able to make him feel this way, and that gave him hope. Hope that sex wasn't impossible.

"Tomorrow?" Skye said, pulling away. "Really?" His eyes danced over River's face again, as if to gauge his sincerity.

River blinked and nodded as he tried to catch his breath. "Yes, Skye, please? The only reason we're not going now is because the courthouse is already closed. But I've been too sick lately to try and plan a wedding. These migraines are so debilitating, and we still don't know if this new medication is even going to work. I want to marry you before they start up again. So, if in the morning I'm still migraine free, can we please go get married?"

Skye took River's face in his hands and kissed him. "Okay," he said, smiling. "You convinced me. I guess I better call my boss to tell him I need a personal day tomorrow. And then I better make a few other phone calls too. I think Jaden and Mom would be pretty upset if I didn't tell them I was getting married."

"And Nick and Jenna," River said, smiling so hard his cheeks hurt.

Skye grinned. "Definitely. If we don't tell them, Jenna will have our balls."

River laughed, and Skye made his phone calls. Jenna and Nick swore they were going to be at the courthouse in the morning to witness the nuptials, even if it got them fired, and they barely slept that night, curled up in each other's arms, smiling, kissing, brushing their faces together, sliding their legs in between each other's, holding each other close, because in the morning, they were getting married.

CHAPTER 24

They were beaming the whole way back from the courthouse the next day. They'd gotten a little dressed up for the occasion. Dress pants, shirts, and ties. Skye's tie was blue, and River's was green. And Skye had a hard time keeping his eyes on the road instead of on his husband as they drove home.

Husband. He couldn't get used to the idea that River was his husband. That they truly belonged to each other. Forever. For always. He was River's and River was his. And he wouldn't have it any other way. He reached over to take his husband's hand, the one that now bore a silver wedding band, and squeezed it gently. River smiled at him, interlocking their fingers together, and holding their hands on his lap.

It had been a simple ceremony, and Nick and Jenna had both cried. Then they had gone out to brunch with their friends who were still very much together and very clearly in love. Skye wondered how long it would be before they tied the knot.

When they got home, Skye went around to River's side of the car before he could get very far and handed his keys to River.

"Here, take these," he said.

River looked at him in confusion but did as he asked, and the next thing he knew his feet were off the ground and he was in Skye's arms. He let out a surprised yelp, and wrapped his arms around Skye's neck.

"You're being way too romantic," River said, smiling up at him as Skye carried him up the front walk.

Skye smiled back. "You gotta open the door," he said, gesturing.

River held on to Skye with one arm and unlocked the door with the other. He opened it and they stepped inside. Skye planted another kiss on River's lips before setting him back on his feet again.

"Hey, don't you have a phone call to make?" Skye said. "The sooner we get you that medication the better."

"Oh, right," River said, pulling out his phone.

"All good?" Skye asked when River got off the phone.

"She called the pharmacy. They'll ship it to me. Should be here in two days. Hopefully I'll still be migraine free by then."

"And you're going to be okay with doing that to yourself?" Skye asked, shivering at the thought.

"You mean sticking a needle in my leg once a month?" River said. "If it gets rid of these migraines, hell yeah."

"More power to ya, angel," Skye said. "No way I could do that."

River grinned. "I know."

They spent the rest of the day together, cuddled up, watching tv, reading, always with their feet touching, or their hands together, or with River's head resting on Skye's shoulder, or in his lap, Skye's fingers stroking through his hair. It wasn't the wedding night that Skye had always envisioned, but that was okay. Because he had River.

And with River's head in his lap, both of them reading their books, Skye smiled softly and continued to stroke River's thick, dark hair, and thought of how lucky and blessed he was, that the man he so desperately loved, not only loved him back, but now called him husband.

~

"No way!" Gwen exclaimed the following day when she noticed the band around Skye's ring finger. "You got married?!"

And all of a sudden the room was bustling with questions.

"Seriously?" Kevin said.

"What?" Ben asked.

"Why didn't you tell us?" Gwen chimed again. "I'm hurt. Wait, is that why we had a sub yesterday?" She raised her eyebrow at him and suddenly there were forty eyes staring at him inquisitively.

"Yes, it is," Skye admitted, and he couldn't keep the smile off of his face. He looked at his ring and twisted it around his finger. It was exactly the same as River's. They wanted their rings to match. For some reason it made them feel like they belonged to each other even more.

"Details," Gwen said. "It's River, right? The super cute boyfriend who brought you flowers on Valentine's Day? That was adorable. You guys finally tied the knot? Who proposed? You or him? Wait, how long have you been engaged? You didn't tell us you were engaged?" Now Gwen was looking highly offended and she crossed her arms over her chest.

Skye couldn't help but laugh. "Guys, look, it's not the time for twenty questions, okay? Yes, I got married to my roommate, aka, the super cute boyfriend with the flowers." He smirked at Gwen. "It was really spur of the moment, so I didn't tell anyone other than my family and a couple of close friends. "

Gwen raised an eyebrow. "Really?" she said. "You're not blowing smoke?"

"Really," Skye replied. "Scouts honor." He saluted her.

"Okay, you're forgiven," Gwen said, a smile escaping her lips.

And Skye noticed that the rest of the class was smiling too. "Thank you."

"Yes, Claire," he said, when the girl raised her hand.

"So, you didn't go on a honeymoon, or have a celebration, or anything?" she asked, somewhat timidly.

"Not yet," Skye said.

She nodded and bit her lip. "Well, congratulations."

"Thank you," Skye said again with a smile. "Now, you guys do have a test at the end of the week, so maybe we should talk about something other than my husband, because unfortunately he won't be on it."

They all chuckled and opened their books.

~

THREE WEEKS LATER

Skye awoke to a gentle arm around his waist and River's chin pressed against his shoulder, his stubble rubbing up against Skye's cheek.

"Skye?" River said, slightly above a whisper.

"Hmm?" Skye murmured, barely awake. He placed his arm over River's and interlocked their fingers together on his stomach as he felt River's nose against his neck. But the minute he heard his husband's breath hitching, his body was on alert.

"River?" he said, as he sat up and turned on the bedside lamp. River was shaking when Skye turned to face him again, tears sliding down his cheeks. "River, what's wrong?" he asked, scooting close to him and stroking the side of his head with his fingers.

"I'm sorry, Skye." River wiped tears away. "I tried to fall back asleep, but I couldn't."

"It's okay," Skye said. "You know it's okay. Did you have another nightmare?"

River nodded. "I haven't had one in a while, but this one was especially bad. It was like I was reliving it all over again." He shook as he sobbed, and Skye took his husband into his arms and held him close, just like he always did when River cried. When River hurt. "Shh," he soothed. "I've got you. I'm here, angel. You're safe."

It was several minutes before River eased his grip on Skye, sniffling and wiping his eyes. "Skye, do you think...do you think you could touch me?"

Skye blinked, and then pulled away and stared down at his husband. "What?" he asked.

"I want you to touch me," River said again, reaching up to place his hand on Skye's chest, and looking into his eyes. "Please?"

Skye's heart was hammering in his chest and he was sure River could feel it. He couldn't breathe. "But, but you just had a nightmare about being assaulted, Riv, you..."

"Exactly. The only time I've ever experienced sexual touch has been by people who wanted to do me harm. Who were being cruel and hurtful, and were taking advantage of me, and...I want to be touched by someone who loves me. Someone that I trust. Someone that I love." He pressed his lips to Skye's and Skye's breath hitched. Tears stung his eyes when River pulled away.

"I want this," River said, stroking his cheek. "I want you. Please?"

Skye bit his lip as his tears fell freely now and he leaned forward, resting his forehead against River's as River rested back on the pillow, smiling up at him. River planted soft, tender kisses on Skye's cheeks as he cried.

"I love you," River said.

"I love you, too, Riv," Skye said. "So much." He let out a deep breath.

"You okay?" River asked, running his fingers through Skye's hair.

Skye smiled. "Yeah, I'm just," he wiped away tears, "I'm overwhelmed, River."

River took both of Skye's cheeks into his hands and kissed his forehead. "Whenever you're ready."

Skye nodded. "You want me to take your pants off?"

"Please," River said with a smile. "This time I'll help you. And maybe it won't be as awkward."

Skye chuckled, thinking about the last time he'd undressed River, and how he'd had to try not to think of his best friend in a sexual manner, and how wonderful it was that he could do so now, that he was meant to do so now. River was his husband. River wanted him to undress him. River wanted him to touch him. He was going to see River naked for the first time. And his hands were shaking slightly as he sat up and gripped the waistband of River's pajama pants, and his briefs, and pulled them down as River lifted his hips.

As soon as they were off, Skye tossed them to the floor and then looked back at his husband, laying on the bed, fully erect, his cock long and thick, surrounded by dark pubes, twitching under Skye's gaze. Fuck, that was beautiful.

His gaze wandered up until it locked with those gorgeous blue eyes staring up at him.

River swallowed. "You're making me nervous," he said. "Please say something."

But Skye couldn't speak. He had more tears filling his eyes as he looked into River's, and kissed him, lying down again and wrapping his arms around his husband, pulling his naked body close, their legs tangling.

"God, River, you're so damn beautiful," he said once they pulled away. He traced a finger down River's side and over the swell of his perfectly round ass. He squeezed his ass cheek and River moaned slightly, pressing his forehead to Skye's, their cocks brushing together. Skye moaned in turn, his cock throbbing at the knowledge that he was about to touch River for the first time.

"Please touch me," River pleaded softly.

Skye was still shaking slightly, and he kept his forehead against River's as he reached his hand down and began to stroke his husband's shaft. The feel of River's cock in his hand was something he thought he would never experience, and it was everything. Full, and thick, and dripping with precum as he continued to move his hand up and down in slow, firm strokes, hearing River's breath hitch and feeling his cock twitch in his grip as River bucked his hips forward, thrusting into Skye's palm. River's moans and whimpers filled his mouth as Skye kissed him and slid his thumb over the slit of his engorged cock.

"Skye," River said, and he was crying now too, his body trembling.

"River, are you okay?" Skye said. "Do I need to stop?"

River shook his head, his hands gripping Skye's face. His hips stopped moving. "No. They're good tears, happy tears, Skye. I'm... oh, God," River closed his eyes and moaned Skye's name. "This feels amazing, and I just...I can't believe how much you love me, and..." he was breathing heavily, more tears falling. He brought Skye's face down to his and kissed him again and again and again even as he cried, and Skye continued to stroke him. River thrust upward again and whimpered into Skye's mouth.

When River released only moments later, they were both crying and smiling, and laughing, and peppering each other with kisses. And Skye knew that he had never experienced anything more beautiful in his entire life. To have River in bed with him, naked, to be holding him, pleasuring him, to be the reason for his orgasm, to hear his name on River's lips as he climaxed. It was everything he could have asked for and more.

"Can I taste you?" he asked, and when River nodded, a slightly stunned expression on his face, Skye didn't waste any time. He lowered himself and lapped up the cum covering River's abdomen, feeling River shudder underneath him, his stomach sinking in. He swallowed, moaning as he did, and didn't miss how River's cock twitched. River moaned again as Skye lowered his face once more and licked the last remaining drops of cum from River's cock.

"Fuck, that's hot," River whispered, his eyes blown wide.

"You taste amazing, baby," Skye said, savoring the saltiness of River on his tongue and letting it slide down his throat. "Fucking perfect." He kissed his husband again and River moaned into his mouth. They kissed for a moment longer before Skye pulled away and collapsed on his back. But River was hovering over him in a second, his smile wide.

"Your turn," he said.

Skye jerked when he felt River's hand in his pants, and his breath hitched.

"May I?" River asked, grinning, and nuzzling Skye's nose with his.

"You don't have to," Skye said, breathless, as River rested on his elbow.

River's gaze was steady, his voice firm but gentle. "I want to." Skye nodded.

River knelt and pulled Skye's pants and underwear off together, and then tugged at the hem of his shirt. Skye took the hint and sat up slightly, slipping the shirt off and tossing it to the floor as well.

River smiled wider as his gaze trailed over Skye's body, taking it in, just as Skye had done with him. "Wow," he said. "You're perfect."

Skye blushed fiercely because there was nothing but sincerity in River's tone.

"Shut up," he said, but he was smiling, and pulling River back down to him.

"I love you," River said, pressing a kiss to Skye's nose as they both lay, moments later, basking in the afterglow of their orgasms, and relishing in the fact that they had made each other come.

The smells of sweat and sex permeated the room, and Skye didn't think he'd ever been more content.

"Does this mean we can change in front of each other now?" Skye asked as River snuggled up next to him and rested his head on Skye's shoulder. He began to run his fingers through River's hair and he heard River humming softly in approval as he did.

"Yeah," he said. "I'd like that. I know this wasn't quite sex, Skye, but it was pretty good, right?"

"It was better than good, angel," Skye said, wrapping his arms around his husband and kissing his hair. "Even if this is all we ever do, I'd be satisfied."

"It won't be, Skye," River stated matter of factly. "I promise. I want more. And I'll get there."

"I'd like that, River. But there's no pressure."

"I know," River said, and he lifted his head and planted a kiss against the smooth skin of Skye's jaw.

Skye reached for his phone and groaned when he saw what time it was. "We should probably get dressed and get some sleep. It's getting late. Or early, depending on how you look at it. And we both have work in the morning."

River stuck out his bottom lip. "But I don't want you to get dressed. I'll miss you." He glanced down at Skye's mostly flaccid cock and then looked back up at his husband with puppy dog eyes.

Skye chuckled. "Sorry, angel," he said with a grin. "Say goodnight to Skye junior. He'll come out to play again later."

River chuckled and looked down at Skye's cock again. "Bye little fella," he said, waving at it. "See you next time."

Skye raised an eyebrow. "Little?" River laughed. He kissed Skye and then slid out of bed, and they finished cleaning off.

Once they were both dressed again, and back in bed, Skye took River into his arms as they drifted to sleep, warm, and sated.

CHAPTER 25

Skye

Skye groaned the next morning when the alarm went off, reaching over blindly to pick up his phone and silence it.

"River." He tapped his husband. "Time to get up."

River groaned and pulled the covers up over his head.

"Come on, angel, I don't wanna get up either, but we gotta."

River's eyes stayed closed as he mumbled something unintelligible and shuffled closer to Skye, burrowing into his side.

"Uh uh, nice try," Skye said, shifting away. "Bet if I take away your warmth you'll get up faster." He climbed out of bed and River pulled the covers down long enough to glare at him before curling up underneath them again.

"Come on, River, we need to hurry. We have to be out of here in forty-five minutes."

"I'll be up in ten," River said, his voice muffled under the covers. "Promise."

"We could shower together." Skye grinned when the covers came off of River's face again and he was smirking.

"Somehow I don't think that will be faster."

"More fun though," Skye said, and winked at his husband.

Skye laughed when River flung the covers aside and grabbed his hand, dragging him into the bathroom.

They were both a little late to work.

~

Skye was on cloud nine the entire day, thinking about the incredible night and morning he'd had with River. The shower had been amazing, washing each other's warm, wet bodies, his gaze trailing over River's body as the water glided down his tan skin, over corded muscles, and his perfect ass, making out before Skye had asked River if he could touch him again. He'd been so damn hard after having his hands all over River's incredible body and his cock had been throbbing. Fortunately, River's had, too, and he'd nodded, letting Skye take him in hand and stroke him as the water rained down on them, washing away the soap and shampoo.

River had moaned and thrown his head back as Skye had pleasured him, his head against the shower wall, and Skye had devoured the sight of the water droplets clinging to his skin, sliding down his neck and pecs. He'd leaned forward and licked them up, sucking and nibbling on River's skin as he did, feeling his husband's cock throbbing and twitching in his grip. He fucking loved the feel of River's hard cock in his hand.

And when River had met his gaze and said, "Both of us, do both of us," Skye hadn't wasted a second. He'd moved closer and gripped both of their cocks in his hand, and they'd both shuddered at the incredible pleasure of having their cocks against each other's, hard and begging for release.

"God, why does that feel so good?" River had rasped as Skye had stroked them, their breaths mingling between them.

"Fuck, angel," Skye had moaned so loudly he thought the neighbors might hear even over the sound of the shower running, "you feel incredible. Love this cock, baby."

River had gripped his face and kissed him deeply, and all it had taken was a few more strokes before they had both come together, crying out each other's names, their releases covering Skye's hand. He'd licked off the evidence of their mutual orgasms and then planted another heated kiss on River's lips.

They had come so far in such a short amount of time, and Skye was incredibly grateful for every moment, every touch, every kiss, he shared with the man he loved.

~

"Hey, babe, how was work?" Skye asked when River got home that evening.

"It was fine," River said, smiling at his husband. "My coworkers seemed confused as to why I was both exhausted and couldn't stop smiling at the same time. I'm pretty sure I'd had six cups of coffee by ten am."

Skye chuckled. "Me too," he said, sliding his arms around River's waist. "I'm beat. It was worth it though."

"Yeah, it was," River said, and pressed his lips to Skye's. "I love being married to you, Skye. And I don't want to jinx it, but I do think that migraine medication is helping. I haven't had a migraine since I started taking it."

"That's good. So is that the best part of being married to me so far?" he teased. "Your migraine medication?"

"It's up there," River said with a grin. "I think last night and this morning top it, though."

"I don't know. If you'd had a migraine we wouldn't have had last night," Skye pointed out, sliding his hands away from River and heading into the kitchen, but not before he planted a kiss on his forehead.

"That's true," River said, following after him. "Would you like me to make dinner?" he asked.

Skye eyed him. "Really? The last time you made food for me it was breakfast, and I got burnt toast and a banana."

River narrowed his eyes and stuck out his tongue. "Fine, I'll never make anything for you again."

Skye grinned. "From the bottom of my heart, thank you." He slid his arm around River's waist and pulled him close enough that their bodies were pressed together, River's hands resting on his chest. His smile widened. "Now, kiss me, and get out of my kitchen."

River grinned, and obeyed, slapping Skye on the ass on his way out.

CHAPTER 26

Skye

"Hey, River?" Skye said, when he got home from work a couple of weeks later. He'd stayed later for parent teacher conferences so he was home a few minutes after River usually was.

"In the kitchen," River called back. "And don't worry, I didn't cook," he added with a smirk when Skye entered.

"Take out," Skye said.

"Yeah, I figured you'd be pretty beat today and I didn't want you to have to cook. And since I've been banned from the kitchen..."

"It's for everyone's safety, angel," Skye said with a grin, stroking River's back and planting a kiss on his temple. "Thank you."

River kissed him and smiled. "How was work?" he asked as he dished their food and handed Skye his plate.

"Good," Skye said, taking a bite of food. "A couple of them came to talk to me at the end of the day, and they had a really sweet idea, but they wanted to run it by me first, and I said I would talk to you."

"Oh," River said, his curiosity piqued. "What is it?"

Skye swallowed his food and then spoke again. "They want to throw a wedding reception for us at the school."

River's eyes went wide. "Really? Wow. That's really sweet of them. These are sixth graders?"

Skye nodded. "It was all their idea. They said they ran it by Mr. Richards already, so if we're up for it, they wanna do it. We can invite whoever we want."

River smiled. "Your students really like you, Skye. That's special. You're really making a difference in their lives."

Skye shrugged.

"Come on, Skye, give yourself some credit. They found out you got married and want to give you a party. Students don't do that for just any teacher. You're special."

"Either that or it's an excuse to meet you," Skye said with a grin. "The cute boyfriend with the flowers."

"What?" River said, tilting his head to the side.

"That's how they refer to you."

River chuckled. "Oh, right. Valentine's Day. Well, either way, we're gonna do it, right? I'd like to meet your students. And I'm sure Jenna and Nick would like to come, and we could invite your mom, and Jaden and Chloe. I don't know if they'd be able to make it, but..."

"No, we definitely should," Skye said. "My coworkers too, although I haven't really come out at work yet, River. So far the only ones who know I am gay are Mr. Richards and this one class. If we announce this, the cat's really gonna be out of the bag."

"Is that okay?" River asked. "I mean, I've been talking about my boyfriend slash husband for months now at work so everyone there already knows, but if you aren't ready, it's a much bigger populace for you, Skye. An entire school. I'd understand. I think your students would too."

Skye took a deep breath and let it out, running his fingers through his hair. "I want to do it, River. For us, and for my students. If I back out because I'm afraid or nervous about what other people will think, then I'm teaching all of the other queer students to do the same thing. And that's not the message that I want to send them. I want them to love who they are, and be proud of who they are. And if this—if *we*—can help them do that, I think we should."

River smiled and closed the space between them with a kiss. "You're amazing, Skyler Mckenzie," he said. "I love you."

River beamed when they walked into the school gymnasium the following weekend and saw it decorated with balloons and streamers, tables laid out with punch bowls and desserts, and Taylor Swift's *Love Story* playing in the background.

"Wow, they really went all out," he said, looking around, his hand clasped with Skye's.

They had arrived a few minutes before the rest of the crowd was scheduled to show up and were the only ones there at the moment. And Skye took the opportunity to steal a kiss from his husband.

River blushed and pulled away, smiling when they heard an audible "Aww," from the doorway.

"Are you guys going to be that adorable all night?" Chloe asked, strolling into the room on Jaden's arm.

"Hello to you too, Chloe," Skye said with a wide grin. "I'm really glad you guys made it. Especially on such short notice."

"Of course," Jaden said. "This is a really sweet thing your students are doing for you. And since we didn't get to be at the wedding, which I am not bitter about at all by the way." He slapped his brother on the shoulder.

"Ow," Skye said, rubbing the spot.

River grimaced. "Sorry about that. That was my fault. We had to do things fast with everything we had going on and..."

"River, I'm teasing," Jaden said, giving him a smile. "I

understand. Skye's kept us up to date on all of your health issues and it sounds pretty rough, what you've been going through. We're just happy you are doing better. Honestly." He pulled River into a tight hug. "Welcome to the family."

"Thank you," River said, once he could breathe again.

Skye laughed, and Chloe joined him.

"Hey, can I get in on this?" Skye turned to see Grace coming across the floor, and they embraced her in a group hug before she gave Skye a hug and then River, tears in her eyes as she did.

"You have made my son the happiest man in the world," she told River, hands resting on his shoulders once she'd pulled away. "He is so blessed to have you, River. And he needs you just as much as you need him. Remember that, okay?"

River looked a bit overwhelmed, and just nodded as Skye pressed a kiss to his temple, drinking in that watermelon and coconut scent. "She's right, you know," he murmured in his husband's ear, then kissed him again.

More guests started to fill the room in the minutes that followed, including Nick and Jenna. Skye introduced his co-workers to his family and friends, as did River, and Skye introduced each of his students to River as well. Some of River's church acquaintances were also there.

"I've heard a lot about you," River said to Gwen as he shook her hand. "It was really sweet of you guys to do this for us."

Gwen blushed. "Not much trouble, really," she deflected. "The decorations were already here from the seventh grade dance. Just asked them to leave them up and told them we'd do the clean up. We did take care of the refreshments, though, and the awesome music."

River smiled. "Well, we appreciate it," he said.

"So, you guys gonna dance, or what?" Gwen asked.

"Are we supposed to?" Skye asked.

"It's a party, isn't it?"

Skye looked around. "No one else is dancing."

"Then you can start them off. You're the guests of honor after all."

Skye smirked at her. "Fair enough." He held his hand out to River, who blushed and handed Gwen his drink before following Skye out to the center of the room.

Skye slid his arms around River's waist, and River wrapped his arms around Skye's shoulders and they danced to the music, slowly, smiling and gazing into each other's eyes.

For a while it was just them. River pressed his cheek to Skye's as they swayed softly, and when the song ended he moved his face and pressed his lips to Skye's, causing clapping and loud cheers to erupt around them. Skye blushed and smiled and so did River. Then more couples were coming to join them on the dance floor.

Skye watched as Jenna and Nick held each other and moved to the music, smiling and sharing subtle kisses.

"Think they'll be tying the knot, soon?" River said, gazing in the direction of the smitten couple as well.

"Definitely," Skye said, and smiled when Nick glanced their way and winked at him.

When Skye looked back at his husband, River had a tear sliding down his cheek. "Hey, angel, what's wrong?" he asked.

River wiped it away and gave a sad smile. "Just thinking about my Aunt Jodi and wishing she could be here to celebrate with us. God, I miss her so much."

Skye pressed a kiss to River's forehead. "Me, too," he said.

Skye stole a dance with Jenna after that, and then River danced with her while Skye made his way over to the dessert table for some punch.

"Mr. Mckenzie?" Skye turned when he heard his name. Claire's mother stopped in front of him. She looked contemplative, like she wanted to say something but wasn't sure if she should, or how to proceed.

"Yes?" Skye said gently.

"I'm Rebecca Wilson, Claire's mom," she started, as if he were meeting her for the first time. They weren't well acquainted but he recognized her and had spoken with her on occasion.

"Yes, of course," he said. And when she didn't say anything, Skye continued. "She's doing very well in class."

Rebecca smiled softly. "Her grades have actually been improving," she said. "Actually, I wanted to thank you for that."

"Me? I'm afraid I don't understand."

"I've been worried about her," she admitted. "She's been very closed off lately. I could tell something was wrong but she wouldn't talk to me. It was affecting her school work, and her social life, and..." tears were starting to fill her eyes now and she fought them. "I'm sorry," she said, wiping at her eyes. "I don't mean to ruin your evening."

"No, no, it's okay," Skye said. "Is everything okay with Claire?"

Rebecca smiled again and looked at him. "It is now," she said. "She told me about a month ago that she's gay, and it was like this veil came off of her face and she could breathe again. Like she had been holding this piece of herself in for so long, so afraid to tell me. And she's been so much happier since then, so much more alive, so much more herself. She still struggles with what her peers will think, and society, you know, but I'm so glad she said something to me, and I don't think she would have had the courage to do that, if it hadn't been for you. She's told me about your class, and the things you guys talk about in there and just the impact it's had on her, that you've had on her. I just want you to know that you are making a difference in those kids' lives. In Claire's life. So thank you."

Skye had to hold back his own tears now. "Claire's a very

special girl," he said. "And she's very lucky to have you for a mother."

Rebecca smiled at that. "Well, you and your husband are adorable together. Congratulations."

"Thank you," Skye said. He watched as she walked away, before wiping away the tear that slid down his cheek.

"Hey," he heard River say, and turned to see his husband standing next to him. "You okay?"

Skye smiled. "Yeah, I'm fine, angel," he said. He took River's hand, interlocking their fingers together.

"Your students have some sort of game planned."

"Oh?"

"I didn't get all of the details but I think it involves us doing a lot of kissing when other people sing songs or recite poems with the word *love* in it."

Skye grinned. "I'll go for that."

It may have been Jaden and Chloe that spearheaded the majority of the songs and poems, which was unfortunate, mainly because Jaden could *not* sing.

But that was okay, because Skye and River *could* kiss. And kiss they did.

~

Skye was lying in bed with a book that night when River climbed in and scooted close to him, a grin on his face and his blue eyes sparkling with mischief. Skye forgot all about his book when River's lips brushed against his jaw, and then down his neck. He chuckled.

"You want something, angel?" he asked. River hummed and Skye jerked when his husband slid his hand into his pants and cupped his hardening cock. He couldn't help the moan that escaped him.

"I don't think I can go all the way tonight, but I would

really like to try something we haven't yet," River murmured in his ear.

Skye nodded. "Anything. I'll do anything." He gripped River's face and brought his lips to his, kissing him tenderly.

Then River was sliding down his body and pulling his pants and underwear off, tossing them to the floor. Skye's cock grew hard in an instant as River nuzzled it, breathing him in, before peppering it with soft kisses. He gasped, and his cock jerked, his breath picking up and a loud moan escaping him when River licked a stripe from his sack to the tip of his cock. "Shit, Riv." His head fell back on the pillow. "That feels good."

River reached over and grabbed the bottle of lube from the nightstand before squirting some on his fingers. Skye was expecting River to stroke his cock, but River surprised him by saying, "Spread your legs for me, baby."

Skye's heart beat wildly and he felt tears stinging his eyes.

"You okay?" River asked, when Skye didn't move.

"You've never called me that before," Skye said. River smiled and leaned forward, kissing him again.

"Baby," he whispered against his lips. "I want my fingers inside you, driving you crazy. I want to feel your ass clenching against me when you come."

"Shit." Skye shivered, and spread his legs wide, giving River a perfect view of his hole. He hadn't bottomed in years, but like he said, he would do anything for River, to be close to River. His cock was aching now, with the need to feel River inside him. "Fuck me with your fingers, angel."

River grinned and slid his lube coated fingers over Skye's pucker, using his other hand to keep Skye's legs apart. Skye jerked and his breath hitched. "Fuck," he gasped. River circled his hole, making him whimper and moan.

"Love the sounds you make," River said, and Skye gasped again when River's finger slid inside him. "Mmm, especially that one."

"Fuck, Riv," Skye cried as he felt his husband's finger moving inside him, driving him crazy, before a second finger entered him, causing his muscles to tighten and his back to arch off the bed. He bit his lip to keep from moaning too loudly but that all went to hell when River pegged his prostate. "Shit, Riv!"

"I want to hear you, baby," River encouraged. "Don't hide from me. You're so fucking sexy."

Why did hearing River curse during sex make Skye even harder? His cock jerked against his stomach, precum leaking out in droves as River pegged his prostate again and again, making him squirm and whimper underneath him.

"Fuck, Riv...I can't," he gasped. "I need to come."

He let out a shout when River leaned over and took his cock in his mouth, sucking on the engorged tip, slipping his tongue into the slit. "Fuck!" He came then, without warning, his ass clamping around River's fingers buried inside him and his cock pulsing his release inside River's mouth, spilling out and sliding down his husband's chin and onto his stomach.

"Shit, I'm sorry," he said, gasping as River gagged slightly and popped off of him.

River just grinned and wiped the cum from his lips and chin before licking it off of his fingers.

"Fuck, that's hot," Skye whispered, his voice hoarse. "Come here."

River climbed up his body and kissed him. And Skye was crying and laughing and kissing River over and over and over again.

CHAPTER 27

River

River was at work a few days later when someone tapped him on the shoulder. He turned around, expecting to see a coworker, and was speechless when he saw Anna standing in front of him.

"Hi Riv," she said, smiling softly. "I hope it's okay that I'm here. I know you are working so I'll make it quick. But, um, I just wanted to say that I'm sorry I couldn't make it to your reception the other night, and I wanted to give you this." She handed him a small white box with a ribbon tied around it.

"Thank you," River said, taking it from her. He reached forward and pulled her into a hug. "Thank you, Anna. For everything. You helped me see myself for who I really was, helped me realize what I really wanted. And you did it with grace and love. And that means everything to me. Thank you."

Anna smiled. "You're welcome, River. I'm glad you are happy."

"And you?" River asked, pulling away. "Are you happy?"

Anna's smile widened. "I am," she said. "We've been missing you at church. And we'd love to see you both there if Skye's up for it."

River sighed. "Thanks," he said. "I'm still struggling to sit down for very long, so that's why I haven't been back. It's too painful. That on top of the migraines... I've been watching the sermons at home. I'd love to come back, if things get better. I'm not so sure about Skye, though. It's not really his thing, and I'm not gonna push him."

"I understand," Anna said, sincerely. "And I hope things do get better. You know our doors are open to everyone." She eyed him as if asking if maybe his relationship with Skye was the reason he'd been staying away this whole time and not his health problems.

"I know," River said. "I do. It's not that, Anna. I feel safe there. I promise. One of the reasons I chose that church was because of their acceptance of the LGBTQ community."

She paused for a moment and then bit her lip. "Pastor Phillips asked about you. I told him you were having some health struggles. I hope that's okay."

River gave her a soft smile. "Yes, that's fine. He actually called me to check and see how I was doing and I filled him in. He said you were praying for me, which I appreciate. And I told him about Skye and the wedding. He was very happy for us and said he'd love to have us both there if I'm doing better in the future."

Anna gave him a slight smile and rested her hand on his arm. "Okay," she said. "Take care, River." She stood on her tiptoes to kiss his cheek and then walked away.

River waited until he was on his lunch break to open the gift from Anna. Inside was a gift card to the movie theater with the reclining seats, which was the only one he and Skye could go to on their dates, along with a Doordash gift card, which meant they could have dinner and a movie in comfort without River worrying about his tailbone.

Perfect date night combo, I thought. Congratulations, River and Skye. Love, Anna.

River was hopeful that he and Skye could take the next step in their intimacy fairly soon. He longed to have Skye inside of him, making love to him. And maybe this date night would be the perfect precursor.

〜

"Hey, Skye?" River said as they lay in bed a few nights later, after enjoying their gift from Anna.

"Hmm?" Skye asked. His eyes went wide when River sat up and straddled him.

"Holy shit," he said, gripping River's hips. He didn't even try to keep the surprise out of his voice.

River smiled. "I had fun with you tonight." He rested his hands on Skye's chest, and looked into his eyes.

"Yeah," Skye said, in barely a whisper. He swallowed. "Me too, Riv."

River reached up and brushed his fingers through the blond waves falling over Skye's forehead. Tears sprang to his eyes. "Remember when we were in college and you told me that I still got to choose who I give myself to?"

Skye nodded. "Yeah." He reached up to wipe away River's tears, and River saw that Skye's eyes were starting to water now too.

"I choose you, Skye," he said. He lowered himself onto his husband, their bodies flush, and kissed his neck, and then his jaw, tears still falling, mingling with Skye's. "I choose you," he said again. "Make love to me."

"Are you sure?" Skye asked. And River nodded.

"What about your tailbone? Will it hurt?"

"I don't know. But I would like to try."

But when River was under Skye a few moments later, his husband pushing inside him for the first time, his heart rate started to spike, and it wasn't for the reason he would have liked. And neither was the sweat that was beading his forehead. He couldn't breathe, and he started to shake as Skye pressed further inside him.

"Skye, stop," he said, barely choking the words out, shame washing over him, tears spilling down his cheeks. He hated this. Everything had gone so well for them so far, and he didn't want to be afraid of his husband. But he was having a full blown anxiety attack right now, in the middle of sex, and he knew it.

"River? What's wrong?" Skye asked. "Shit, did I hurt you?"

River shook his head. "Please get off," he said, hating himself even more, the tears falling even harder now. He wanted to curl up in a ball and pretend none of this was happening. That he wasn't asking his husband to pull out of him when he'd finally decided he wanted to try and bottom for the first time. He'd felt so ready. He'd wanted this, needed it, even. Skye inside him. Wanted to feel this closeness and connection to his husband, but as soon as Skye's cock pushed inside him it was like he wasn't in control anymore, his memories were. And instead of being in bed with the man he loved, sharing the sweet, beautiful connection that he'd craved, he was back in that dark alleyway, pressed up against a rough, brick wall, gagged, hands clasping his wrists and pinning him in place even as he struggled, and cried out, sobbing as he heard those familiar voices, the taunts, the laughter, felt his pants being unbuttoned and tugged down, the humid air against his bare skin, knowing he couldn't stop what they were about to do to him.

Cold fingers pressing against his hole, making him sob and shake his head. A rough hand gripping his cock, making him squirm. Bile rising up his throat.

We're going to make you feel good, righteous boy. You'll thank us later.

"Okay." River felt his husband sliding out of him, and then the warmth of Skye's body lying next to his. "You're okay," he said, rubbing his hand up and down River's arm. "You're safe."

We're doing you a favor.

River was trying to breathe, his body still shaking, tears still falling as Skye scooted closer and held him close.

Fuck, you feel that, righteous boy? You feel yourself getting fucked? Feels good, doesn't it? I'm gonna make you come. Right after I come inside you.

"Was it a flashback?" Skye asked.

My turn. Hold him down.

Fuck, he's hard.

Knew you would like it, virgin boy.

Not a virgin anymore.

Laughter.

River nodded. "I'm sorry, Skye. I'm so sorry."

"Oh, River," Skye cooed, "don't apologize." He kissed the top of River's head as he held him close, and River clung to him.

"I can still feel them, Skye," River sobbed. "They were laughing. I can still hear them whispering in my ear. I can still feel them pressed up against me, holding me down, their weight on me. I can feel them inside me, their breath on my skin, the way they smelled." River shook as he continued to sob.

"I begged them to stop. I cried and screamed through the gag but they wouldn't listen. And I hated myself when I came, because it felt like proof that I'd enjoyed it, or that I'd wanted it, even though I knew I didn't. And they left me there, gagged and half naked, covered in cum, and I couldn't stop shaking and vomiting and crying. And I wanted to rip my own skin off, so that I didn't have to live in what they had touched, or look at it. I couldn't stand to be in my own body. I felt so gross, so violated and ashamed, and I hated myself. I still do sometimes."

River felt another kiss against his hair. "You are beautiful, River," his husband said. "Inside and out. You shine so bright, baby. And you are not tainted. Not by what they did to you.

Not by anything. You are so strong and amazing. And I love you. I'm so sorry that that is a part of your story. I wish to God it wasn't."

River soaked up Skye's words and let them wash over him, let them wrap around his heart and absorb some of the grief and pain that had been eating away at him for so long. He'd never told Skye his whole story before. But getting it out, sharing it with the person he loved more than anything, the person he longed for, trusted and felt safe with, was allowing those broken pieces of him to heal, bit by bit.

"I don't want to be reminded of what happened when I'm with you," he said. "I want you in me, Skye."

"We'll figure it out. And if we can't do it on our own, and you really want me in you, then there's always counseling like we talked about, right? It's probably not a bad idea for me to talk to your therapist anyway. It might help both of us. I'm on your side, angel."

River nodded, sniffling, and wiped away tears. "Yeah," he said. "You're right. I kinda hate the idea of talking about our sex life with someone, though."

Skye chuckled. "Trust me, angel, they've heard it all."

"I know. And if it helps me get closer to you, I'll do anything."

TWO MONTHS LATER

Skye

"Look at me," Skye said, gripping River's face in his hands and gazing into his sapphire eyes. "You're doing great. Breathe." He took a deep breath in and held it, and River followed, before they both released. "Again," Skye said, and they breathed in, held it for a count of five, and let it out. Skye stayed inside him, his cock not fully sheathed, but farther than it had ever been before. He grabbed his cologne off the night-stand and held it under River's nose. "Breathe," he said again, and River inhaled the scent of him, his body relaxing a bit more. "I've got you, angel. You're here, right now, with me, and you're safe. Breathe." Another breath in and out.

After several more attempts at bottoming and having minimal success without his anxiety spiking, River had decided to see his therapist again and explain the situation to her. Skye had joined him for the session in order to support his husband, but also because he knew it would benefit him as well. This was about both of them, not just River, and he wanted to know what he could do to help.

She had been kind and attentive, and had assured them both that what they wanted was achievable, but might take some time. She had applauded River for his openness and honesty with Skye, saying how important it was in the healing process to communicate his wants, needs, and fears with his partner, that it would help build the love and trust between them and strengthen their emotional bond, which would in turn help with their physical bond.

Then she had reminded River of the tools he could use when his anxiety attacks surfaced, encouraging him to use them when he wasn't having an attack so that they would be more readily available to him in the moments where he felt anxious or out of control. Skye knew River knew all of this after having been in therapy for a while, but it seemed like it was helping him to have a refresher, to remind him that he had tools to use when he needed them, and to have Skye by his side this time as well, absorbing everything he could.

She'd touched on coping mechanisms, such as breathing exercises, grounding techniques, like focusing on the senses, what he could see, touch, smell, taste, and hear in the moment, but had also given him some techniques specific to Skye, such as smelling Skye's cologne or body wash, or even his deodorant, to help bring River back to the present, and to the fact that he was safe, and with the man he loved. She explained that smelling something familiar was actually the quickest way to access happy memories as the part of the brain connected to the sense of smell was also the one closest to the part of the brain responsible for memory. She had also recommended having something nearby of Skye's to touch, that would help him when he was triggered, be it Skye himself, or something that reminded River of him, and their bond.

Other methods such as wiggling his toes or clenching and unclenching his fists could prove helpful as well. Or having a candy like a jolly rancher or a sour patch kid to suck on to help stimulate his salivary glands again, which halted when a person was afraid. This process could reactivate those glands, and remind River that he was in fact, safe.

Skye had purchased the sour patch kids, as River was most fond of them, and kept the bag on the nightstand in their bedroom, so they would have it when and if River needed it. He'd also placed his cologne there to give them quick access.

River had been using his coping techniques more and more over the past several weeks when he wasn't having an attack, and Skye could tell he was determined to make this work. To have Skye inside of him, making love to him.

Practicing with the tools in his toolbox had fallen by the wayside for the past several months because of his health issues, but he was doing better now and seemed to have the time and energy to put towards this goal.

Skye had seen River gripping his wedding ring and twisting it around his finger like he used to do with his "Rise" ring, and realized it was because he was practicing grounding himself. The ring, its coolness, weight, and probably the fact that it was a reminder of his union to Skye, seemed to ground him most of all.

They had tried penetrative sex two or three nights a week now for the past several weeks and River had made slow, steady progress. He'd lasted longer and longer each time Skye had entered him, by using the techniques their therapist had suggested, Skye coaching him when necessary. It wore River out, each and every time, but Skye knew they were getting there, and he was so damn proud of River.

"Should I keep going or come out?" Skye asked.

River took another deep breath, opening and closing his fists, then reached around and gripped his ring over Skye's back. He looked into Skye's eyes a second later. "Keep going," he said, determination in his voice.

Skye didn't argue. He pushed forward, his gaze locked with River's as his husband continued to take deep breaths in and out. Skye had tears stinging at the corners of his eyes when he finally bottomed out.

"You okay?" he asked, and River nodded. He still looked like he was having a hard time, but he was focused, present, and breathing in and out calmly.

"I'm safe," River whispered. He breathed in and out again. "I'm safe."

Skye rested his forehead against River's and sighed. "You're safe." He could feel River still playing with his ring over his back, could feel his chest rising and falling underneath him steadily. "I love you so much, baby. And I'm so freaking proud of you."

River smiled softly as tears filled his eyes. "I love you, too," he said. He reached up to brush the hair back from Skye's eyes.

Skye smiled. He pressed a kiss to River's forehead, which was slick with sweat. "I'm gonna come out now. You look exhausted." His husband had done so well, but he was clearly worn out from everything, and Skye didn't want to push him, emotionally or physically. So he pulled out slowly and they held each other as they drifted to sleep.

River

It was three days later when they tried again. River clung to Skye as his husband moved inside him, feeling the warmth of Skye's skin against his, inhaling his scent, his fingers gripping Skye's hair as he soaked up the pleasure, the connection, the oneness of their bodies coming together, tears sliding down his cheeks, because with every thrust, every kiss, every orgasm, from Skye, he felt loved, safe, and cherished. Skye was his home, his heart, his breath, and he never thought they would be here, that what had once been used as an act of cruelty, to break him, destroy him, was now being used to make him whole again. He'd never thought that having sex with the right person could help him heal, that being with Skye could mend the shattered pieces of his soul and turn them into something beautiful. He was healing a little more, every single day, because of Skye.

They came together, moaning each other's names. Skye inside of River, with River's legs wrapped around him, and River in Skye's hand.

River held Skye, his husband collapsed on top of him, both of them sated, and crying tears of joy, their bodies soaked in sweat, and as he stroked his fingers through Skye's hair with one hand and along his bare side with the other, he smiled warmly and sent up a silent prayer, thanking God for Skye, and for marriage, and for the beautiful gift of sex, and that he finally knew what it was like to be one, in every sense of the word, with the person he loved most in all the world.

CHAPTER 28

Skye

3 MONTHS LATER

"Hey, can I join you?" River asked, sitting next to Skye on the sofa, both of them with reading materials in their hands. This had become a regular routine for them, spending time during the weekends or evenings reading together, sometimes to themselves and sometimes to each other.

Skye smiled and lifted his arms so that River could lay down and rest his head on his lap.

"What's that one about?" Skye asked as he stroked his fingers through River's hair, gazing down at him. He had another *National Geographic* magazine in his hands. He was such a dork.

"*Secrets of Whales*?" Skye said with a grin, when River turned the cover so Skye could read it. "You're adorable, you know that?" He leaned down and pressed his lips to his husband's.

River smiled through the kiss and gripped the back of Skye's neck, kissing him back.

They read for a while, Skye stroking his fingers through River's hair, before River set his magazine aside and stood.

But he was sitting back down in an instant, his hand over his heart.

"River?" Skye said, when he noticed the glazed look in his husband's eyes, and his face growing pale.

"Shit," River said, closing his eyes. He rested back against the sofa, seeming to gather himself.

"Riv?" Skye said again, his heart racing now. "What's wrong?" He rested his hand on River's arm. His husband looked exhausted from having been on his feet for less than three seconds.

"It was my heart, Skye," River said finally, eyes still closed, his hand resting on his chest.

"What?" Skye said in surprise. "I thought that was better. I thought the medicine was working. You haven't had an episode in months."

River opened his eyes now and bit his lip, glancing at his husband.

Skye narrowed his eyes. "River," he said, his tone dripping with accusation. "You haven't had an episode in months, right?"

River glanced away. "They, uh...they started up again, a few weeks ago," he admitted.

"What?" Skye almost shouted. He couldn't remember a time when he'd ever been more upset with River. "Are you kidding me?! This has been going on for weeks, and you didn't think to tell me? What the hell, Riv?" There was more anger behind his words than he'd intended but he couldn't help it. "Were you ever planning on telling me or were you going to just pass out on me one day, or let me get a phone call telling me you were in the hospital again and that's how I was going to find out?" His jaw was clenched when he stopped speaking and River's eyes were wide.

"I'm sorry, Skye," he said. "I didn't want to worry you..."

That just made Skye angrier. "Didn't..." he clenched his jaw to keep from losing it on River again, standing up and running his fingers through his hair. He took a deep breath and let it out. "Damn it, River," he said, finally, looking back at his husband, his voice calmer but still stern. "What do you think I'm doing now? You can't keep this kind of stuff from me. I need to know if you've got something going on, *especially* when it has to do with your heart."

"I guess...I guess I was hoping it would go away again on its own, and...I wouldn't have to say anything. And I think I thought that maybe telling you, somehow would make it more real. And maybe ignoring it would make it easier to handle. And I'm frustrated that it's happening again, Skye. Things have been going so well. Our sex life has been amazing, and my health has been good, aside from my tailbone and hip pain, but I'm living with it. I just didn't want to accept that we had one more thing to deal with. I didn't want you to be burdened with one more problem."

Skye sighed. "I get that, River. I do. But this is a big deal. And I'm your husband. I want to know when you aren't well. That's what marriage is. We take care of each other, and carry each other's burdens."

River's eyes blazed. "God, Skye, it's not that easy!" He almost shouted, but there were tears stinging at the corners of his eyes too. "Especially when I'm the one in the relationship with all the problems. I'm the one with the mental health issues and the physical health issues, and what do I carry for you, or even with you? Nothing, because your life wasn't a hell hole before we met." Tears slid down his cheeks now. "It's not like I *have* a burden, for fuck's sake. I *am* the goddamn burden! And I'm tired of it! I just want to be normal. Healthy. I want to be okay, and not have you worrying about me, or taking care of me all the time. I just..." He growled and grabbed a pillow off the couch before throwing it across the room, hard and then stood up from the couch and walked into the bedroom, slamming the door shut behind him, making Skye flinch.

Skye ran his fingers through his hair and sat back down on the couch, letting out a heavy sigh. Three months. They'd had three months of relative normalcy. River had had some headaches but no full blown migraines, thanks to the medication he was on. His tailbone still bothered him and he still carried his seat cushion everywhere he went. They couldn't travel far but they'd managed a week long trip out to a state park nearby. They'd rented an RV so that they'd be more comfortable, and enjoyed fishing, swimming, sitting out by the campfire, stargazing, and just relaxing and getting away from it all. And it had been wonderful.

The best part was that despite the issues with River's tailbone he was still able to enjoy anal sex. He was sore afterwards but he said it was worth it, and he did stretches and iced if necessary, or had Skye massage his glutes which seemed to help.

River's flashbacks had been less and less frequent, his nightmares had been almost nonexistent, and he was right. Their sex life had been pretty great. Things had been good over the last few months. And now to have this staring them in the face again. No wonder River hadn't wanted to tell him. They'd had so little reprieve and he wasn't ready to say goodbye to it. He couldn't face that things were going downhill again so soon.

"Skye," he heard, and looked up to see River standing in the doorway to their bedroom. He had tears drying on his cheeks and his hands stuffed in his pockets, and he wouldn't meet Skye's gaze.

"Hey, Riv," Skye said, softly.

"I'm sorry," River said, still crying. "I didn't mean to get so angry. But I guess I just am, Skye. I am angry. I just...I shouldn't have taken it out on you. I just don't know what to do."

"Hey, come here," Skye said, and stood, and River went to him and they hugged, and River cried into his shirt. "It's okay," Skye said. "It's okay for you to be angry, angel. And sad. It's okay for you to feel whatever you feel. This sucks. I get it."

River sniffled. "I'm sorry I didn't tell you," he said.

"I think I get it now, why you didn't," Skye said, rubbing his back. "But please, promise you won't keep secrets from me anymore."

River sighed. "I promise," he said, as Skye pulled back and wiped the tears from his eyes.

"Will you let me drive you to work?" Skye asked. "I really don't like the idea of you being behind the wheel, River. It scares me."

"Skye, I don't..." he started. But then his eyes met Skye's, and he nodded. "Okay," he said, reaching over to stroke his cheek, and Skye relaxed.

"Okay," Skye said. "And if it gets worse you are going back to the cardiologist."

River nodded and Skye kissed him.

~

3 MONTHS LATER

Skye

River had gone back to the cardiologist after the palpitations hadn't gone away, and had actually grown more frequent. He'd had them happen a couple of times at work, and had had to find a place to lie down in the middle of a session with a client before he passed out, and Skye knew he was becoming increasingly frustrated and worried about losing his job if it kept up. So far he'd been able to hide it from his boss, but he didn't know how much longer he'd be able to. If his episodes lasted longer than a minute or happened back to back he would be in trouble.

Unfortunately the cardiologist said there wasn't much they could do other than trying a different medication. They ran all of the same tests they'd done previously over again just to make sure nothing had changed, but when those all came back the same as before, they were back to not having any answers.

River seemed to be developing new symptoms every other week that had Skye worried and confused, and River becoming more upset.

Along with the palpitations he was also having nearly constant chest pain that couldn't be explained, along with dizziness, brain fog, nausea, lightheadedness, even when his heart wasn't acting up, and he was exhausted all the time no matter how much sleep he got. He felt weak, and had developed an intolerance for exercise. Just being on his feet all day for work was exhausting.

His thermoregulation was off. He'd be freezing cold one minute and frying hot the next, even though the temperature in the house hadn't changed a bit. He'd lost his appetite and Skye was more than aware of how much weight he'd lost in the last couple of months. His toned, muscular body had become frail and thin.

His body was falling apart in front of them, and neither of them knew why, or what to do, and neither it seemed, did the doctors.

They'd gotten River in to see the neurologist again, and they'd done more blood work and muscle tests, and nerve tests, but hadn't found anything that could explain his symptoms. They visited a rheumatologist next who did not have any answers for them either and River was beside himself with grief and frustration.

Next was a colonoscopy and an endoscopy just to make sure the reason for River's lack of appetite wasn't anything internal or parasitic, or cancerous, and it wasn't. And for that Skye was grateful of course, but he felt so helpless. Like his hands were tied, and all he could do was watch as his husband suffered and withered away.

Each time he took River into his arms and felt how thin he had become, he had to keep himself from crying. And he had to tell himself that he wouldn't break River if he hugged him too tightly.

"Skye, you won't hurt me," River said, as they stood in the kitchen one day after coming back from an appointment with a nutritionist. They'd decided they needed to do something to get River to gain some of his weight back. He'd lost thirty pounds in two months, and Skye was really starting to worry.

Tears fell down his cheeks as he tightened his grip around River and felt his husband's hair tickling the side of his face.

"I'm scared for you, River," he said.

"I know," River said. "Me, too, Skye."

~

River

River did his best to force himself to eat but he couldn't stomach food, so Skye started making him smoothies for breakfast and dinner. He would have the occasional banana or granola bar, but sometimes he wouldn't even finish them. Other than that he survived mostly on protein shakes, because drinking was easier than eating. Still he ended up losing another five pounds.

He'd started feeling even more lightheaded and foggy, and it got considerably worse when he went from laying down to sitting or from sitting to standing. It got to the point where he would have to sit up or stand very slowly so that he didn't risk toppling over again once he did get back on his feet, and it made him feel like a ninety year old, especially when he had to grab on to the wall or the counter or whatever other sturdy structure was nearby for support to help him walk the first few steps until he got his bearings straight. Being on his feet for any length of time at all was exhausting and only made the lightheadedness and dizziness worse.

But it wasn't until he passed out at work that he knew he was in real trouble. And when it happened three times in one month he knew that he couldn't keep up with the workload anymore, on top of all of his symptoms. So it wasn't a surprise when his boss called him into his office one afternoon and with sympathy in his eyes, told him that he was being let go.

River knew this was coming. It wasn't fair to his clients or his coworkers to keep him on, he knew that. He really wasn't doing well, and he didn't have any business being there. His boss didn't seem upset with him, just concerned. But River still felt sick to his stomach when he finished up for the day and thought about how he would tell Skye that he was no longer employed.

How would they afford their home on just Skye's salary? How would they pay for all of the medical bills they had piling up?

He kept himself together during the drive back to their condo. Skye kept glancing at him and River was fully aware that Skye knew something was wrong and was waiting for him to talk, but he didn't.

He couldn't. Not yet.

When they got inside Skye kissed his temple. "I'm gonna make dinner," he said, then walked into the kitchen. River was grateful that Skye wasn't pushing him.

He nodded and went to the bedroom, shutting the door behind him, and as soon as his head hit the pillow, he began to cry.

Skye

"Hey, Riv," Skye said, poking his head into the room a half an hour later. He moved into the room and sat on the edge of the bed next to his husband. "Dinner's ready. You wanna talk first or eat first?"

River sniffled and wiped his eyes. "I'm not very hungry."

"I made you a smoothie," Skye replied, hoping he could get River to consume something, especially if it was already made. They'd had to buy him all new clothes in the past couple of months because of all the weight he'd lost, and the arms and chest that once felt so firm and strong against him were so thin and frail.

"Can you tell me what's wrong?" Skye asked, resting a hand on River's hip.

"I've lost everything, Skye," he cried. He closed his eyes tightly as the tears slid down his cheeks and his shoulders shook with sobs.

Skye reached up and stroked his fingers through River's hair. "What do you mean?"

"My independence, my freedom, my health, and now my..." River's breath hitched as he tried to choke out the words. "They....they let me go, Skye. I don't have a job anymore."

Skye's heart was hammering in his chest. He couldn't deny the panic that was filling his mind, but he had to do everything he could to keep River from seeing it. Right now his husband needed his support and comfort. He'd find time later to freak out about their financial situation.

"I'm so sorry, Skye," River said, wiping tears from his eyes. "I know this puts us in a horrible situation. I don't know how we're going to manage—"

"Shhh," Skye interrupted, moving his fingers to stroke River's cheek. "Not right now, angel," he said. "We'll worry about that later. This isn't your fault. You have nothing to be sorry for. I can't imagine how hard this is for you. I know how hard you worked to get your degree, and how much you love your job. I'm so sorry, baby."

River looked him in the eyes for the first time since he'd sat down. "Will you hold me?" he asked.

Skye leaned over and kissed him on the cheek and then crawled around and laid behind him and scooped River into his arms.

"You haven't lost me," he whispered, and he felt River pressing even closer to him, and held him even tighter.

~

River

River awoke that night feeling unusually cold, and when he reached behind him, he realized why. Skye wasn't in the bed. He rubbed his eyes and sat up, noticing that the bedroom door was closed and there was a light on on the other side. He picked up his phone and squinted at it.

Two-thirty am.

What was Skye doing up at this hour?

River slid his glasses on before slowly sitting up, then standing. His vision started to blur and he swayed, but gripped the dresser for a moment, before his vision cleared again and he felt well enough to walk.

He pulled his robe on before opening the door and shuffling out to find his husband sitting at the dining room table with the laptop open.

"Skye?" he said groggily. He wrapped his arms around himself and squinted at his husband.

Skye's head jerked up at the sound of River's voice and he had a look on his face like he'd been caught with his hand in the cookie jar as he bit his lip.

"Hey, Riv," he said, closing the lid to the laptop and running his hand over his thigh. "What are you doing up?"

"I was gonna ask you the same question," River said, stepping closer to Skye and running his fingers through his hair. "I woke up 'cause I was cold and you were gone."

Skye sighed and wrapped his arm around River's waist, pulling him gently onto his lap. "I'm sorry, angel," he said. "I guess I just couldn't sleep."

"What are you doing?" River asked, gesturing to the computer.

Skye shrugged. "Just stuff." He pressed a kiss to River's cheek.

"Skye," River eyed him, still stroking his fingers through his husband's hair. "Be honest with me."

Skye sighed again. "I'm looking at our finances," he admitted. "I was hoping I could do it without you noticing. I didn't want to stress you out."

River frowned. "You were going to have to tell me eventually."

"I know, but I was hoping to have a plan of action before I brought anything to your attention."

"How's it look?"

Skye bit his lip again. "Not good," he admitted. "Your salary was a big chunk of everything. You made more than I did, and with all the medical bills and the school loans still needing to be paid off...I don't know."

River's frown deepened. "I'm sorry. I feel like this is all my fault."

Skye shook his head. "River, we've been over this." His voice was gentle but stern. "It's not your fault. I'm not trying to make you feel guilty. I'm just stating the facts, what's going through my head, so we can figure it out, okay?" Skye pressed a kiss to River's shoulder and nuzzled it with his nose.

"I just feel bad, Skye," River replied, not looking at his husband. "It's all my medical bills, and my school debt, and you wouldn't have any of it if you hadn't married me. And now you're stuck with trying to figure out how to pay it off on your own."

"River, stop," Skye said, in a way that made River turn to him, their eyes locking. "You know what, you're right. I wouldn't have any of those things if I hadn't married you, and I wouldn't have to deal with it, but you know what else I wouldn't have if I hadn't married you? *You*, River. And I wanted *you*. And everything that came with you. The day we got married those bills and debt became ours, remember? *Ours*, not yours. And we're going to figure this out. Feeling bad isn't going to help the situation. And I don't regret marrying you. You damn well better know that."

River bit his lip. "Yeah," he said. "If it helps, I think I can apply for disability. And my boss did say that if I start feeling better they'd be happy to take me back, but I don't think we can count on that."

Skye nodded.

River stroked his husband's hair again and kissed the side of his head. "Can we deal with the rest of this in the morning? I'd like to go back to bed, with you. It's cold and lonely in there by myself."

Skye grinned. "Okay."

"I love you, Skye," River said as they snuggled up together under the covers.

Skye pressed a light kiss to River's jaw and then nuzzled his neck with his nose. "I love you, too, angel," he said.

CHAPTER 29

River

Three weeks later, Jenna and Nick, along with Anna and a few members of River's old Bible study, were helping River and Skye move into their new apartment. As much as they hated leaving their condo, they'd realized they just couldn't afford it anymore on a single income, and River was taking it the hardest, trying not to beat himself up, trying not to see it as being his fault that they had to leave the home they'd loved, that they'd fallen in love in, and shared for the last six years, that they'd built so many memories in.

Their new place was nice enough. Smaller, with only one bedroom and one bathroom, and a smaller kitchen as well, but a decent sized living area and a nice neighborhood. And their neighbors seemed friendly too, so as hard as it was, they were trying to keep their heads up and focus on the good, and what they had to be thankful for. Even with all the bad, they still had amazing friends who were helping them move, putting their furniture together and hauling away the things they couldn't bring with them, neighbors who were welcoming them to the building and bringing them brownies, and even a housewarming present from Jaden and Chloe.

Skye opened the large box once everyone else had gone and

it was just them, Nick and Jenna left. He grinned when he pulled out two large, very soft blankets. One in rainbow and the other in blue, pink, and purple.

"What's that?" River asked from his spot on the sofa. He'd been resting on the couch for the majority of the moving, and although he'd longed to help and feel useful, his heart had acted up several times and his lightheadedness and nausea had kept him from doing much of anything, so he'd had to leave it up to the others to handle.

"Our colors, angel," Skye said, and handed River his.

Jenna sat next to him and petted the large blanket as Nick stood nearby chugging some water. "Oooh, it's so soft," she cood.

She was right. It was so plush and warm. River loved it. He had never had anything representing his sexuality before. Except Skye.

"That was really nice of Jaden and Chloe."

"Yeah, it was," Skye agreed. "Why don't I order some pizza and we can watch something on the laptop while we eat dinner. Unpacking can wait til tomorrow. I'm beat."

Jenna turned her gaze to Nick, and then back to them when he nodded. "Actually, before we do that, Nick and I have an announcement."

River's eyes widened as did Skye's. Jenna and Nick were both beaming now, and River thought he had noticed them being a little bit more touchy feely than normal throughout the day, exchanging kisses as they passed each other, and at one point he recalled them being missing for several minutes.

Jenna thrust her hand forward and River almost squealed at the large diamond band on her ring finger.

"Oh my God, you guys are engaged?" Skye said. They nodded and River hugged Jenna as Skye hugged Nick. River was forever grateful when Jenna moved aside to allow Nick to sit so he could hug him without standing.

"I'm so happy for you," he said. "Do you have a date?"

"Not yet," Nick shrugged. "Sometime in the spring."

"Fuck, you guys," Skye was doing a happy dance when he hugged Jenna and she laughed. "This is the best news ever."

"We want you both to be in the wedding," Jenna said, pulling away and gripping Skye's hands.

"Oh, um, yeah, we'd love to. I don't know if that's a good idea for me, though. I can't really stand up for that long." River bit his lip. He hated to let his friends down, but passing out during their wedding wasn't going to help anyone either.

"We can have you sit," Jenna said, nonplussed. "You have a handicap, River, like a lot of people. It's not going to keep us from wanting you in our wedding."

"You want me sitting up there the whole time?"

"Sure. Why not? What if you had a wheelchair? It wouldn't be any different."

River hadn't thought of that, except that sitting was still painful for him, but there was no way he would miss out on Nick and Jenna's wedding.

"It'll be a short ceremony anyway, 'cause we want to get to the reception," Nick said with a grin. "We know you might not be able to be there for long but we can't get married without you, River." Nick's big hazel eyes were so full of hope it made River's chest ache.

"I'll be there," he said, giving his friends a smile. "You might have to put me in a wheelchair, but I'll be there."

Jenna kissed River on the cheek and Skye ordered their pizza.

River unwrapped his new blanket completely and couldn't keep the smile off of his face as he draped it over himself. It was amazingly comfortable and covered his entire body, and it made him feel whole and safe, and like maybe this little apartment could actually be their home.

"Looks good on you, angel," Skye said, grinning at his husband, and leaning down to kiss him again.

They spent the evening with their friends, surrounded by

boxes, watching *Star Wars* on their laptop, and huddled under their pride blankets, holding hands.

~

Skye

"Hey, you wanna turn on some Christmas music for us?" Skye asked as he fluffed the tree.

River was sitting up length wise on the couch, his pillow propped up behind him for support. He was bundled up in a hoodie, flannel pajama pants, slippers and his pride blanket from Jaden and Chloe and was still shivering. Skye had already turned the heat up once to try and accommodate his husband but River's thermoregulation was so out of whack he knew he'd be turning it back down again in thirty minutes anyway when his husband got too hot.

River picked up his phone and swiped, and soon there was classical Christmas music filling the space. Skye swayed his hips a little to the tune as he continued to decorate the tree.

"You want something warm to drink?" he asked. "Coffee, tea, hot chocolate?"

"Sure," River said as he shivered some more. "Tea sounds good."

"Peppermint okay?"

River nodded. "I can get it, Skye."

Skye eyed him. "I'll get it," he said, and pressed his lips to River's temple. A few minutes later Skye handed River a warm mug of peppermint tea, and watched as he breathed it in and sighed contentedly.

"What's with the blue lights this year?" River asked as Skye strung the lights.

Skye looked over at him and smiled. "It's my favorite color," he said, and gave his husband a wink.

River blushed and grinned. "Shut up."

River watched as Skye decorated the tree with the ornaments next and raised his eyebrow when he saw Skye pull one out that didn't match the others.

"What's that?" he asked. It was flat and oval shaped, and River could only see the back of it.

"This, I was kind of hoping you could hang with me," Skye said, and he knelt next to River and showed it to him. On the front of the ornament were two chibi figures that looked like them, dressed in tuxedos and holding hands. "River" was wearing a green and red scarf and "Skye" had reindeer antlers on his head. Underneath them it said "Our first Christmas together."

River smiled and laughed a little. "That's pretty adorable," he said.

"I thought so," Skye said, grinning. "You feel well enough to stand long enough to help me find a prime spot for it?"

"I think so." River set his drink aside and climbed out from under his blanket. He stood slowly, and when he did he had to brace himself on Skye for a moment.

"You okay?" Skye asked.

River nodded.

They made their way over to the tree and hung the ornament up together, front and center, and then Skye took River's face in his hands and kissed him tenderly. He wished it could have been longer but he knew that the longer River was on his feet the worse he felt, so he let his husband go and helped him back to the couch.

Skye's phone started buzzing before he made it back to the tree and when he took it out of his pocket he saw that it was Grace.

"Hey, Mom," he answered.

"Hi, sweetheart," Grace said. "How are you guys?"

"We're okay," Skye said. "Hanging in there." He honestly didn't know how to answer that question anymore. 'Okay' seemed like the best response. They certainly weren't good. They were far from good, but they were doing their best. Most days, though, it felt like they were barely keeping their heads above water. Skye tried, really tried to find the good in their situation, and he knew River did too, but it was hard sometimes. Really hard. Sometimes it felt like they were drowning and then being handed a baby. He missed the life they used to have before River was so sick. He missed the life he thought they would have together, and trying to stay hopeful and be optimistic took every ounce of strength and energy he had. It was hard to find moments where they could smile and laugh in the midst of all the hurt and confusion and anger over not understanding what was going on with his husband and why he felt the way he did or how to help him. Overwhelmed didn't even begin to describe it.

"Well, I was calling about Christmas," Grace said. "I know River hasn't been feeling well, and he's not really up for traveling, so I was wondering what you thought about Jaden and Chloe and I coming to you guys this year?"

Skye's breath caught in his throat and he had tears filling his eyes. "Really?" he asked.

"Unless you'd rather have Christmas to yourselves this year," Grace said.

"No, no, we want to see you guys, we just didn't think it would work," Skye said. "I mean, we don't have space for guests to stay overnight since we moved, Mom."

"I know. I called Jenna and she said we were welcome to use her and Nick's place since they would be out of town."

"Oh, wow, that's great," Skye said, and he was crying now. "I don't know why I didn't think of that."

"You've got a lot on your mind, Skye," Grace said. "You and River have had a rough year. How's the new place?"

"It's not bad," Skye said. "It's an adjustment, but it could be worse. I'm just... I'm really glad you guys are coming, Mom. River and I were both getting pretty depressed about the idea of spending Christmas alone, actually. And I know he felt pretty guilty about me missing Christmas with my family."

"Well, he does know that he's your family, right?" Grace said.

Skye smiled and laughed a little. "Yeah, I told him that too."

"Well, we'll be there whenever you want us. And please let River know that we don't expect him to be up serving us or anything. He doesn't even have to get out of his pajamas. We just want to be with you guys, whatever that looks like this year. Even if we're just inside watching movies and eating cookies all day. We don't need any special plans. We just want to be together. Okay?"

Skye smiled. "That sounds pretty great to me."

"Good," Grace said. "I'll try not to burn the pie this year."

"I'll eat it anyway."

"I know."

"Thanks, Mom. I love you."

"I love you, too."

"Your family is coming for Christmas?" River asked as soon as Skye got off the phone.

"Yeah," Skye said, and he was smiling and wiping tears from his eyes.

River smiled. "I'm glad."

Skye had never realized just how thoughtful and caring and compassionate people could be until you needed them to be, and his family and friends were really coming through for him right now at a time when he needed them the most, and he had never been more grateful.

He glanced up at the clock. "Shit," he said. "I gotta get to work, babe." He hurried into the bedroom to change and came back out in the khakis and polo shirt he wore for his new part time job. He'd had to take on some extra work since River had lost his job, and he'd been working at an auto parts shop on Saturdays for the past few weeks. He didn't mind it, except that between it and grading papers and making lesson plans he felt like he rarely got time with River any more, and he missed his husband. Still, at least it was a job he enjoyed, so he had that to be thankful for.

"See you tonight," he said, and gave River a kiss before heading out the door.

~

"Hey, I thought you would be asleep," Skye said when he got home late that night and saw River sitting up in bed with his laptop open in front of him, his thumb nail in his mouth and a look of concentration on his handsome face.

"I've been thinking," River said, looking up from his screen. "I want to do something, if I can, to help out financially. I hate that you are working as much as you are and I am so bored most of the time. I was trying to think of things I could do from home, and I think I could get my medical transcription certificate and start earning money again."

Skye continued to strip as his husband talked. He changed into pajama pants and a T-shirt, and then made his way over to his side of the bed and climbed in. He glanced at River's screen and then looked at his husband. "You know you don't have to do that. I don't want you pushing yourself if you aren't well enough."

"I want to," River insisted. "It will take some time to earn the certification and I wouldn't be making nearly as much as I was before, but, it'd be something."

Skye smiled despite his fatigue, and leaned over to press a kiss to his husband's lips. Truth be told he was getting more and more stressed about their financial situation and if River could handle working, even part time, it would really help them. But he wasn't going to say anything to his husband about their finances because he knew it would only make River feel worse, and he dealt with enough guilt as it was. "You know I will support whatever you want to do, angel."

River grinned and Skye kissed him again.

God, he loved that smile.

~

6 MONTHS LATER

Skye

Skye couldn't get over how incredible his husband looked in his tuxedo. He'd never seen River this dressed up, and it suited him. His black framed glasses just added to his sex appeal. It had taken him far longer to get ready than it used to. Showering was difficult now, because he couldn't risk passing out and getting injured, so they had purchased a stool he could sit on. It worked well enough, but just the process of showering was enough to wear him out most of the time, so he would have to rest when he was finished, then style his hair and brush his teeth, then rest again, before getting dressed.

Skye had helped him as much as he could, and now River sat on the bed, reclining against the wedge pillow he still used on a regular basis. He looked pale and exhausted, but Skye knew he wouldn't miss this wedding no matter what.

"You look amazing, even if you feel like shit," he said, and gave his husband a small smile. River smiled back softly as Skye pressed a kiss to his forehead. That damn bow-tie was what was really doing it for him. Why was it so damn cute? It made him want to undress River and fuck him right here and now, even though they had literally spent the last hour getting him dressed. Maybe fuck him with the bow-tie still on?

"I'll be ready soon," he said. "Rest."

It was an hour later when they arrived at the outdoor

236

wedding, set in a beautiful botanical garden. It was late morning and the air was filled with the scents of flowers. There were white chairs set up for the guests and a gorgeous arch in the front.

Skye had rented a wheelchair for River so he had it if he needed it but could stand if he wanted to.

The ceremony was beautiful, and Jenna was absolutely stunning. Her gown was form fitting and strapless, covered in lace and sparkling under the mid morning sun. Her dark hair had grown longer over the months and was in a gorgeous updo. A simple tiara was placed on top of her head, no veil.

Nick was in tears when she walked down the aisle, and Skye was crying too. He couldn't believe his best friends were getting married.

When she reached the front, Nick took her hand and pulled her to him, and even though it wasn't "time" yet he pressed a kiss to her lips, making everyone laugh and "aww." He blushed and Jenna smiled from ear to ear.

Their vows were simple but beautiful. And when it was officially time for Nick to kiss his bride, he scooped her close again, and tilted her backwards, making everyone cheer.

Skye kept his eyes on River, who was seated behind Jenna in his wheelchair. They had questioned her choice of "maid of honor" but she had said she didn't give a flying fuck what people thought. It was her and Nick's wedding, not anyone else's, and River was her closest friend, so she wanted him to be in her bridal party, while Skye had been Nick's best man.

River seemed okay, and when the newlyweds walked back down the aisle, Skye met River in the middle of the aisle and pushed him towards the reception.

"Any chance you feel up to having a short dance with me?" Skye asked his husband after the cake had been cut and he and River had given their speeches.

River's eyes sparkled and he nodded. "I'll try."

He stood, slowly, and held Skye's arm as they walked to

the dance floor, joining the other guests. Nick and Jenna stood nearby, swaying to the soft music, smiling endlessly.

Skye took River in his arms and supported him as best he could while they danced, slowly. He knew it wouldn't last long but he wanted this moment with his husband. "I love you," he said sincerely, gazing into sapphire eyes. "I love you so much."

River gave a small smile and kissed him. "I love you, too," he said.

CHAPTER 30

Skye

"Skye is that you?" It was late afternoon and Skye had just returned home from work. He slipped off his tie and untucked his shirt, starting to unbutton it.

"Yeah, babe, I'm home," he said. He was exhausted, like always, but he was glad to hear River's voice, and happy to be home. "You okay?" he called into the bathroom.

"Yeah, I'm fine," his husband called back. "I'll be out in a minute."

Skye finished unbuttoning his shirt and slid it off, before slipping into sweatpants and a T-shirt, then propping up some pillows and positioning himself on the bed. He rested his head back and closed his eyes. A second later he heard the door to the bathroom open, but his eyes stayed closed.

"Hey," he heard his husband say, in a tone he hadn't heard in a very long time. And that got his attention. His eyes opened and his jaw dropped at the same time that his cock began to twitch, and instantly harden. There was River, leaning against the doorframe, one knee bent and an arm above his head, in nothing but the skimpiest, tightest, bright orange silk bikini underwear he'd ever seen in his life. Skye's mouth was watering and his heart was racing. Goddamn this was the hottest thing he'd ever seen.

Their sex life had been almost non existent the last several months. River had been so sick and in so much pain he rarely felt up for doing anything, and Skye never pushed him. He'd gotten used to pleasuring himself when the need got too severe, but it was, of course, not the same as indulging in his husband. Having River's hand on his cock, River's lips on his bare skin, their naked bodies pressed together. Burying himself inside his husband and hearing the sounds he made. Feeling River tight and warm and wonderful around him. God his cock was getting harder just thinking about it.

He knew River missed him too, wanted him, but pain had a way of dulling all the other senses and River was dealing with so many things that made it difficult for him to want sex, to enjoy sex. It was yet another thing that his chronic illnesses had robbed them of. And it sucked.

"Please don't tease me, because this is not funny," Skye said, his gaze roaming over River's body, his cock throbbing now, already leaking precum. And from the looks of it, River's was doing the same. "God, you're beautiful."

River laughed. "I'm not teasing you," he said walking closer to his husband slowly, his gloriously hard cock barely contained in his skimpy underwear. He climbed onto Skye and straddled him. "Like what you see?" he asked when he noticed Skye staring not at his eyes, but at his crotch.

"Jesus, yes," Skye said, and River laughed again.

"Kiss me," he said, and Skye did. He let River pull his shirt up and off, and they kissed again. Skye slid his hands under River's silken underwear, feeling the warm, firm, soft skin beneath the material, and God it was heaven. They both moaned, and River pressed further into him, their cocks grinding against each other's, both seeking friction.

"I want you naked," River whispered, his voice low and husky. He rolled off his husband and onto the bed, sliding his underwear off and waiting for Skye to undress, and then he was back on top of him.

Skye took River into his arms and kissed him tenderly, rolling River over slowly onto his back and drawing their bodies close, feeling his husband's hard on pressing against his, and moaning once more into his mouth, shaking as their naked bodies melded.

"Oh, River," Skye whispered. And he was almost in tears. "I've missed you so much."

"Me, too, Skye," his husband replied, as they continued to kiss.

It wasn't long, though, before River had to pull away, out of breath. "Sorry," he said. "It doesn't take much for me to get worn out."

"It's okay," Skye said, stroking his arm, and pressing their foreheads together, keeping their bodies pressed close, their dicks still touching, their legs wrapped around each other. "We can slow down."

River smiled. "I'm sorry it's been so long, Skye," he said softly, catching his breath.

"What? No, it hasn't been that long," Skye said, waving him off.

"Skye, I know you haven't been asking because you know I feel like crap," River said. "And I do feel like crap. But I also know it's been almost three weeks. And I am sorry."

"It's okay, Riv," Skye said sincerely. "I know you love me."

"I do," River said. Then he took both of their cocks into his hand and began to stroke them in tandem as he kissed Skye again and again.

~

River

River's heart soared as he heard his husband whimper and moan over and over and press against him, saying his name and sliding his tongue into his mouth. And God, it felt so. Damn. Good. River hadn't been this turned on in a long time, and he missed his husband so much.

But it was over in an instant as his heart started racing, and he gasped, pulling away from Skye and closing his eyes, trying to take deep breaths in and out to calm it.

"Your heart?" Skye asked.

He nodded, took a few more breaths in and out, and waited.

And waited.

And waited.

Finally, after what seemed like forever, and feeling like his heart was going to leap out of his chest, it stopped.

"It's over," he said, opening his eyes.

"God, that scares me every time," Skye said, leaning in to kiss him. "Do we need to be done?"

"I don't want to be," River said, gazing into his husband's eyes, earnestly. He was so over this. So over not being able to have sex with his husband as often as they wanted to. As often as they needed to. They needed each other. They needed this time to connect, to be intimate, and River hated that his illness was taking it away from them. That he had to deny Skye what he needed yet again. What they both needed and wanted. And this time it didn't have anything to do with his sexual trauma.

"I don't want to hurt you," Skye said, stroking his cheek.

"The sex isn't what caused it, Skye, it happens randomly. I could be sitting here, and it wouldn't matter."

"But it wears you out. How are you feeling?"

"Like I want to keep trying."

"Okay," Skye said. And he kissed River again. His lips, his jaw, leaving marks on his neck, his collarbone, and making his way down his body, licking and sucking on his nipples, River moaned as his husband worshiped his body.

"Oh God." His hips jerked as Skye traced his fingers along his pelvis and then took River's rock hard cock into his mouth. "Oh, Skye," he moaned, breathlessly as Skye sucked and licked, taking him deeper, moving his hand down to stroke his balls gently and then even further, down to his hole. River gasped and trembled as Skye traced the outside of his hole while he continued to bob up and down on his cock. He came off for a brief second, just long enough to squirt some lube on his hand, and then went back down on his husband, and River watched as Skye locked gazes with him, and slid a finger into his hole. He shook and gasped, arching his head back and groaning as he felt Skye's tongue in the slit of his cock and then his husband's warm, slick mouth covering him once more as Skye took him deep once again, and then River was thrusting, fucking his husband's mouth while Skye finger fucked him, and God it was glorious.

"Skye...oh, baby, I...you keep that up, I'm gonna..."

"Yeah?" Skye asked, coming off of his cock, but adding a second finger to River's hole. River's thighs trembled and his mouth fell open as he felt Skye's fingers pegging his prostate over and over, sweat beading his skin, his cock throbbing, precum sliding down his shaft.

River brought his hand down to his cock and began to stroke himself as Skye worked yet another finger into his hole and he gasped, shaking even more, his body trembling as his orgasm built. He was hovering on the edge now. So very close to coming.

"That's it, sweetheart," Skye said, smiling. "Touch yourself. God, you're so beautiful." He nudged River's prostate again. "I want you to come for me, baby."

River couldn't hold it back any more. He came. And he came hard. Shouting. His neck and back arching, the veins bulging, his cum shooting out in spurts over his stomach and chest. His body shook as his hole tightened, and then spasmed on Skye's fingers as he trembled. Then he was tugging at Skye's arms and pulling him up, kissing him, and breathing heavily.

He was exhausted but so damn happy. "I...I'm fairly certain, that might be the death of me," he breathed out, and then smiled.

"Not such a bad way to go," Skye said. "God, Riv, you were beautiful. I miss seeing you come."

River smiled and blushed, still in a daze, coming down off the high of his orgasm. "You're sweet," he said.

"You gonna be okay?" Skye asked, using a tissue to wipe the cum off of River's torso. "Or did I wear you out too much?"

"I'll be fine," River said, smiling again. "Give me a minute and I'll repay the favor."

"You sure?"

"Absolutely."

~

Skye

A few minutes later, Skye was under his husband, his cock in River's mouth, and Skye was moaning, and thrusting, and so very very close to coming, when suddenly River grunted and stopped moving, and his gaze caught Skye's and eyes were filled with pain.

"Riv?" Skye said, in earnest. "What's wrong?"

But River wasn't talking, just slowly, very slowly trying to come off of him, and it looked like he couldn't open his mouth any further, and he was clearly in a lot of pain. Skye winced slightly as River's teeth scraped against his dick.

When he finally did get all the way off he had a hand on his jaw and his eyes were filled with something other than pain. Fear. And he still wasn't talking.

"Riv, what happened?" he asked.

River just shook his head and pointed to his jaw. He looked close to tears.

Oh God.

Skye scrambled out of the bed and grabbed a sock from the dresser drawer and ran into the kitchen. He filled it with rice and tied it at the top and then threw it in the microwave for a minute and brought it back to River and handed it to him. "Try this," he said. "It should help relax your jaw."

~

River

River took the makeshift heating pad and rested it against his jaw, closing his eyes, trying to breathe. He was trying not to freak out. It hurt so bad. He'd never had his jaw lock on him before. And of all times for it to happen, it just had to be while he was giving his husband a blow job.

Goddamnit. He felt like he couldn't do anything right. And the tears started falling once again, which just made his jaw hurt more.

"Riv," Skye said next to him. "It's gonna be okay." He rested a hand on River's shoulder but River jerked away, his tears coming harder now.

Skye sighed. "Should I leave you alone?" he asked.

River didn't know what he wanted. He didn't want Skye's pity. He just wanted to be a fucking husband and give the man he loved pleasure and he couldn't fucking do that because his fucking body wouldn't fucking work! And he was so fucking angry and done with all of it, but there was nothing he could do. What he wanted was to be better, to be whole. But Skye couldn't give him that. So what was he supposed to do?

He nodded.

Skye got dressed and left.

And River cried.

When Skye came back to the bedroom half an hour later and climbed into bed, River was still awake.

"Hey," Skye said softly. "Your jaw doing better?"

"Yeah," River replied, facing away from his husband. He was depressed and angry and didn't know what to do with his emotions. All the good memories from the sex they'd had earlier were mired by the fact that he felt like he'd let Skye down. He still hadn't been able to give his husband an orgasm. Skye had probably rubbed one out in the living room while River had been in the bedroom feeling sorry for himself.

"Do you want to talk about it?"

River shook his head.

"K," Skye said. And River could tell he was disappointed. "I love you," he said. "Goodnight, Riv."

A few minutes later he heard Skye snoring, and he closed his eyes as more tears slid down his cheeks.

CHAPTER 31

Skye

It was a few days later when Skye crawled into bed next to his husband and River sidled up next to him, planting kisses on his shoulder blades, and then his neck, before nibbling and licking his ear, that Skye wondered what was going on. They hadn't talked about the other night still and they hadn't had any other sexual encounters, just soft kisses and casual touches, and River had seemed aloof and somewhat distant. Skye had wanted to talk to him, but he didn't know how to bring it up again, and he'd been so exhausted.

"Hey," he said, turning to face his husband. "What's going on?"

"I'm sorry about the other night, Skye," River said. "Can I make it up to you?"

"What do you mean?" Skye asked.

"I want to pleasure you. Please?"

Skye bit his lip. He wanted this, sure, but he didn't want River to be doing it for the wrong reasons. "Riv, you don't have to do this because you feel guilty, okay? I'm fine. I don't—"

"Damn it, Skye," River snapped. "This isn't about guilt, okay, this is about me wanting to do something that I can actually do. One thing, to make life a little better, a little easier for you, because you do a million things for me. Yes, I hated that I couldn't finish what we started the other night and I was mad as hell at my body for failing me again, but I don't want those limitations to keep us apart any more than they have to. So maybe I can't use my mouth, and maybe anal sex is too exhausting for me, but I can give my husband a goddamn hand job because he fucking deserves it and because I fucking love him and I want to touch him, and be close to him, and this is the only way I know how. I can't cook, or clean, or work, but I can do this! I can give back to you, and I can take care of you, like you take care of me, every single day." River's anger was giving way to tears and he was sobbing now. "So, please, Skye, please let me touch you. Not out of guilt or obligation. Out of love. Please."

Skye gazed at his husband for a brief moment and then he kissed him fiercely and nodded. "I'm all yours, angel," he said, and rested back on his pillow.

~

River

River smiled and his hand found Skye's cock. He'd almost forgotten what it felt like to hold Skye in his hand, to hear his husband moan and feel his body shaking as he came, to feel Skye's lips pressed against his as his cock spasmed in River's hand and the warm cum filled his palm, leaking down his arm and onto the sheets. And God, he couldn't wait to do it again.

~

Skye

Skye was exhausted. He'd had a long week of teaching, and had spent the entire weekend at the auto repair shop. The last year had been especially rough for them financially, and he'd had to pick up some extra hours and was working non stop at this point, it seemed. He was hoping he would be able to cut back soon. River had earned his certificate for medical transcription just a few months ago and was starting to bring in some money again, which was a huge relief, as their medical bills kept piling up and their rent had been raised as well, but it would be a while still before Skye would be able to quit his weekend job. And not only was he exhausted, but he was depressed, and he missed his husband. River was still sick, and they didn't have any more answers than they'd had a year ago. He was pretty much bedridden at this point. He got up to go to the bathroom and get himself the occasional snack or drink, and shower, but that was it. Fortunately he could do his job from bed and it gave him something to focus on during the day, and had lifted his mood a bit, knowing that he was back to contributing financially. But his husband still struggled every day and Skye knew how hard it was for him to have lost everything he had over the last couple of years; his job, his health, his ability to function, his dignity and purpose. Skye didn't see it that way of course, but he knew his husband did.

River was depressed too, and lonely, Skye knew. He missed his work, he missed being able to go places and do things with friends, or by himself. He still missed church and his friends there, and going to Bible study.

They only saw each other during the evenings, and Skye spent most of those evenings making lesson plans, grading papers, and answering emails, and he was so wiped out from working 70 hour weeks that he often fell asleep on the couch, or in their bed next to River with papers spread around him, and would wake in the morning to find that River had moved his things aside and tucked him in.

They had managed to make it to a movie the previous week, which was really the only thing River could handle since he couldn't stand or sit anywhere that didn't have reclining seats, at least not for long. It had been their first date in months.

Fortunately they still had their game nights with Nick and Jenna, or Skye didn't know what they would do. They both needed it desperately, and River's tailbone was okay enough that he could sit at the table for a shorter game. If not he would curl up on the sofa and they would play on the coffee table in the living room, or even have Jenna and Nick join them in their bedroom and spread the board game or cards out on the bed so River could sit where he was most comfortable and still participate. Even after all this time, Nick and Jenna had been so gracious and accommodating, and Skye was forever grateful. They even spent their Saturdays visiting River while Skye was at work so he wouldn't be alone so much, and it meant the world to him. Anna was even coming by with meals and visiting when she could.

Their friends were the one thing Skye felt was keeping them sane in all the madness. That, and the fact that Jenna and Nick had announced they were having a baby. Skye couldn't wait to meet the little bundle. Jenna was just getting out of her first trimester, so it would still be several months, but it gave both he and River something to smile about, and to look forward to, and they needed that desperately.

River

River still missed going for runs and rock climbing, though those things seemed to be a far distant memory now. He'd been sick for so long, he'd forgotten what it felt like to be well.

And more often than not, after tucking Skye in, he would climb back into bed, and cry himself to sleep. He hated what this illness was doing, not only to his body, but to his faith once again. He so desperately wanted answers. Wanted to believe that there was a reason for all of this, but he couldn't see it. How could this be good? How could it be valuable? How could any of what he and Skye were going through be making them better or be bringing God glory or strengthening them? It sure didn't feel like it. If anything, River felt like his faith was weakening day by day. He was growing angry, and bitter, and even more confused than he'd been when he'd been dealing with the migraines a year and a half ago. He'd always thought trials were supposed to bring people closer to God, but this was doing the exact opposite. He was trying so hard to be positive, but he just couldn't anymore. He was grateful for his job, that he could at least do something now to help Skye with the financial side of things. The fact that he was contributing made him feel like less of a burden on his husband, but he still grieved what he had lost. What he had worked so hard for, for years, only to have it ripped out of his fingers. Being a physical therapist had brought him so much joy, and he hated that he didn't have the capacity to do the job he loved.

There was just so much pain, and grief. So much loss. And River just needed a break. Skye needed a break from working so much, trying to take care of him, and of their home, of everything. And he was worried about Skye's health if he continued to have to work so hard. His husband was burned out, he knew, and it broke him to see how exhausted he was. They needed time together again, where they were both healthy and happy, and River was starting to wonder if that would ever happen, or if this was just the way things were going to be for them from now on.

Please, God, he prayed as he lay in bed one night, crying softly into his pillow, Skye snoring next to him. *We need help. Please.*

∾

It was a few days later while Skye was at work, that River's phone rang from its place on the coffee table next to him. He picked it up, but when he didn't recognize the number he decided to ignore it. He was depressed and exhausted, and in no mood to deal with a spam call.

A moment later his phone chimed, letting him know that he had a voicemail. He put the phone to his ear and listened, and as he did, tears slid down his cheeks.

"Hi, River, it's Pastor Phillips," the deep, but kind voice said. "It's been a while since we spoke. I just wanted to say that we miss you, and how sorry I am that things have been so rough for you and Skye. I can't imagine how hard it has been. Anna has been keeping me informed somewhat but I wanted to call and check on you myself and let you know we haven't forgotten about you and want to see if there's anything we can do to help. I would like to have my secretary set up a meal train for you guys, if that's okay with you. It wouldn't last forever but I think we could provide you enough meals to get you through a few months anyway, so please call me back and let me know if that's okay." There was a pause, and River thought the voicemail had ended, before he heard, "Don't be afraid to be honest with God about how you feel, River. It's okay to be angry and confused, and God can handle your hurt. I hope you know that."

∾

River had tears sliding down his cheeks as he set his Bible down. It was like those words from the Psalms were coming straight from his soul. They described perfectly his sorrow, his loneliness, and his pain.

The Psalmist, David, had certainly had his share of struggles, and he'd laid everything open before God. His anger, and grief, and doubt, and fear. And River tried to do the same, but it wasn't enough. He didn't just want to talk to God, or know that he could be honest with Him about his anger and grief. He wanted answers. He wanted healing and wholeness. He knew life didn't owe him anything, God didn't owe him anything, but surely, he felt, no one was better off with him being chronically ill. This was something he just could not understand. Sure he was alive, he was surviving, but he didn't want to just survive. He wanted to live. Life was slipping away in front of him, almost laughing in his face, telling him that this was just one more wasted moment, one more blip in eternity that he would never get back. A moment that had so much potential but was never fully realized, and it made his chest ache, made his soul scream. Why?

He pulled his pride blanket up around him as he sat on the balcony of their apartment, sipping his coffee. It was spring once again, the second one they'd had in their new apartment. He used to love spring. But now it felt like the flowers and trees and birds only taunted him with their signs of new life, reminding him of how long he'd been sick, of what he no longer had, and all the things he could no longer enjoy. He heard them, and saw them, but he couldn't go for walks anymore, or bike rides, or runs. Couldn't go on camping trips, or go swimming, or kayaking, or climbing. Couldn't enjoy nature the way he used to. So many well-intentioned people kept telling him to remember everything that was still good in his life, all the blessings he had, everything he had to be thankful for. But it was getting to the point where he just couldn't think of anything.

Skye was amazing, and he'd stuck by River's side through all of it. He was the best partner River could ask for, his bright spot in all of the darkness; his comfort, joy and courage. But he was overworked and exhausted trying to keep up with all of the bills and the housework.

Their sex life had dwindled to practically nothing because River felt too sick most of the time to engage. And when he did, he felt worse afterwards. His jaw pain had only gotten worse ever since it had locked up on him during the blow job he'd given Skye, and so they hadn't tried it since. Skye could give them to him, but River always felt badly that he couldn't reciprocate, and it just added to his feelings of guilt and inadequacy.

Nothing was going right.

"River?" he heard, and looked up to see Skye standing there, sadness etched on his face, and behind his eyes. He looked exhausted. "You okay?"

"Does He see us anymore, Skye?" River asked, tears sliding down his cheeks. "Does He even care? It's been so long. And nothing good has come from it. Nothing. I feel like He's abandoned me. Abandoned us. I don't know how to do this anymore. Live like this. I just can't...I miss you, Skye. I miss us. And I miss my work, and being able to just get out and do things. And I'm so lonely."

Skye sighed and went over to River, wrapping his arms around him, and River slid his arms around Skye's waist, his head resting against his abdomen.

"I know, River," Skye said softly, rubbing River's back. "I know."

∽

Skye

Skye climbed out of his car and shut the door. He took a deep breath, stuck his hands in his coat pockets, and headed up the sidewalk to the church.

River was desperate. He was desperate. And he needed someone to talk to.

CHAPTER 32

Skye

Skye couldn't help but feel nervous as he sat in the pastor's office, waiting for him to enter. His leg was bouncing up and down and he found himself biting at the inside of his cheek. God, he must really love River to be doing this. He hadn't been at a church since River's Aunt Jodi's funeral and that hadn't really been the same type of experience. Sitting in a pastor's office, waiting to talk about personal stuff... but he did love River. And he would do anything for him. Even this. Even if it made him squirm and fidget and maybe even want to puke in his mouth a little. He knew he shouldn't be this nervous. This was River's church after all, and if he felt safe here, so should Skye, right? But Skye had never stepped foot in this building before. And River hadn't been back in ages.

Still, River had told him about the voicemail from his pastor, and he felt like he owed the pastor a visit. He could tell how much it meant to River, to have his church family still beside him through everything, even when he wasn't attending anymore. They hadn't taken the pastor up on his offer of meals yet. He didn't know why. Probably his pride. But Skye was losing every ounce of that as the days went on, and he knew he needed to humble himself, for his sake and his husband's.

"Hello," he heard, and turned to see a middle aged man entering, wearing a button down shirt and slacks. He seemed very casual and that eased the anxiety in Skye's mind just a little. "I'm Pastor Phillips," he said, reaching out to shake Skye's hand.

"Skye," Skye replied.

"Nice to meet you, Skye," Pastor Phillips replied, taking a seat in his large black desk chair. "If you don't mind my saying so, you seem a little agitated. Is everything okay?"

Skye flushed. "I'm not really used to being in churches," he admitted. "Not really a religious person."

"I see," Pastor Phillips said, smiling softly. "What brings you by today then?"

Skye rubbed his neck with the back of his hand. He could do this. For River. And let's face it, for himself, too. They both needed some guidance. Some help. Anything.

"You talked with my husband a few days ago," he started. "He's been sick the last few years, and we're both struggling, not knowing what to do. He lost his job a while back, and we had to move, and things have just been really hard for us financially and emotionally, and for him, spiritually, I think."

Skye saw the moment where it dawned on him, and the older man's eyes brightened. "You're River Dawson's husband. Is it still Dawson?"

Skye gave a soft smile. "We hyphenated our last names, but yes, that's him."

"It's nice to officially meet you," Pastor Phillips said, and Skye could sense how genuine he was. "We've been missing River. I'm so sorry to hear that you guys are struggling. I didn't realize he had lost his job on top of everything else. I can't imagine how difficult that must be."

"Thank you," Skye said, his throat closing up. He took a deep breath.

"What can I help you with today, Skye? I don't know if River told you but we would like to set up a meal train for you guys if that would help."

Skye nodded. "He did. I uh, I think that would be very helpful."

Pastor Phillips nodded and smiled. "Of course. We can get that going as early as tomorrow."

"Thank you." It really would be nice not to have to worry about cooking after he got home from a full day's work. Anna's meals were helpful but that was only a couple of times a month. He was always so exhausted, and maybe it would give him more time to spend with River. Even if it was just twenty minutes. He'd take what he could get.

"One other thing I'd like to offer is free counseling for both you and River. Only if you want to, of course, but it sounds like you could both use someone to talk to on a more regular basis. It can be both of you together or separately, however you want to do it. And it won't be with me. We have professional counselors on staff who can help you process everything you are both going through right now."

"I'll talk with River about it," Skye said with a nod.

"I sense there's something else," the other man prodded gently when Skye didn't move to leave or speak. "What else can we do for you, Skye?"

Skye ran a hand through his hair and sighed. "I need some advice, I guess. I'm not really into all the Jesus and God stuff, but River is, and he's been having a hard time lately."

Pastor Phillips nodded. "I think it's normal for someone in River's position to struggle with their faith, but that doesn't make it easier."

"Yeah," Skye said. "I uh...I guess I just wanted to talk to someone who shared his faith, since I don't, and try to figure out ways to help him. I hate seeing him struggling so much. I uh...I just want to know how to encourage him. His faith is really important to him, and I don't want him to lose it, you know?"

"That's very honorable of you, Skye. Trying to strengthen your husband's faith even when you don't share it. That's an admirable quality. I can see how much you love him."

"I do," Skye said.

"My biggest advice, Skye, though it may be hard for you, would be to pray for your husband. It really is the most powerful weapon we have against everything we face on this earth. Jesus doesn't take any of our hardships lightly. He is so familiar with rejection, suffering and sorrow, you can trust that he will not abandon you in yours. But taking action is important too. In that respect, I would encourage you to remind River of God's promises, of what Scripture says. And if you aren't familiar with them, then it might be time to brush up on some Scripture yourself. Make some note cards with Bible verses on them that you can put up around the house for River to see. Or even just some encouraging quotes. Do you think that would help?"

"Maybe," Skye said. "It's worth a shot I guess."

"Is there anything else I can help you with?" Pastor Phillips asked genuinely, arms resting on his desk, his hands folded together in front of him.

Skye hesitated for a moment, biting his lip, and then said, "Um, actually, yeah. Sorry if this is TMI, but we're kind of struggling in the sexual intimacy department, and I know you aren't a therapist, but if you have any tips on how to get us to be more connected we could use some help. It's not that we don't want to have sex, but River's so sick and in so much pain all the time it makes it difficult, and it's making things hard for us both. I think we need to find other ways to connect, and we've kind of lost sight of how to do that with everything going on."

"I can only imagine that's been a source of frustration and grief for both of you," Pastor Phillips said. "And you don't have to be embarrassed about mentioning it. I talk with couples about that kind of thing more than you'd probably think." He smiled softly. "Sex and intimacy is an important aspect of marriage. And when one of you is chronically ill and the other is working two jobs just to pay the bills, that puts a lot of stress and strain on something that's already got its fair share of complications. I have no doubt though that you and River love each other, and that's what is important. You both want what is best for the other person. Even if you can't have sex as much as you would like, there are things you can do to maintain intimacy with each other, even from a distance, when you are at work and he's at home and you can't be together. Like leaving those notes for him. Maybe you want to make some of them more flirtatious and sensual. Or maybe you guys can text each other throughout the day and be playful in that sense. Try to make it fun. Buy each other some playful or silly gifts, either things that turn you on or make you laugh. Intimacy doesn't have to be just about sex. Intimacy can be laughing together, or having a good conversation. It can be about just enjoying each other, too and having fun. Maybe he can't have sex but he can do something less involved, like a game that gets you two close or maybe instead of penetrative sex if that's too much for him you stick to something simpler. Maybe you want to find funny videos to share with each other to make each other laugh. Whatever gets you two stealing those special moments with each other. Because let's face it, life does suck a lot of the time, but if we hold on to those rare moments it can make it all worthwhile."

Skye gave him a soft smile. "Thank you," he said. "You've given me some things to think about."

"I'm glad you came in, Skye. We all need help sometimes. And our doors are always open. Please let us know if you would like to take us up on the counseling, and my secretary will be in touch with you about the meals."

Skye stood and shook the Pastor's hand.

"I sincerely hope that you find answers, and if not, that you at least find strength and encouragement. We're here for you."

"Thank you," Skye said. And for the first time in a long time, he did have a little bit of hope.

~

River

River was overwhelmed when Skye told him about the visit he'd made to the church. He knew it took a lot for his husband to admit when he needed help. They were both like that, and River was proud of him for accepting the pastor's offer. Especially since it would give them more time together in the evenings and hopefully make Skye less exhausted.

And when he started seeing the note cards that Skye left up throughout the house, his spirits began to lift as well. Partly because of the Bible verses themselves, but honestly more because it was Skye who was taking the time to write them down and put them on his pillow, or on the coffee maker, or even on the toilet seat. Somewhere he knew River would see them. And River found himself looking forward to it every day.

Today when River found it, it was on the bathroom mirror.

Psalm 73:26

"My flesh and my heart may fail, but God is the strength of my heart and my portion forever."

Love you, angel. Can't wait to kiss you when I get home.

. . .

River smiled. He loved his husband so much. Members of his old church had been bringing them meals for a few weeks now, and it had been amazing. Skye had committed to using the time when he wasn't cooking to just cuddle up with River in bed and not do any school work either. It was short, but it was their time together, and they cherished it.

He had decided to take the church up on their offer of free counseling. He didn't have any excuse not to, and he hadn't been able to see his regular therapist because of their financial struggles.

Talking with the therapist was helping him process his pain and grief, and loneliness, and giving him ideas of how to socialize even from home. He'd connected with groups through social media, and met other people who dealt with chronic pain, and it had helped him feel like he wasn't alone, and even given him people to connect with and talk to during the day. They shared some about their illnesses but mostly they talked about their families, their hobbies, recipes, books, or tv shows they enjoyed, and it was wonderful to have connections with people who understood what he was going through. His counselor had recommended some books that had helped as well. Nothing was a permanent fix, and he still fell into bouts of depression and discouragement, but he was having more decent days, and fewer miserable ones.

As he closed his laptop after finishing with his counseling session, he heard his phone go off, signaling a text message, and he smiled when he saw that it was from Skye. His husband had been texting him more lately and it was really starting to make a difference in his mood as well. They had both been so depressed and exhausted for the last couple of years that it had taken a toll on their relationship, but things had improved since Skye's visit to the church, and River wondered what the pastor had said to him. They'd been flirting a lot more, bantering back and forth, tossing around more euphemisms and using a lot more sexual innuendo in their conversations, and it was fun. Really fun. River had lost sight of how much he enjoyed just being Skye's husband, and his friend, and it was like they were getting a piece of that back again, instead of focusing on everything that made life hard right now, and it made River smile.

Sometimes he'd get a funny joke from Skye, and sometimes it would be more sexual in nature. Either way, he enjoyed it. The messages Skye left around the house were the same. Which always had River waiting in anticipation, never knowing what he was going to wake up to, and honestly, it was arousing. But more than that it made him feel wanted, and loved.

He would do his best to respond to Skye's text with something equally as humorous or erotic in nature, depending on what Skye sent to him. And more and more often in the last few weeks, their evening cuddle sessions would turn into them making out and giving each other hand jobs with the television on in the background.

River smiled and blushed when he read Skye's message.

Can't stop thinking about you, angel. Some parts more than others. Wink emoji

River typed out a reply and hit send. **Can't wait to feel that big strong hand on my cock, baby. Miss you.** It was only a few seconds later that River got Skye's response and it was the best one ever.

Great. I guess I'll be teaching the next class from behind my desk. Jerk.

River chuckled. **Do you have a situation?**

Oh yes, a pretty good sized situation thanks to you.

You started it. Smile emoji

I did. Smile emoji

Wanna finish it? Devil emoji. There was a pause before Skye replied.

Come again?

Exactly.

River, you do know I'm at school, right? In my classroom?

Do you have to be? Can you go to your car?

River?

What?

Are you serious?

Am I serious about getting you to rub one out in your car over the phone? Hell yeah. You have a condom?

Another pause. This was risky, they both knew it. Skye would have to be discreet as hell, but it was also turning River on like nothing had for a long time, and he assumed the same was true for Skye. And God they needed this.

Yes, came Skye's reply a moment later. **God, I can't believe I'm even considering this. I am so getting fired.**

River stroked himself as he thought of his gorgeous husband and what they were about to do. **God, Skye, I'm so hard right now. Please.**

Jesus, Riv. You're killing me.

Wish I was stroking you instead. Or had your gorgeous cock inside me. God, Skye, I want to touch you.

River!

You in the car?

Jesus, yes. Don't text me for a minute. I told my boss I needed to run a quick errand during my lunch break so I could find somewhere besides the school parking lot to have phone sex with my husband.

You didn't tell him the phone sex part did you?

Eye roll emoji.

Laugh emoji.

River?

Yeah?

I love you.

Got your condom on?

Yes.

Are you touching yourself?

Fuck, yes.
How hard are you, Skye?
Riv, don't torture me.
Skye?
Hard, Riv. Throbbing, aching, for you, baby.
Show me.

~

Skye

Three seconds later Skye's phone rang with a facetime call and he answered, his face flushed and breathing heavily, but a smile splitting his face as well when he saw his husband's grin.

"Hey, beautiful," River said, his voice sultry and seductive, sapphire eyes sparkling. "You look good." Skye was propped up against the driver seat window, trees in the background.

"Shut up," Skye muttered. "You're evil."

River chuckled. "I'm sorry," he said. "Now show me that sweet cock, baby."

"You gonna show me yours?" Skye asked, raising an eyebrow. "Two way street here, angel."

River smirked smugly and surprised Skye by slipping his shirt over his head first, which only made him swallow, his cock twitching and throbbing painfully, and then he watched as River leaned back on his wedge, resting one arm behind his head, and held his phone in the air, giving Skye the most beautiful full view of his face, torso, and groin, gloriously hard.

"Oh, River," Skye breathed. He could barely stand it. He didn't think he'd ever seen River look so beautiful before, splayed out like that, just for him. He must be using a selfie stick to get that incredible angle. Even with all the weight and muscle mass he'd lost, he was still gorgeous. He was thin, but not sickly so, and he still had some definition in his arms and chest. The same high cheek bones as always, the same full lips.

And those sapphire eyes of his were sparkling mischievously, his dark hair tousled, and his cock twitched. He didn't think he'd ever been so turned on in his life. And it was an incredible feeling to know that he could do this to River. That River could do this to him. Make him come so undone with his words, with his body. But it wasn't just that. It was everything they were to each other. Everything they shared. Everything they had been through. It was their love and commitment and devotion and friendship and loyalty that made this so erotic on top of everything else. The sex was just the icing on the cake. But damn if Skye wasn't going to lick that icing off and taste it for all that it was worth.

"Your turn, baby," River murmured as he stroked himself slowly and Skye watched, making more precum leak out of Skye's engorged cock. It was twitching like crazy now and pressing painfully against his zipper. "Show me how hard I make you. Show me what I do to you, sweetheart."

Skye couldn't give River the same view, but he slid his pants further off, along with his boxers, and pulled up his shirt, then angled the phone at his dick, trying so hard not to touch himself. "This what you want, Riv?" he asked, panting, his voice raspy.

River growled through the phone. "Shit, yeah, that's what I want. Touch yourself, Skye. I want to see you come for me."

Skye didn't have to be told twice. He wrapped his hand around the base of his shaft and started stroking.

"River?" he said.

"Hmmm?"

"Are you touching yourself too?"

"Yeah, Skye, I am. I'm so fucking hard for you right now, baby."

Skye groaned and stroked himself harder.

"That's it, baby," River cooed. "Fuck your fist for me. Such a pretty cock."

Skye moaned as his body shook with pleasure. Who knew his husband had such a dirty mouth?

"Wanna get my hands all over you, baby," River said. "You're gonna come so hard for me, aren't you?"

Skye nodded, panting, though River couldn't see it. "Are you close?" he asked.

"You wanna see?"

"Yes," Skye said, barely able to breathe as he continued to stroke himself. He was so close now.

"Okay."

Skye took his phone away from his crotch so he could watch River, and he was not disappointed. His husband's eyes were closed, his knees bent, his back and ass lifted slightly off the bed, legs parted. His face was flushed and he started making the most incredible sounds.

"Oh, Skye," he moaned. "Skye, I want you."

"Fuck, River," Skye whimpered as he stroked himself harder, his body shuddering. Everything in him wanted to jump through the phone and shove himself against his husband, and yet it didn't, because this was what was so erotic about it, the fact that they were having sex this way, and couldn't touch each other. There was something about being limited, being bound, using their imaginations, and their words, that was such a turn on.

"Picturing you on me, Skye," River said, his chest rising and falling as he continued to stroke himself. "Holding your dick against mine, stroking them together, watching us come together, you releasing all over me."

"Fuck, River," Skye moaned, "I'm gonna come. Fuck, I'm so close."

"Come for me, baby," River said, his voice deep. "Say my name. Scream for me, Skye."

"Oh, God," Skye let out one final guttural moan and then howled River's name as he came hard in his condom, his back arching and his head falling back against the window of his car.

"Fuck, that was beautiful," he heard his husband say, and he smiled, his eyes still closed, shoulders and chest rising and falling, still coming down off his orgasm.

"Did...did I miss yours?" Skye asked, and he opened his eyes to look at his husband.

"Yeah, sorry," River said, a guilty smile on his face. "Hearing you scream my name like that pushed me over the edge."

Skye smiled too. "Understandable. It was pretty hot."

"This whole thing was pretty hot."

Skye blushed and his smile widened. "Probably can't make it a regular thing though, or I really will get fired."

"I know," River said. "First time I've had phone sex though, and hopefully it won't be the last."

Skye smiled and blushed again. "Definitely won't be the last."

River grinned. "I love you, Skye."

"Love you, too, Riv. See you later."

"Bye."

"Bye, baby."

~

4 MONTHS LATER

River

Hey, I'm coming over! Jenna texted River as he was sitting in bed trying to do some exercises to keep his body from completely wasting away. **Dr is worried about me going into preterm labor so they've put me on bed rest for the next six weeks. We're gonna be bed buddies!!!!**

Everything okay? River texted back.

It's fine. Baby is healthy. I'm 3cm dilated but that's not totally abnormal. They're just taking precautions. See you soon!!!

River smiled. Having Jenna's company for the next six weeks would be wonderful. He couldn't wait to see her.

She entered the apartment without knocking and made her way into the bedroom, her baby bump leading the way. She was ginormous, but glowing, and River smiled widely when he saw her. She propped the pillows up and then climbed into the bed on Skye's side and rested her head back, letting out a sigh.

"All this extra weight is killing me," she said, then rubbed her belly. "I am ready for this little guy to come out."

River laughed. "I bet. You all set with babyland?"

Jenna grinned. "Nursery is all set up. Nick is fussing over me like crazy, which is really sweet, and slightly annoying."

River grinned. "Sounds like him."

Jenna gasped suddenly and River startled until she rested her hand on her bump and smiled. "He's moving. Wanna feel?"

River nodded and she took his hand, resting it on her stomach. It was a moment before River felt a knock against his hand. "Oh, God, that's so cool."

"Yeah, in the middle of the afternoon it is, but not at three am," Jenna remarked with a grin, and River laughed.

"You must be exhausted, growing another person in your body."

"Fuck, you can say that again." She jumped and River felt the baby moving again at the same time.

"Active little guy. You pick out a name yet?"

Jenna shook her head. "We're still deciding between a few. I never realized how hard it would be to choose a name, but we've vetoed so many for different reasons, it's ridiculous.

Finding any that we both like has been a nightmare. I must have spent hours on babynames.com."

River chuckled again.

They talked and laughed and watched tv, and played games, before they both decided it was time for a nap.

〜

Skye

It was late afternoon when Skye walked in the door to the apartment. He'd seen Jenna's car in the driveway so he knew she was here with River, and that made him happy.

When he made his way into the bedroom, he couldn't help the wide smile that split his face. River and Jenna were asleep, curled up in each other's arms. Jenna's baby bump pressed against his husband. They looked absolutely adorable together.

Skye pulled out his phone and snapped a picture before sending it to Nick with the caption, **Our sleeping beauties**.

Aww, Nick replied shortly. **Hey, what if I bring dinner over to your place and we can hang out for a bit?**

Sounds good, Skye replied. **See you soon.**

CHAPTER 33

Skye

1 YEAR LATER

I will rejoice and be glad in your steadfast love, because you have seen my affliction; you have known the distress of my soul (Psalm 31:7)

4 years. It had been 4 years and River was still sick.

Nothing had changed.

And everything had changed.

They still didn't have answers. And River was still bedbound. Not only that, but River's jaw pain had gotten exponentially worse over the years. Not only did it lock on occasion but it hurt just to talk, or chew, or sing, or laugh, or even to kiss Skye. When he'd asked his dentist about it they had recommended seeing a TMJ specialist who had told him that not only did he have TMJ dysfunction, which meant his jaw could lock at any given moment, but he also had arthritis and mild dislocations in both sides of his jaw.

Skye couldn't believe it. River was only 32, and his body

271

was falling apart bit by bit, year after year. What the hell was going on?

The TMJ specialist had told him that chewing gum on a regular basis would help with the jaw pain, and gave him medication to help him sleep at night and relax his jaw so he wouldn't clench as much, and also recommended a splint for him to wear at night. Unfortunately that wasn't covered by insurance and would cost $1200. Their financial situation was a bit better than it had been a year ago, now that River was making a steady income, and Skye had quit his job at the auto parts store, but things were still tight, and if their medical expenses didn't slow down he'd have to pick up more work again, and he just didn't know if he could do it. Not when he was finally spending more time with River and feeling less exhausted. The fact that River was making enough money for Skye to quit his second job had been a huge boost for his husband emotionally, and Skye hated the thought of taking that away from him.

He of course insisted that River get the splint because he wanted River to do anything and everything he could to feel better, to be better, but the thought of going back to working weekends on top of his teaching job made him break out in a sweat, his heart racing, and he found himself sitting in his car after work one day, tears sliding down his cheeks, unable to make the drive home.

He felt so hopeless once again.

He was exhausted, physically and emotionally. He felt like every ounce of energy he did have got poured into his work, and into River, and keeping their home together. And he just didn't know if he could do it anymore. Not that he would ever leave his husband. God, of course not. He loved River, and when he'd promised to stay by his side 'in sickness and in health' he'd meant it. But once again he found himself in desperate need of help.

He picked up his phone and dialed and then held it to his ear, wiping tears from his eyes.

"Hey, sweetheart," Grace answered.

"Hi, Mom," Skye said, and his voice was shaking, and more tears were falling.

"Oh, Skye," Grace said, softly. "You sound like you aren't doing so well."

Skye sniffled. "Yeah, I guess you could say that."

"I'm so sorry. What's going on? Is it River?"

"I mean, yeah, it's River. But it's me, Mom. It's just me. I'm falling apart. I'm stressed, and exhausted."

"You sound overwhelmed, Skye," Grace said, concern in her voice. "My poor baby."

"Yeah," Skye admitted, wiping more tears from his eyes. "I'm sorry, Mom. I don't mean to call you just to cry and complain."

"Yes you do," Grace said softly once again. "And that's okay, Skye. That's more than okay. That's what I'm here for. It's okay for you not to be okay. And I want you to call me when that's happening. You're my son, and I love you. And it breaks my heart to see you hurting so much. There's nothing wrong with tears, baby."

Skye was sobbing now, his head resting against the steering wheel.

"It's okay," Grace said. "It's okay, Skye. I'm here. I'm here. And I love you. And you love River so much. I know. That's what love is. When your partner is going through hell, and you walk right through the flames with them."

"Mom, I just don't know what to do," he choked out. "We are doing a bit better financially, but things are still tough and I'm worried I might have to go back to work at the shop, and I just don't think I can. I'm so fucking exhausted."

"I know," Grace said. "Skye, I've been thinking about you guys a lot, actually, and how I might be able to help. And the truth is, I don't feel like there really is much I can do from Kansas."

"I know, Mom."

"So, I was thinking I should move out there."

Skye's heart stopped. "What?" he asked, picking his head up off of the steering wheel.

"I miss my boys, Skye. I have ever since Jaden went away to college. And if I can be near you and River and help you out, I'd really like to do that. Mind you, I'm not much of a cook, but I could help out with groceries, and laundry, and dishes, and cleaning, and just being there. And I'd really like to do that. And just being able to see you guys on a regular basis would be wonderful."

Skye's heart was pounding. "Are you serious?"

"Very," Grace said, a hint of a smile in her voice.

"But, what about the beer company? I mean, you started that with Dad. That's everything to you."

"No, Skye, you are everything to me."

Skye was crying all over again.

"I have a friend who's going to take things over for me. I'll still own it but I don't have to be here all the time. It'll take me a month or so to get things in order but then I can be closer to you guys and be helping out. Does that sound okay?"

Skye was speechless for a minute. He closed his eyes tightly as tears continued to fall.

"Skye?" Grace asked. "Are you there?"

"Yeah, Mom, I'm here. That, uh, that sounds amazing. Really. Are you sure?"

"I'm sure, Skye."

~

River

I see your pain, and it's big. I also see your courage. And it's bigger. ~Glennon Doyle

You'll always be the bravest and best person I know.
  Love you, angel. XOXO

River smiled despite his pain and exhaustion. A year later Skye was still leaving him these encouraging notes and Bible verses. This one was on the coffee pot.

He made his coffee and carried it back to bed where he sat propped up on his wedge that Skye had gotten for him all those years ago when he'd first started having tailbone pain. The beginnings of his journey with chronic pain and illness. Who knew then that it would last this long? He felt like he should be grateful really, that it wasn't life threatening. He didn't have cancer. He wasn't dying. But even though it wasn't life threatening, it was still life altering. It changed things, big time, for him and for Skye. And the hardest part was never knowing if he would get better or not. Still not having a diagnosis. Still not having answers.

~

Skye

Skye was wiping off the white board after school a few weeks later when he heard a knock on the door. His eyes widened when he turned and saw who it was, a smile spreading across his face.

"Claire," he said.

"Hi, Mr. Mckenzie." Claire's smile lit up her face. "Can I come in?"

"Of course," Skye said. He couldn't believe how grown up

Claire looked. He hadn't seen her in several years and she was becoming a young woman now. Her blonde hair fell loosely down her back and over her shoulders and she wore tight jeans with holes in the knees and a T-shirt with a zip up hoodie over top. She was wearing makeup now, light pink lip gloss and dark eyeliner. It suited her.

"How are you?" Skye asked as he sat down and gestured for her to do the same.

"I'm fine," she said, somewhat shyly. "I'm good, actually." She blushed a little and smiled more. "I have a girlfriend."

Skye beamed. "That's great."

"Yeah, thanks," Claire said. "Anyway, I uh, I actually came to talk about you."

"Me?"

"Yeah, word's kinda been getting around about your husband not feeling well, and I wanted to say how sorry I am," Claire said, her blue eyes conveying sympathy.

Skye swallowed. "Thank you, Claire," he said. "That's very sweet of you."

"Yeah, well, Gwen and I have been talking, and we were kind of hoping that you would let us set up a Go Fund Me account for you guys. We really want to help, and I don't think we're the only ones. But we wanted to run it by you first, of course. My mom said we could do it if we had your permission."

Skye swallowed again. He was overwhelmed. He couldn't believe one of his former students was sitting in front of him, expressing sympathy for him and his husband and at the same time offering to set up a way to get them financial assistance. But he didn't know if he could take it. He was not used to accepting money from people. He felt like taking care of River, of the medical bills and the school debt, was his responsibility, not anyone else's.

"That's really generous of you guys, but I don't think—"

"Come on, Mr. Mckenzie," Claire interrupted. "We can't

help you at home, or make River feel any better physically, and I don't cook worth a damn, but we can do this."

Skye smirked at her. "I understand that, and I really appreciate it, but there's so many people out there who probably need the money even more than River and I do. I just don't feel right about taking it."

"Mr. Mckenzie, we can't help the other people out there who need the money. We don't know them. We know you. And we can help you. And you need it. Can you honestly tell me you don't need it?" Claire eyed him and Skye couldn't believe how stubborn she'd gotten, or maybe she was just allowing this side of herself to finally show through.

He sighed. "I'll talk with River about it."

Claire narrowed her eyes. "Like, you'll actually talk to him, or you say you'll talk to him and then you'll go home and I'll never hear from you 'cause that's your way of avoiding it?"

Skye grinned slightly. "I'll actually talk to him."

Her eyebrows furrowed. "Promise?"

"Promise."

"Okay. I'm gonna be back here the day after tomorrow just to make sure. Do your homework." She pointed a finger at him.

"Yes, ma'am."

~

River

A month later, things were looking up slightly. River was still bedridden, but Grace was settled into her new place only ten minutes down the road from them, and Skye and River had decided to take Claire up on her and Gwen's offer of setting up a Go Fund Me account (even though it still made Skye feel uneasy) and they had been once again overwhelmed by the generosity and kindness of their friends, community and even strangers who had donated to help them. And River had seen the difference it had made. His husband was significantly less stressed, and had the sparkle back in his beautiful green eyes.

They were curled up in bed watching tv when River's phone rang. When he picked it up he saw that it was Anna, and swiped to answer. Skye continued to run his fingers through River's hair as he held the phone to his ear, nuzzling a little closer into his husband's side.

"Hey, Anna," River said.

"Hey. How are you guys?" Her voice was sweet and thoughtful as always.

"Okay. Surviving."

"Well, I'm calling with what I'm hoping will be good news."

"Oh?" River said. "What's that?"

"I was out to lunch with a friend today, and she was talking about how her sister was really sick and had been for a long time, and finally got a diagnosis. And I thought that her symptoms sounded really similar to yours, so I wanted to pass on to you guys what doctor this girl's sister saw, 'cause they're about an hour away, and it seems like it's been helping her, and maybe, I don't know... I don't want to give you false hope, 'cause I know you have been to hell and back for years with this crap, but I thought it might be worth a shot. I mean it might not be what you have, but I thought it was worth a try."

"Yeah, it might be. What's the diagnosis, or treatment, or whatever?"

"It's called POTS," Anna said. "That's what my friend's sister has. It took her years to get a diagnosis but she has pretty much all of the same symptoms that you do. Except for the tailbone pain and the arthritis stuff. But I mean, the palpitations, and the nausea, and lightheadedness, and fainting, and dizziness, and she was bedridden for years too. But she found this doctor, whose daughter I guess also has it, so she knows a lot about it, and anyway, she's been doing better. She's gotten to the point where she has a part time job now."

"Wow," River said, and he couldn't help but feel a little bit hopeful again. "That's awesome."

"It's called what, again?" River asked, and he could feel Skye's fingers stalling in his hair, his interest clearly piqued.

"POTS," Anna said. "It stands for Postural Orthostatic Tachycardia Syndrome."

River grabbed the pen and paper that were sitting by his nightstand and wrote the name down and showed it to Skye. His husband blinked at him and pursed his lips, then shrugged, indicating that he'd never heard of it before.

"So, some of the things my friend suggested were drinking coconut water and other things with lots of electrolytes to stay hydrated, and eating lots of salty snacks. Apparently that's what her sister does. They also said you could try compression socks. If you want to check out the doctor's website I can send you the information."

"Yes, please, that would be amazing."

"Okay. I'll send it now. Let me know how it goes, if you can. I really hope this helps you, River."

"Thank you," he said. "I really appreciate it. Goodnight."

"Goodnight."

"That sounded like good news," Skye prodded as River set his phone aside.

"Yeah, Anna thinks she may have found a doctor who can help me."

"Really?" Skye said, sitting up more.

River filled him in. They took a look at the website Anna had texted to him, and sent an email asking for a consultation, and then Skye took River back into his arms, holding him tight.

"Skye," River said, his hand resting on his husband's chest. "Thank you."

"For what?" Skye asked, tilting his head slightly to look down at him.

"For everything," River said. "For sticking with me through all of this. I know it's been just as hard for you as it has been for me. Just in a different way. I know how hard you have worked, and how stressed and tired you have been. You have always put me first. And I know this isn't what you thought marriage would be. So thank you. I know I have complained a lot, and cried a lot and you've had to be the strong one. I just want you to know that I see you. I see how much you love me, and everything you sacrifice, and how hard you work. And I appreciate it more than you know. And I love you."

Skye shifted away from River slightly and loosened his grip. He put his fingers under River's chin and lifted his face so that River was looking him in the eyes. And then he kissed him soundly.

River rested his hand on Skye's cheek and kissed him back, falling onto his back and pulling Skye on top of him, his husband's tongue sliding into his mouth, and they both moaned as their kissing intensified and their cocks began to harden against one another's.

It wasn't long before they were both naked and River had his legs wrapped around his husband as Skye slid inside him. They let out a string of curses as they came together, and then held each other, basking in their post orgasmic bliss.

"I love you, Riv," Skye said.

"I love you, too, Skye," River whispered. They touched their lips together a few more times and then slid under the covers and snuggled up together once again.

And with Skye by his side, River knew that he would be okay. They didn't have all of the answers about life, or faith, or about anything, really, but they had each other, and that was enough.

River

EPILOGUE

SEVEN MONTHS LATER

"Oh, fuck. You feel so damn good, baby." Skye had taken River on a date and ended it by driving him out to a secluded location for a moonlit picnic. They were tucked back in a clearing, with a beautiful lake in front of them and trees on all sides.

After their meal they had made out until they were both horny as hell, and then climbed into the car to head home so they could fuck each other senseless.

They hadn't made it that far, though. River had slid across the seat and straddled his husband's lap, knocking into the car horn and making it blare, startling them both, but then causing them to laugh heartily afterwards, before he'd pressed his lips to his husband's again.

"Want you," he'd said, "right now." Skye's eyes had blazed with heat and he'd moved River off of his lap so they could strip. It had been a bit awkward trying to get their clothes off in the car, but they had managed, and now River was straddling his husband's lap as Skye thrusted into him over and over. River mewled with pleasure, his own cock slapping against his stomach as he bounced up and down on his husband's cock, Skye's hands gripping his hips tightly, sweat covering their bodies.

"Fuck, you feel amazing, baby," Skye breathed. "So fucking gorgeous, riding me." His voice was raspy and deep and it sent a shiver down River's spine, making his balls tingle and his cock weep, more precum leaking down the sides.

"Nnnggg," he whimpered, his head thrown back as Skye's cock pegged his prostate with each rise and fall of his body.

"God, I want to make you come so bad," Skye rasped. "Fucking come for me, baby. I want to see that gorgeous cock spraying all over me."

River gripped his cock and stroked furiously, and seconds later he was howling Skye's name as his cum covered his husband's chest and slid down his torso.

Skye growled and started thrusting even harder. "Fuck, yes. So fucking hot, angel." He thrust two more times and then he was coming with a shout, emptying his release in River's hole and filling him up.

River collapsed on his husband, drinking in the smells of leather, sweat, and sex.

"Best date ever," River murmured, and Skye laughed.

It had been seven months since River had seen the doctor Anna had recommended, and after listening to his symptoms she had suggested a tilt table test, which had been rather uncomfortable, as it exacerbated River's symptoms of light-headedness and dizziness, but thankfully he'd managed not to pass out, and she was indeed able to diagnose him with POTS as a result.

She explained that the condition was a dysfunction of the autonomic nervous system, which meant his nervous system wasn't balancing his blood pressure and heart rate when he changed positions, particularly when he went from sitting or lying down to standing. This could cause a variety of symp-toms and looked different with each patient. She recommended a new medication for River to try, along with the things he'd been doing already, such as drinking a lot of water, getting a certain amount of protein each day, and wearing compression stockings to help pump the blood up from his legs in order to reduce his symptoms. Because some patients experienced POTS as a result of their sympathetic nervous system being hyperactive, she also recommended River start meditation if he wasn't doing it already, and focus on mindfulness in general. This would help his parasympathetic nervous system re-engage.

He'd been on the medication since then and had started meditating, and while he wasn't cured, he'd noticed some improvement. He'd been able to get up and move around the house more, do some chores, or exercise a small amount before he got worn out again and had to take a break. He was spending more and more time out of bed in small bursts and it felt good. He couldn't be on his feet for long periods of time still, but he was thankful for the small amount of progress that he'd made.

They were back to having anal sex at least twice a week, which was River's favorite part of feeling better, and he was pretty sure it was Skye's too. After being too sick and worn out to engage in anything other than handjobs or frotting for the longest time, they were able to have the connection they both craved once again. He knew how much his husband loved being inside of him, and River couldn't deny that he'd noticed a shift in Skye's mood as a result, and he was so glad that this was something he could give to his husband again after everything Skye had given him.

He still dealt with the tailbone pain and the issues with his jaw, and being in pain every day was exhausting, there was no doubt about it. He still struggled, still cried sometimes when it all felt so overwhelming, still hated that he couldn't do so many of the things he loved. But every time he looked at his husband he was reminded of how blessed he was. How loved he was, and that he had an amazing partner going through this life with him. He knew that no matter how difficult things got, he would always have Skye. The man who meant the world to him, the sunshine in his darkness and the rainbow after his storm.

River felt Skye kissing the top of his head before he lifted it, his chest now sticky with his own release from being pressed up against his husband. He ran a finger through his cum and lifted it to Skye's lips. His husband smirked and took River's finger into his mouth, licking and sucking, making River's dick twitch as it tried to rally again at the sight. "Not tonight," Skye said with a smile, popping off of his finger and pressing another kiss to River's lips. "We should get home and get some sleep. We have a party to get ready for tomorrow, and that means getting up bright and early."

Skye was right. They had a big day tomorrow and needed to get home. River would have to stretch for a while before bed to relieve the ache in his hips and tailbone after their fuck session, but it had been worth it.

"Ooh, yes, I want baby cuddles," River said, shifting off of his husband and handing Skye some wipes from the glove box to clean himself off.

Skye chuckled. "If you can get the little monkey to let you hold him for more than three seconds. That little dude is a whirlwind."

River laughed. Josiah was eighteen months old and looked just like his father, with Nick's hazel eyes and brown hair, but he had Jenna's fiery, outgoing personality. The little guy never stopped moving, but he was adorable as hell and they all loved him to bits. The fact that he was starting to talk and was calling them "Wiver" and "Kye" was the best part of all and it made River's heart melt every time. He was in a constant battle with Josiah to stop stealing his glasses right off his face every time he held him, though. The little thief.

River couldn't wait to see everyone. They were having

their friends over tomorrow, along with Grace, to celebrate River's health improving, and they were going all out with decorations, food, and games. River had balked at the idea when Skye first brought it up, saying it wasn't necessary, that parties were for birthdays and anniversaries, not something like this. But his husband had convinced him otherwise, telling him that life was full of so many difficult moments, and that every victory, every achievement, every milestone, deserved to be celebrated with the people you loved. River hadn't been able to argue with that, and their friends had been ecstatic about the idea.

So tonight they would go home and rest, and tomorrow they would party, because celebrations didn't happen nearly enough, and life deserved to be celebrated.

The End

Thank You

Thank you so much for reading Skye and River's story. If you enjoyed it please consider leaving a review!

PLAYLIST

These are songs that resonated with me in telling the story of these amazing men - https://spoti.fi/3WjBWMx

About the Author

I live in sunny Florida with my husband and three children. I love reading and writing mm romance and am an advocate of mental health and chronic pain awareness. I love rainy days and sunshine and curling up with a good book or watching my favorite tv shows. I'm a big fan of the tv show Supernatural and believe that Starbucks is a form of self-care :)

You can follow me on social media, join my facebook group Felicity Snow's Followers, sign up for my newsletter, see my Pinterest storyboards, and find my other books here: https://linktr.ee/felsnowauthor